EAT, BRAINS, LOVE

JEFF HART

HARPER TEEN
An Imprint of HarperCollinsPublishers

perCollins Publishers.

ove

 For information address HarperCollins Children's Books, a division of HarperCollins Publishers, 10 East 53rd Street, New York, NY 10022.

www.epicreads.com

Library of Congress Cataloging-in-Publication Data

Hart, Jeff (Jeffrey Alan), 1983-

Eat, brains, love / Jeff Hart. – First edition.

pages cm

Summary: New Jersey teens Jake Stephenson and Amanda Blake are turning into zombies and, having devoured half of their senior class, they are on the run, pursued by teen psychic Cass, a member of a government unit charged with killing zombies and keeping their existence secret.

ISBN 978-0-06-220034-1 (pbk. bdg.)

[1. Zombies–Fiction. 2. Psychic ability–Fiction. 3. Fugitives from justice–Fiction. 4. Horror stories.] I. Title.

PZ.H25682Eat 2013 2012045521

[Fic]–dc23

CIP

AC

Typography by Torborg Davern

13 14 15 16 17 CG/RRDH 10 9 8 7 6 5 4 3 2 1

❖

First Edition

For Deborah

JAKE

FIRST SEMESTER OF MY SENIOR YEAR, THE GUIDANCE counselor at Ronald Reagan High School gave all us new seniors this lame career-aptitude test. It was one of those deals where you have to fill in a bubble to indicate whether you strongly agree, agree, disagree, or strongly disagree with statements like "I take pride in helping others make photocopies" or "I used the money from my summer job to make sound financial investments." Apparently, it was supposed to help us figure out what we'd be good at when we enter the adult world next year, or at least let us know what majors to be looking at when we applied to colleges.

This was before I turned into a flesh-eating monster, by the way.

I swear I was the last person in my class to get my results. Most kids just got an envelope in homeroom that said something like "Congratulations! You'd make an excellent zookeeper or a very good prison guard!" I didn't get an envelope. Instead, I got called down to the guidance office for a one-on-one with Mrs. Snyder, something that's usually reserved for the weirdos who set fires inside their lockers or spend gym class crying behind the bleachers.

"Jake, I'm not sure how to put this," Mrs. Snyder said, studying my test results while I pocketed as many Jolly Ranchers from the dish on her desk as possible because free candy is awesome. "I've never seen a score quite like this. There are more than fifty different career recommendations possible on this test and you scored equally in almost all of them."

"That's good, right?" I asked, feeling sort of proud that this dumb test had finally discovered my true jack-of-all-trades nature. Maybe my future career could be one of those dudes that companies hire when they need to fix whatever, you know, goes wrong with companies. I could, like, streamline and synergize and whatever—and oh, fix your plumbing too because, yeah, I'm also good at that.

"Equally *low*, Jake," Mrs. Snyder clarified. "You scored equally low in all areas. So low, in fact, that the test is unable to make a recommendation."

"Oh."

"Have you considered liberal arts?"

Mrs. Snyder suggested that I take the test again, but what good would that do? It's not something I could study for, like if I tried harder I could make sure I picked all the right answers so my result would be "awesome bass guitarist." Whatever. Basically, I forgot about that test as soon as I left Mrs. Snyder's office.

Of course now I know for sure that test was total bullshit.

There weren't any questions about cannibalism, or fleeing government hit squads, or picking the perfect sound track for a road trip/car chase. Of the fifty possible career recommendations, none of them was "undead fugitive."

You can't figure out life from a Scantron test. I devoured a good portion of my graduating class during lunch in the cafeteria. That sucked for me and I'm aware that it sucked even more for the students at Ronald Reagan. I don't feel good about it. No test could've predicted that.

But I don't know—there have been some unexpected perks to all this too. Some silver linings. And that's life, right? "Once in a while you get shown the light in the strangest of places if you look at it right." That's from a Grateful Dead song. I'm not a Dead Head, it just came on the radio. See? Great road-trip music. I'd never know that if I wasn't running for my life.

I found my calling. That'll show you, Mrs. Snyder.

I spent my last night as a bona fide human being in pretty much the best possible way. I mean, I was just hanging out by myself in my basement, playing video games and whatever, but it was cool. I finally prestiged on the new *Call of Duty*; I was totally in the zone, just *pwning* my way through hordes of terrorist scum, their squealed complaints and guttural curses piped over my Xbox headset, fueling my kill streak. I had Severed Lung blasting on the stereo, and the couch was so comfortable, and it was like one of those times where you're just like, *Shit, life is great.*

If I had known that was going to be it, as in *it* it, I don't know if I would have done anything different. Maybe I would have snuck some of my parents' brandy or something—whatever you're supposed to drink for special occasions. Maybe I would've said good-bye to my mom and dad, thanked them for being pretty cool most of the time and pretending to believe me whenever I told them that smell coming from my room was incense. I guess I could have woken up my little sister and said, "Hey, Kelly, you're the best." I don't know, though. I probably would've just hung in the basement, because all that seems way too dramatic.

The one thing I *do* wish is that I'd hit up Wendy's or Popeyes or Taco Bell. Just for one last combo meal. Actually, maybe I would've hit up all three of them to get a combo at each. You'd be surprised how much you end up thinking about that stuff when you don't really eat anymore. Not the meat, really. I get plenty of that. It's the spicy crispy breading or the hard taco shells you miss. Raw human flesh just lacks the finer preparation techniques of fast food.

The next day started out the same as ever. I woke up way too late, chugged some Hawaiian Punch, and stuffed a fistful of Froot Loops into my mouth before screeching out of the driveway in my trusty, falling-apart Honda Civic with Kelly putting on her lip gloss in the passenger seat, making stupid little kissy-faces in the passenger-side mirror. The one tiny sign that anything was off was that as soon as I turned the key in the ignition, my stomach let out probably the loudest rumble I'd ever heard.

Kelly looked over at me and made a gagging noise, but that was nothing new; Kelly spends half of her life being disgusted at one thing or another. She's twelve. It's her hobby. And it's not like my stomach's never made insane sounds before, so I didn't think too much about it.

I had bigger fish to fry than a stomachache. I was supposed to be giving an oral presentation on some book called *The House of Mirth* in seventh-period English, and I hadn't even started reading it.

These are the things I used to worry about.

I dropped Kelly off and heard the first bell ring as I shut the car door in the RRHS parking lot. I was racing to biology when I went slamming right into Chazz Slade, who was standing inconveniently in the middle of the hallway with his girlfriend, Amanda Blake. My copy of *The House of Mirth*, which I'd been trying to read while I ran, dropped right at his feet. He looked down at it. I looked down at it. Amanda Blake looked annoyed.

Chazz Slade was built like Captain America if, instead of fighting Nazis, Captain America spent all his time drinking powdered muscle shakes and working on his obliques. He probably could've been the captain of the football team if he wasn't getting suspended all the time for skipping classes. In fact, this was the first time I'd seen Chazz around school in a while. He wore a spotless white hat that matched his spotless white tee that matched his spotless white sneakers. He bared his spotless white teeth at me.

"I gotta get the name of your dentist sometime, Chazz," I said with a weak smile.

Chazz wasn't amused. He grabbed me by the collar and yanked me toward him. "What the hell?" he fumed.

The toes of my sneakers squeaked against the linoleum tiles. "Who do you think you are, you little scrub?"

"Uh, last I checked I was Jake Stephens," I said. "The scrub thing is debatable, I guess."

Chazz let out a disgusted snort and released me. I took a deep breath; he'd sort of been choking me.

Don't misread the situation here. I didn't exactly *like* being picked on by Chazz Slade, but I wasn't scared of him either. He talked a big game, but he was sort of like one of those grizzly bears that do those bluff charges and only actually maul you if you show fear. Chazz would've made total sense on the Nature Channel.

His girlfriend, Amanda Blake, on the other hand, scared me a lot—mostly because of her ridiculous hotness. Right then, she had her arms folded over her chest, pushing her boobs up in a way that was hard to ignore. She was looking back and forth between me and Chazz with an expression somewhere between sympathy and disgust. I couldn't tell whether it was meant for him or me.

Unfortunately, Chazz wasn't done.

"You little shit," he was saying, gathering himself into his full height—he had to be at least six four—and puffing out his chest as he backed me against a locker. "You think you can just go running into school like an asshole, crashing into whoever you want?" He raised a fist.

I closed my eyes. Was the bear actually going to attack this time? This was going to suck—a black eye for sure, maybe worse. But if there's one thing I've learned from my many hours of playing video games, it's that there is nothing to fear in defeat. You just respawn at the last checkpoint.

And anyway, getting beaten up would totally get me out of school for the day, which meant another day to prepare my presentation. Ignoring the possibility of permanent brain damage, maybe getting punched in the face wasn't such a terrible idea.

It never happened, though. Instead, Amanda Blake spoke up.

"Oh, quit being so cliché, Chazz."

My eyes flew open. Amanda had grabbed Chazz's arm, and he slowly lowered it, scowling first at me and then at her. "Stay out of this," he mumbled at her under his breath.

I looked at Amanda in sheepish surprise. Why was she taking my side? She barely knew me, and Chazz was her boyfriend. But then I noticed that her eyes were a little red and her makeup was all smudged. Maybe they'd been fighting or something.

Maybe, I thought, just *maybe* this was my shot with Amanda. If they were breaking up, I could start laying the groundwork now.

"Hey, Amanda," I said. "You're in my English class,

right? Any chance you read that *House of Girth* thing? I've got my oral presentation this afternoon."

"Really?" She gave me a pitying look.

I shrugged. "Help a guy out?"

She sighed and rolled her eyes. "Listen," she said. "Just say something about women's place in society at the turn of the century, and maybe something about witchcraft. Crap like that. Ms. Moonbeam will eat it up."

Ms. Moonbeam was what everyone called our English teacher, Ms. Mueller, because she always wore those really long, flowy skirts and dangly earrings and was constantly talking about something called the "sacred feminine." Amanda was right—all I had to do was spout a bunch of stuff about fairies and goblets and Susan B. Anthony and our teacher would do backflips.

"Thanks," I said. "I'll get you back for it. Just let me know if—"

"Could you go now?" Amanda interrupted. "We're trying to have a *talk* here."

Then, for the second time that day, my stomach let out a freakishly loud rumble, this time even more extreme than the one in the car. Great.

"That's the last time I eat Mexican for breakfast," I said, giving my best shit-eating grin.

I thought it was at least worth a smile—maybe even a laugh—but Amanda folded her arms tighter and scowled. Chazz's face twisted into a furious mask—like I'd chosen to make my stomach growl as a deliberate insult to his dainty sensibilities. This time he grabbed me by my neck and swung me against the locker.

"Did you not hear her, retard? She told you to fuck off."

"Mr. Slade, please unhand Mr. Stephens."

Chazz and I both jumped. Neither of us had heard Assistant Principal Hardwick creeping up on us. That's the way it went with Hardwick; she was gnome-size and ninja-like. There were jokes about her springing out from within lockers to accost unsuspecting kids. Legend had it that Hardwick had once been headmistress at some all-girls Catholic boarding school upstate but had been banished for being too severe. Everyone knew she was really in charge at RRHS, steam-rolling hippie-dippy Principal Oakenfeld, who mostly stayed hidden in his office.

"Gentlemen"—Hardwick's voice was barely above a whisper as Chazz released me—"have we chosen fisticuffs instead of first period?"

I picked my book up off the floor and tried to slink away, but Hardwick's steely gaze held me in place. She glanced from me to Chazz and, when neither of us answered, turned toward Amanda.

"Ms. Blake, is the male gaze really worth such debasement?"

"Huh?"

Hardwick grabbed a pen out of her silver bun and poked Amanda right in the cleavage.

"If I had a check box for harlotry I would use it," said Hardwick, pulling out her pack of citations. "Instead, it will be tardiness."

I mouthed *harlotry* at Amanda, rolling my eyes, but she and Chazz just glared at me.

I stumbled into first-period biology a few minutes later, clutching my write-up, and saw that I'd gotten lucky for once. We had a substitute and were watching some documentary about the migratory patterns of fruit bats, narrated by Oprah Winfrey.

It was perfect for figuring out what the hell I was going to do about my Enid Wharton presentation. But the unlucky part is that for some reason Oprah's voice makes me very, very relaxed. I was asleep within five minutes.

By the time I slid into my seat in the cafeteria for lunch, my stomach was feeling even iffier than before. I was a little worried; I had made it this far in life without ever hurling in front of anyone except my parents and I really wanted to keep it that way.

"Yo, Jake," my friend Adam DeCarlo said. "Where's your head? You didn't pull another wake and bake, did you? We all know how that turned out last time."

"I'm fine," I said. "Just feeling a little queasy. And hungry, I guess."

"Your stomach's upset *and* you're hungry," repeated

Adam, smirking at me. "You're a mess."

I looked down at my plastic tray full of questionable cafeteria food. *Was* I hungry? That was the weird thing. I felt like I could puke at any second but I also felt like I could eat my own hand. In fact, I felt like I could eat anything except the meat loaf and fruit cup that were sitting right in front of me, both of which looked about as appetizing as the piece of week-old bologna I once found under my bed.

"Man," I said, shaking my head. "I think this *House of Mirth* presentation is stressing me out."

Our friend Henry Robinson dropped his tray on the table and slid onto the bench next to Adam. He looked me over and made a face, then turned to Adam.

"What's wrong with him?"

"Stressed out about some hilarious house presentation," replied Adam, shrugging. "That or possibly Ebola."

"Oh, cool," said Henry, and immediately moved on. "You guys want to help me hang these up after school?"

Henry opened a folder filled with MISSING flyers for his golden retriever, Falafel.

"What is with this town and missing dogs lately?" asked Adam, picking up one of the flyers. "It's like some voodoo cult is abducting them."

"Please, only positive thoughts for Falafel, guys," replied Henry, staring sadly at the photocopied picture of his panting dog.

"I'll help," said Adam. "Don't know about Jake, here. He looks like he might be keeled over by then."

"Falafel," was all I could manage. I put my head down on the cool surface of the cafeteria table.

Adam and Henry quickly lost interest in me and started a discussion about things you can eat to make your pee smell really bad. It's a topic I normally would have been interested in, but I tuned them out and tried to make myself focus on *The House of Mirth.*

Instead of suddenly coming up with a brilliant presentation topic, I was distracted by my aching stomach. And I don't know why, but it somehow reminded me of this girl Janine. I saw her face in my mind and then I was remembering the night a month ago that I'd met her at the Black Bolt.

My parents had been out of town that night and Kelly had gone to some seventh-grade kegger at her friend Annika Golden's house, and after sitting around for an hour drinking 40s, listening to old Captain Beefheart LPs, and feeling like real losers, Adam and I had decided it was time to actually do something fun for once.

So we'd taken the bus to this dive bar in Princeton called the Black Bolt, where Adam had heard they never carded. We just figured we'd have a couple of beers, see what kind of trouble we could get into.

The place was more crowded than we'd been

expecting. There was some dumb-ass band playing, and there were all these chicks with tattoos and little black glasses hopping up and down and rocking out like it was GWAR, even though the band sounded more like the kind of music my dad listened to while doing his crossword puzzles.

Adam was in heaven; he loves those alternative librarian types. Give him a girl with bangs, glasses, and a tight little cardigan and he goes nuts. I lost him within minutes of stepping into the place.

So I had a beer by myself, just hanging out at the bar, and then another, and after that I decided I was bored with warm Bud, so I ordered a piña colada. The bartender gave me a funny look but what's wrong with wanting a tasty frozen drink every now and then? I had nothing to apologize for.

Anyway, after I was done with that, I was feeling a little loopy, like I needed some air, and Adam was nowhere to be found. So I went outside and leaned against the brick wall next to the alley, just getting my bearings. I'd been standing there for about a minute when a girl slid right up next to me and lit a cigarette.

She was tall and curvy, in black jeans with a studded belt and a tank top. Both of her arms were covered in tattoo sleeves. Her hair was Kool-Aid red. She was actually kind of hot. I looked away; I didn't want her to think I was some creep.

"Hey," she said.

"Hey," I said.

"I'm Janine," she said.

"I'm Jake," I said.

"It's too much in there," she said. "I don't know what that band is but they need to grow a pair. It sounds like *Sesame Street* or something."

"Tell me about it." I paused, not sure what to say next. "Have you ever heard of The Puppy Bladders?"

"Nah," she said. "Cool name, though. You go to Princeton?"

"Uh, no," I mumbled.

"I was there for three semesters but it was, like, enough with the dead, white heterosexual men already. So boring. Now I have my own Etsy store selling crocheted pot holders with portraits of feminist heroes. I'm actually doing pretty well. The Tura Satana is my best seller. So where do you go?"

"Oh," I said. It dawned on me that I probably shouldn't tell her I was seventeen and in high school. "Um, Rutgers."

"Cool," she said. "That's, like, so much *realer* anyway."

I shrugged and smiled. Janine gave me a cocky pout and exhaled a cloud of smoke right in my face.

"So," she said. "Wanna come back to my place? It's just a couple of blocks from here."

"Um," I replied. I was about to come up with an excuse

when I realized I had no reason not to go. My parents were gone; Kelly was probably passed out in Annika's rec room until at least the next afternoon. There was Adam, yeah, but he could fend for himself. And the truth was, it had been a while since my ex-girlfriend, Sasha Tremens, had dumped me. Let's just say a little female company was long overdue.

"Sure," I said. "Let's go."

It was actually a good night. Janine was kooky, and her apartment was kind of scuzzy, but she wasn't all hung up and formal over the sex stuff, and we had fun. I was like, *So this is what being a grown-up is like.* For the first time, it seemed pretty cool.

There was only one thing. One stupid, fucking thing.

I hadn't worn a condom.

Ever since then, I'd been off-and-on paranoid that maybe I'd picked up an STD. There had been no dripping, no weird sores, but you never know. And now I had this crazy stomachache. But who's ever heard of a sex disease that gives you a stomachache?

Whatever it was, something was definitely wrong. I sat up straight, leaving a forehead-sweat imprint on the tabletop. I looked back over to Adam and Henry and realized I had no idea what they were saying anymore. They sounded like they were talking backward.

I was dizzy; my vision was a little fuzzy; the world had suddenly taken on a pinkish tinge. I made a mental note to look up the symptoms of syphilis when I got home.

And then a bunch of things happened all at once. There was an ear-piercing scream from across the room and when I looked up, a bunch of Amanda Blake's bobblehead friends had all stood up from their usual lunch table and were staring at something. Then there was another scream, but this time it was low and rumbly.

No. It wasn't a scream. It was a roar.

"Holy fucking shit," Adam said. His voice sounded garbled and far away and I couldn't tell what he was talking about. Everything was moving in slow motion and then the bobbleheads weren't staring anymore, they were running for the door, pushing one another out of the way, jumping over empty chairs.

That's when I saw it too. Amanda Blake was hunched like an animal on the floor next to the table. She was eating something, devouring it really, snarling and spitting. The something looked an awful lot like Amanda's best friend, Cindy St. Clair. I could tell from the twitching red soles of the designer heels she was always bragging about.

Or at least, I think that's why they were red.

Blood was squirting everywhere, and now everyone was screaming and racing for the exit, and the thing eating Cindy stood up and it looked like Amanda Blake gone totally rancid.

She was standing there, swaying on her feet, seeming unsure of what to do next. Her face was gray and dried out, like it was covered in one of those mud masks Kelly's always doing, except where the mask cracked, thick, dark blood oozed out.

She roared again, then dove for another girl who was cowering a few feet away, and plunged her fingers right into the girl's stomach, ripping out a big chunk of flesh that she began to chow down on.

"Dude," Adam said, grabbing my arm. "Come on! We have to get the hell out of here."

My stomach growled yet again, and then Adam's eyes widened in shock. He dropped my arm and began to back slowly away from me.

"There's another one!" someone shouted, pointing at me. I didn't know what that meant and I didn't care. My head was throbbing, and my vision had completely clouded with red. I felt a weird emptiness in my chest and realized that my heart had stopped beating. When I looked back up at Adam, who was a few feet from me now, still steadily backing away, all I could think about was how tasty he looked. How satisfying it would be to rip into one of his fleshy biceps and finally have a decent meal.

Apparently, that's exactly what I did.

CASS

ABOUT A MONTH AGO, I STARTED DEVELOPING THIS theory that the zombies were evolving. The gore-drenched scenes my unit of the Necrotic Control Division responded to didn't seem as messy as they once had. The dismembered limbs, the arterial blood spray, the chewed-up faces—they started seeming neater somehow, like the zombies were taking greater care with their eating habits. Not exactly tying bibs on and putting down tablecloths, but not totally savage either.

Eventually, I realized it wasn't the zombies that

were evolving. It was *me.* I was getting used to the job. The gore was starting to look normal.

I work for the government, hunting down zombies, keeping the public safe and unaware. Most people my age work after school at the Gap or at Cinnabon, and I can't say that doesn't sometimes appeal to me.

Then again, I already know what that's like. Before all this started, I was a hostess at an Italian chain restaurant on Carmel Mountain Road, which is not as appetizing as it sounds, and it was basically the worst. They had rats in the kitchen, everyone was always slobbering for refills on their endless salad, and one time my manager grabbed my butt. So maybe this job isn't actually so bad, even if I'm a little worried it's turning me into the poster girl for desensitized teenagers.

At least I'm helping out with this whole zombie thing that's happening—even if most people don't know about it. There's a big map of the country in the Washington command center covered in little red lights that blink on whenever there's a known zombie attack. I take way more pride in snuffing out those lights with my team than I ever took in slinging garlic bread sticks. And besides, our team leader, Harlene, keeps promising me that we'll kill them all soon and I'll get to go home . . . at which point I better not have to go back to the land of endless breadsticks.

My team got to New Jersey about an hour after the

zombie attack happened. Harlene went to the high school first, along with our combat specialist, Jamison, to make sure the scene was clear of any undead threats. In most cases, especially if it's a first-time necrotization, the zombie just hangs around the scene afterward, wondering what the hell happened and what they have stuck in their teeth. That is, if they ate enough to get their heart beating again. Either way, that's when our guys show up with guns and pick them off.

No such luck at Ronald Reagan—our zombie had peaced out. In cases like that, we send in the quarantine team. They round up witnesses, talk to the local cops, and basically make sure nothing slips through the cracks. We don't want to start a nationwide panic, right?

And then, finally, there's me and Tom, the investigation side of our unit. We aren't even combat trained and weren't going to be blowing any heads off, so we had a little more room to dawdle on the way.

This time we stopped at the Wawa for magazines, and then got cheesesteaks at this place Tom had read about on some foodie website. But then we were running *really* late, so Tom said we could turn on the siren, which I always love, and we made it to the zombie site before anyone noticed we were slacking.

Tom was busy checking out the rest of the school while I tried to get a read on the cafeteria. It was a disaster, really. I had to step over a girl with her face chewed off and skip around a puddle of entrails just to get to the Pepsi machine. Yuck. But I was really thirsty after that cheesesteak.

Gore aside, it was weird being back in a high school again. Minus the blood and the corpses it could have been my old school back in San Diego: same long, folding tables with the fake wood veneer, same weird gray light reflecting off the tiles. That chicken-nugget-and-milk smell that even the stink of fresh guts couldn't totally cover up.

I popped a couple dollars in the Pepsi machine and pressed a button. The machine beeped and blinked: INSERT .50. Seriously? Two fifty for a Diet Dr Pepper?

The last time I'd been inside a high school, I was just a regular student. I had friends; I got okay grades; I dated this guy named Jason Roth for two weeks before he dumped me for some annoying girl with a nose ring.

Then one day, these people in suits came and everyone had to take these weird aptitude tests where you had to guess what pictures were drawn on the back of cards. It seemed like a complete joke except for the fact that I got every one right. Every single one, and I wasn't even trying.

They hadn't told us what the tests were about or why they were doing them. But the next week, a bunch of people from the military—big shots, in uniforms with medals and stuff—were at my house making my mom sign all these forms releasing me to their care.

They started throwing around the word *telepath* a lot.

I'm not supposed to reveal this, but my mom also received a phone call from the *actual* president of the United States, telling her how patriotic she was and how special I am, and how much good I'm going to do for the country. And I'm *really* not supposed to reveal this part, but there's a special, secret Executive Order just for me. Because normally you're not allowed to join the military if you're under eighteen.

Next thing you know, I'm waving good-bye to my mom and my big sister and getting my official NCD field uniform and going to this training camp with a bunch of grown-ups who weren't nearly as good at the whole mind-reading thing as me. And now here I am: seventeen, the youngest official high-clearance US military operative of all time. I've been doing it for about a year and a half, but it feels like a lot longer. I don't even remember the name of the girl with the nose ring.

Sometimes I do miss my mom and my sister, though.

Anyway, you can't think about that stuff. I was thirsty. I sighed and dug through the pocket of my contamination suit for a couple quarters and popped them into the machine. When Tom stumbled in, I was sitting at a cafeteria table—one of the ones that wasn't all gross—drinking my Diet Dr Pepper. I couldn't help but laugh when he burst through the door and nearly tripped over a corpse, steadying himself just in time to avoid flying face-first into a puddle of blood.

Tom refuses to wear the contamination jumpsuit, and today was sporting a skinny black tie and a designer suit that was cropped a little at the ankles to show off his hot-pink paisley socks. I'm always telling him to just wear the stupid containment suit or at least dress down; one drop of blood on those socks and they'll be ruined. They're probably cashmere. But he never listens to me.

I can see why he hates the jumpsuit, I guess, but I think I look good in it. It's that Ellen Ripley, *Alien* look. Sexy but tough.

"Whoa," Tom said, taking a digital camera out from inside his jacket as he surveyed the carnage. "This is pretty bad."

"Yeah," I replied. "Harlene said she thinks it's the highest body count she's ever seen."

Tom shrugged, snapping a pic of the nearest body. "I don't know. There was that football game back in Cleveland last year. That one was bad too."

"Not this bad," I said. "Nothing like this." I chugged my soda. "There's got to be twenty dead. Thirty? It's hard to even tell."

"Yeah, it's a doozy. Considering how many exits there are in here I'm surprised so many of 'em got chomped."

"Harlene and Jamison are out on the football field," I said. "I guess our zombie dropped leftovers all the way out there."

"Dropped leftovers," repeated Tom, shaking his head

and giving me a reproachful look. "Who are you? Quit sitting around being morbid and get a handle on this thing, will ya?"

I'd been putting off my work with my Diet Dr Pepper, but with Tom here, it was time to get down to it. It'd be easier while the corpses were fresh anyway.

I bit my lip and scanned the room.

It's not that the bodies and blood don't bother me. All the death. You get used to it, but it never gets cute. And there was something about this scene that was particularly rough. Maybe it was just the fact that the victims were my age. They were like me. Could've been me. But the only way to do a job like mine is to put all that stuff aside.

A few feet away from me, a girl was dead on the floor. She was relatively unmaimed—just a few bites taken out of her here and there—but one of them caught the carotid artery and that was it for her.

I looked at her face, studying it. It feels more respectful to the dead not to let yourself get too grossed out by the way they look, so I try to think of them the way they were before. I can usually see it pretty clearly if I focus a little, even when they're totally torn up. This one wasn't so hard to imagine alive. She had a few splotches of acne around her chin and forehead, but she was pretty, with dark hair and big blue eyes. She looked like someone I could have been friends with. You know, in our past lives.

I reached into her pocket and pulled out her phone.

It was a crappy old flip phone. I wrapped my fingers tight around it and closed my eyes.

Then the real details started coming. Even dead, the girl's psychic residue was still here. Her name was Sarah. She'd just gotten her driver's license. (Lucky her—I still don't have one.) She had two younger brothers and she loved pizza.

That part was a little depressing. Who loves pizza so much that they leave a mental imprint about it when they die?

On the other hand, I shudder to think about what my own deathprint would look like, so I guess I shouldn't be so judgey. Considering that these days I have no life of my own, the inside of my head probably just looks like a bunch of clips from movies.

I pushed past Sarah's love of pizza, looking for something more relevant to the situation. It took a little digging but then I saw the whole scene through Sarah's eyes. Right before she died. It was like watching a horror movie with someone else's annoying play-by-play narration dubbed over the action.

Everyone's running. I should be running. Is that the fire alarm? Is there a fire too? What if I run into a fire? I just have to get to the door and—

Oh god. There she is.

Just turn and run. Do it now! No. Him too? Oh my god. Oh my god!

I looked up at Tom. "There were two."

Tom stopped photographing corpses and looked over at me. "Two?"

"Two zombies."

He let out a whistle and his eyes widened. "Now *that's* interesting. Two zombies don't usually necrotize at the exact same moment. Quite a coincidence."

"Yeah, I know," I said. "I've been doing this as long as you have, remember?"

Tom rolled his eyes. "Simmer down, Psychic Friend. I'm just saying."

Tom's nickname for me is Psychic Friend, which supposedly has something to do with some old TV commercial. I never really got it. But Tom *is* pretty much my only friend.

It's a little weird: one, because he's about fifteen years older than I am. Two, because taking care of me is basically his job. Tom's a smarty-pants; he was a medical examiner in some small town when the CIA recruited him, his double major in forensics and behavioral psychology making him ideal for work with psychics. He spent a couple years doing research in psychometrics before the NCD came along and assigned him to be my official military liaison, which is partly how they got away with drafting me when I was sixteen. Sure, he's supposed to document the carnage for further study of zombie-eating habits or whatever, but his main job seems to be making sure that I'm not losing it.

Sometimes I wonder if he just pretends to be my friend because it's his job, and he feels sorry for me. But then I remember that time we watched *Terms of Endearment* together and both cried at the same parts. That has to count for something, right?

I stood, left Sarah, and walked across the room to a green backpack that lay soaking in a puddle of blood. Sometimes objects almost seem like they have a personality—at least to me—and I could feel the backpack trying to talk to me somehow. I know that makes me sound completely crazy, but if you ever develop psychometric powers you'll understand.

I knelt by it, touched my palm to the JanSport logo, then unzipped it.

"Anything good in there?" Tom asked. "In suburbs like these I bet all the kids do their homework on iPads."

"Sorry, dude. Just this," I said, pulling out an old copy of *The House of Mirth*.

Tom made a face. "No thank you."

"No, it's good," I said. "I read it for summer reading once. It'll make you think twice before you ever go work in a hat shop."

"Damn. There goes my secret life's ambition. After killing zombies, of course."

Before I could say anything else, things started spinning. The book was linking me to someone else.

Stupid Edith Whoreton. I'm never going to finish this presentation. Janine, man, she was hot. Why am I so hungry? Brains. Delicious brains. Wait. What?

Oh shit. Are my hands turning blue? No . . . gray. Weird. Why is Adam yelling? What's his problem? Oh shit, Adam looks so tasty.

Hungry.

Eat.

When I came back to my own mind, Harlene had joined Tom, and Jamison stood a few feet off, watching the containment team as they started zipping kids into body bags. He was in his special battle armor that covered him from chin to toe in lightweight plates of superdurable metal and pierce-resistant fiber. He was scowling as usual, probably disappointed he didn't get a chance to use the shotgun slung over his shoulder. Even for a guy that ordinarily communicates in grunts, Jamison was being especially quiet.

Harlene and Tom stood over me, watching me expectantly.

"Hey, Sweet Pea. What'd ya see?" Harlene asked in her sugary drawl. Like Jamison, she was dressed for a fight: a handgun hanging from one hip and a sheathed machete from the other. She's probably the world's only former Miss Georgia Peach with flawless marksmanship and a penchant for really big knives.

Still, even though Harlene's been a trained government killer for almost twenty years, some habits die hard. She may spend her life lopping the heads off zombies, but she never goes into battle without a full face of makeup.

Sometimes right after I have a flash like that I'm a little disoriented; I have trouble picking out the important details from the stupid ones. So as I recall what I've just seen I spend a lot of time telling them about *The House of Mirth* and some missing golden retriever. My team listened patiently as I muddled through; we've worked together long enough that they all know this is how it goes.

When I was done, Harlene's eyes were cold and resolute. "Two of 'em!" she said. "Let's hope they stick together, make things easy-peasy. Okay, baby girl. Find me the bastard."

Clutching the book, I started to reach out with my mind, across New Jersey, past the strip malls and the power lines and the landfills, through the messy web of highways and into the grid of the suburbs. I skimmed over the echoes of thoughts I heard, floating past half-frosted windows of lives I could peek into if I wanted to. But I didn't.

There was only one person I was looking for.

And I would find him.

JAKE

"JAKE! C'MON, MAN!" I WAS LYING ON THE GROUND, and Amanda Blake was shaking me.

The first real thought I had was, *Dude, Amanda Blake knows your name.*

The second thought I had was, *What the hell is going on?*

I didn't know where we were or how we'd gotten there. I didn't know why I was with Amanda Blake either, although for some weird reason, I wasn't really surprised by it.

I sat up on my elbows and looked around. Amanda

and I were in a parking lot somewhere.

The sun was bright, the sky that rippling, swimming-pool color, and we were surrounded on all sides by barbed wire and chain-link fence. The view in every direction was blocked by warehouses and crappy, low-slung industrial buildings. Little brown weeds were poking up through the cracks in the concrete.

Amanda was standing over me, glancing nervously over her shoulder every few seconds. "Listen," she said. "We have to get the hell out of here. Now."

I stood too. "Um," I said. I felt weird talking to her like we were friends or whatever. My head was pounding. "Where are we? How did we get here?"

She looked at me impatiently. "Think," she said.

I thought. Then I thought some more. I rubbed my tongue over my teeth and found they still had that satisfying Hawaiian Punch stickiness to them. I shrugged.

"I dunno. What?" I asked. Just as the words were out, I let loose a huge belch. Gross. What was that taste? My stomach had really been acting up today.

Then I remembered.

I mean, sort of remembered. It was like remembering a dream, or remembering a movie your parents let you stay up late to watch when you were really little but you kept falling asleep.

Still. Even *sort of* remembering was bad enough.

"Holy shit," I said.

Amanda didn't say anything. She just nodded, like, *Uh, yeah.*

I sat back down, and put my head in my hands. "Holy shit," I said again. "Did that really happen?"

"Well, if you remember it and I remember it . . ." Amanda said.

"Okay, so wait. Is what *you're* remembering something that has to do with us turning into monsters and eating all of our friends?" I asked. I was rubbing my forehead, squinting to keep the sun out of my eyes. I felt a little faint.

"Bingo," Amanda said.

My heart sank. "What the fuck is going on?"

"A better question," Amanda said, "is whether we really want to *know.*"

I looked at her like she was nuts. "Of course we want to know," I said. "Something truly fucked up just happened here. I want some answers."

Amanda sighed and looked down at her red tank top. I had a vague recollection that it had been white when I'd seen her earlier. "Ugh, I'll never get this blood out," she mumbled to herself.

"Boo-hoo," I said. "Maybe you still have the receipt somewhere. Forget that! What do you think happened?"

She opened her mouth to speak, but hesitated. "You're going to think I'm crazy."

I stared at her. "Amanda. We're in a strange parking

lot covered in blood. I'm pretty sure any explanation has to be crazy."

Amanda tossed her hair and looked me right in the eye. "Fine," she said, all matter-of-fact, "I think we're zombies."

She stared at me, waiting for me to respond. I stared at her, waiting for the punch line.

"Okay," I finally said when it was obvious that there wasn't going to *be* a punch line. "You're insane. I don't know what the hell is going on here, but you're crazy and I'm going back to school to figure out what happened." I stood up again and began to dust myself off.

"Just listen," Amanda said. "It seems crazy to me too, but then again, here we are, covered in blood, with weird bits of food in our teeth. And I don't know about you, but I *always* brush after lunch." For the first time, I looked down at my own shirt. Like Amanda's, it was so soaked with blood that you couldn't tell what color it had been originally.

"Yeah, well . . ." I said.

"Look," Amanda said, "my older brother talks about creepy stuff like this all the time. . . ."

"Is your brother really into *Resident Evil*?" I asked.

"No," she said. "I don't know what that is. What he *is* really into is conspiracy theories and this crazy radio show called *Coast-to-Coast AM*."

"Is that like Rush Limbaugh?"

"It's like Rush Limbaugh if Rush Limbaugh believed in UFOs and the Illuminati and that the United States was secretly being overrun by an out-of-control zombie menace."

"Um," I said, "Rush Limbaugh might believe those things."

Amanda rolled her eyes. "The point *is*, my brother's been saying for at least a year that zombies are real and the government's covering them up. He's convinced that the reason Aunt Ellie in Colorado Springs stopped sending us birthday checks is because she's one too. Well, either a zombie or eaten by zombies; he can never make up his mind which it is."

"Uh," I said. "Okay? So you're crazy *and* your brother's crazy. I don't see what that proves, except that insanity runs in families."

Amanda shrugged. "Do you have any better theories?" she asked. I tapped my chin and gave it some actual thought.

"Vampires?" I ventured.

Amanda pointed up at the midday sun. "We're not bursting into flames, dummy. Or glittering."

"But look," I countered, deciding I would humor her for now. "Zombies aren't real. Vampires, maybe–zombies, no. Even if there was such a thing as zombies, we aren't them. I've watched a lot of zombie movies. A *lot* of zombie movies. Sure, zombies eat people, but they also turn other people into zombies. And there are always, like, thousands of them. I don't totally remember what happened, but there were just two of us today. And do we look like zombies to you? Zombies walk around with their arms all—" I stretched my arms out in front of me and made a zombie face, then dropped them again and relaxed.

"See?" I said. "Not zombies!"

But then I looked at my arms again and shuddered, suddenly picturing them gray and rotting. And was that blood caked under my fingernails?

Amanda and I just looked at each other. We didn't say anything. Then something occurred to me. I slapped my forehead.

"Fuck! My *House of Mirth* presentation! That's twenty-five percent of my grade! It would be one thing if I got an F, but a *zero*?"

Amanda groaned like, *You've got to be kidding me,* which I guess is understandable. Let's just say I was having a hard time wrapping my head around all this shit.

"I wouldn't worry too much about your high school transcript at this point," she said. "I think both of our chances of getting into Harvard just went out the window."

"Maybe if I did a couple years at community college first . . ."

"More like a couple years in prison. Or life in prison. Or worse."

I stared at her, mouth hanging open stupidly.

"Jake, we just killed, like, a ton of people. What do you think—that they're going to send you to juvie for that, like that creepy kid Frank who set the janitor's closet on fire?"

"Technically, I don't think what we did was our fault," I said weakly.

"Yeah, that's a good one. Maybe your parents can find a lawyer who specializes in the zombie defense. But I'm getting the fuck out of here. And I think you should come." She held her hand out for me. I didn't take it.

I pictured my mom crying in the front row of a courtroom while I stood before a judge wearing one of those scary powdered wigs—because apparently my court fantasies take place in England—banging his gavel and declaring me guilty of, like, eighty counts of cannibalism.

Amanda walked over to the gate at the edge of the parking lot. She rattled it, forced it open, and peeked out. "Come on," she said. "Coast is clear. Seriously, we have to keep moving." She turned, put her hand on her hip, and waited for me to follow her.

At that moment, I realized that I had never really looked at Amanda Blake before. Okay, obviously I had *looked* at her—whenever I possibly could—but the thing about her is you never got the chance to look too closely. You checked her out from the corner of your eye in class, and you glanced at her in profile when she walked down the hall, but you never really got a good look at her.

But now it was just me and her and I didn't have a choice except to really see her, and fuck, was she beautiful. Even covered in blood she was more beautiful than I'd ever even realized.

The sun was shining on her hair; her eyes were sparkling. Her makeup had mostly come off—other than a little bit of smeared eye-whatever—and she was biting on her lower lip nervously as she waited for me. She looked like something out of some painting, like one of those ones by one of those artists. Whatever, I'm not an art guy.

"Jake!" Amanda snapped her fingers in a circle around her face. "Come. On!"

I didn't really want to follow her. Or, I did want to follow her, but I didn't want to leave this parking lot. I wanted us both to stay here. It seemed safe, and I still wasn't feeling like myself. Would it be such a bad thing to rest here forever?

Tired of waiting for me, Amanda was already moving, though. So I jogged after her into the street.

The block outside the lot was desolate and abandoned, the kind of area that seems dead and colorless until you notice a little piece of electric-blue tape on a broken window or a moldy baby sock in a gutter. A faded red pickup truck sat a few feet away, its back wheels wedged on the curb. *Uh, nice parking job, loser.*

Then I looked down at my feet. There was a bloody

corpse lying there, mangled and barely recognizable. Its ears were ripped off and this pinkish sludge was dripping from where they should have been. The weird part was that it wasn't even gross to me. I mean, it was disturbing, but it didn't make me want to puke or anything.

"Did we do this?" I asked.

Amanda glanced at the body, but her face didn't register any emotion. She stepped right over it like it wasn't even there, not saying anything. She was just going to pretend it didn't exist.

I followed her lead. It was too much for me to handle anyway.

"So, maybe an obvious question, but how did we get here?" I asked. "I actually have no idea where we are. The last thing I remember we were in the cafeteria, and, you know. Everything went sort of fuzzy after that."

"Yeah," Amanda said. "For me too. I remember chasing someone across the football field. . . ."

A flash of memory came back to me. "It was Henry! Oh man, Henry . . ."

I could only remember bits and pieces of what happened that afternoon, like once I'd gone zombie—if that's really what happened—my mind had just shut down. What parts I could remember, like chasing a screaming Henry across the football field, seemed like a really bad dream.

"I think we climbed up the hill behind the field and

got onto the road behind the school," said Amanda, her face scrunched up as she tried to remember. "Did we run here?"

I pointed down at the dead guy. "Did we chase this guy?"

Amanda looked at the body, finally acknowledging him. "Bad luck, I guess."

In the distance, a siren wailed. Were they coming for us? Amanda and I both stopped talking, listening until the siren faded into the distance.

"Whatever happened," said Amada, "we can't hang around here. The cops'll be looking for us. We need to go on the run."

"The thing is I'm sort of tired," I said. "We might've run from school when we were all undead and whatever, but I don't know how far I can run *now.* I'm not exactly your boyfriend the genetic specimen here."

"Pfft," Amanda said. "We're not going to actually *run* run. We're going to drive. Duh."

Drive. In a car. I felt a twinge of pain in my heart as I thought about my own car. No, fuck it—a pain in my *soul.* Would I ever see my beloved Honda Civic again?

"Drive in what?" I asked.

"In the car we're going to steal." Amanda seemed oddly pleased with herself at the suggestion.

She waltzed over to the red pickup truck—a Chevy Silverado, I noted from the insignia on the fender—pulled a bobby pin out of her hair, and jiggled it in the lock for all of thirty seconds before the door popped open.

"Ta-da," she said. I was standing there dumbfounded, but Amanda had already slid into the driver's seat like it was no big deal and was fiddling with something under the dashboard. The engine turned over and the car began to hum. "Bet you didn't know I knew how to do that, huh?"

Uh, no.

"Well?" she said. "Come on!"

I hesitated for a second, but then I heard a distant thrumming sound. A helicopter. And it was getting louder.

Amanda heard it too: her eyes went right to the sky. "You drive," she said, hopping over the gearshift into the passenger's seat. "I hate driving stick."

I'm not much of a stick man myself but there wasn't time to argue. The whirring noise was pounding in my head and I could see the helicopter approaching as a speck in the distance. It was growing closer by the second. I jumped in the car, shifted into gear, and tore off, the engine balking.

"Where should I go?" I sputtered, suddenly panicking as I sped down the block, fumbling with the gearshift.

"I don't know!" Amanda said. "Anywhere! Just make it fast."

I still had no idea where I was, much less which way

I should turn or where I should head. But there was no slowing down now.

So I floored it straight past the warehouses, slamming through stop signs. There were no cars on the streets anyway; whatever part of town we'd found ourselves in was all but abandoned.

The *chop-chop-chop* sound was basically overhead now. I heard a screech of tires and glanced in the rearview mirror. A black SUV was bearing down on us. Shit! Where did that come from? I pumped the gas and shifted up. Were we seriously in a *car chase*? I looked over at Amanda and her face was expressionless. She was just staring straight ahead, gripping the side of her seat, white-knuckled.

The helicopter was screaming, and the SUV was gaining on us fast, way better suited to high-speed chases than this clunker Amanda had picked out. All its windows were tinted so I couldn't see inside, but whoever was driving was real serious about running us down. If I let them catch us, I had a feeling what happened next would be a lot worse than red-faced judges in powdered wigs.

"Fuck, fuck, fuck!" I said, slamming on the brakes to bang a left down an alley.

Amanda turned to me.

Her face had gone pale. "Um," she said. "I'm, like, kind of *hungry*."

CASS

TOM SNAPPED HIS FINGERS IN MY FACE. "HEY. WHERE are you?"

The literal answer was that I was strapped into the backseat of our tricked-out NCD SUV as Jamison swore to himself and bore down on our targets. But that's not what Tom wanted to know. He was really asking, *Whose head are you in?*

Tom knows me well enough by now to recognize when I've checked out of my body to take a spin around the astral plane.

Let me describe it this way: every mind has a unique sort of signature that I can pick up on. The thoughts can definitely be ugly, but the minds themselves have a homey glow. They're beautiful and inviting. Even a letter-jacket douche that you'd swear would be completely brainless has a singular essence that calls out to me like a warm house after a day spent playing in the snow. Except once you're inside sipping hot chocolate, it's all boobs and beer pong.

It's not like that with zombies, though. Imagine tearing that warm house down and replacing it with a kitten graveyard. Their minds are cold, empty places. They don't have thoughts, just instincts, and usually only one of those: eat. It makes picking zombies out of the psychic crowd pretty easy, especially if I have a trail to follow.

The zombies I'm used to tracking tended to be of the rampaging and starving variety. We learned in training that the first necrotization lasts the longest, the zombie needing to eat early and often to feed the virus burning inside him. Usually, we were able to catch up with the zombies while they were still shambling around, hunting their second batch of victims.

Except it wasn't that way in Jake's mind. His mind was warm. Panicked, sure. But still a place where I wouldn't mind kicking my psychic feet up for a while.

"He's not like the other ones," I told Tom.

Jamison glanced at Tom. "What's she saying?"

"He feels alive," I explained.

Tom mopped at his forehead with an argyle pocket square. "You saw how much they ate back there. He's probably through the first stage already. Probably got his heart beating again. Until he turns again, he would seem almost human."

"Fuck that," growled Jamison. "They're far from human."

"He's thinking of the stars," I said, and slipped out of my skin and onto the astral plane.

Stop chasing us. Stop chasing us. Amanda doesn't look so good. I hope this car doesn't stall. I can't believe there's a fucking helicopter after us. This would be like four stars. I'm in a four-star chase!

"Oh, not *the* stars . . . stars! From *Grand Theft Auto*." I couldn't help but laugh. "Only a boy would be thinking about video games at a time like this."

Jamison stepped on the gas. "He isn't a boy."

Jake. His name was Jake.

Tom was giving me a funny look. "Maybe you should stay out of that zombie's brain for a while."

"Why? I'm trying to help."

"It feels, uh, inappropriate."

I realized that I'd just broken one of the unspoken rules of NCD: don't humanize the targets. Normally, it was easy. The zombies we encountered were more animal than human. All biting teeth and clawing fingers. Totally gross.

But Jake was the first one who was kind of cute. In that skuzzy James Franco sort of way. At least, that's how it felt like he should look based on the inside of his mind. I hadn't actually seen him in person.

Oh man. Get it together, Cass. He's a zombie. Don't check out the zombies.

Outside, we whipped past abandoned row houses.

I was used to speed; even when we weren't chasing zombies, Jamison liked to take advantage of his military credentials by going at least thirty miles over the speed limit.

Now he had us riding the back bumper of Amanda and Jake's stolen pickup truck. In a few seconds, we'd plow right through them.

Harlene's voice drawled from our dashboard communicator. "Jamison, honey, stand down now."

"Are you kidding?" he replied. "I've got them."

"Need I remind you that you've got noncombat personnel on board? Your orders are to pursue but not engage. Plenty of time for that later. Containment's already got a mess to clean up at the school. We don't need another big public brouhaha."

Jamison slowed the SUV. Tom glanced over at me, looking relieved. I smiled back—I can't say I was really looking forward to running these two kids off the road and watching Jamison blow their brains out, zombies or no. I mean, it had to happen eventually, obviously, but I didn't want to watch. Hello? Noncombat personnel here.

Jamison turned off the communicator.

"What're you doing?" asked Tom.

In answer, Jamison raised a middle finger toward the sky, where Harlene floated in the safety of her helicopter.

He floored it.

"Jamison?" asked Tom, his voice a little shaky. "What the hell?"

"You saw what they did back there," said Jamison, his voice cold and determined. "You want to leave them on the loose so they can do it again?"

Our SUV rumbled forward, closing in fast on the pickup once again. It didn't take psychometric powers to know what Jamison had planned.

"He's going to ram them," I said.

Tom looked stricken. "You heard Harlene! We're not combat authorized!"

"Then stay in the fucking car," growled Jamison.

Jamison nudged the back of the pickup just enough to send it spinning out of control, careening to a stop wrapped around a telephone pole. Amazingly, he kept the SUV steady, like he'd run cars off the road at high speed a million times. We pulled up just a few yards from the wreck.

Jamison grabbed his shotgun and stepped into the street.

"Oh Christ," whispered Tom.

I watched as Jake staggered out of the pickup's cab, blinking and disoriented. He was checking on the girl when he saw Jamison striding toward him. *Run, you idiot,* I thought, then grimaced as I realized I was rooting for a zombie. What was wrong with me?

Instead of running, Jake put his hands up.

"Whoa, dude," I heard him say. "Read me my rights."

Jamison shot him in the stomach.

Oh, Jamison. Always go for the head shot. It's the first lesson in NCD training, even for personnel like Tom and me. But Jamison had a reputation. He never made it easy.

Tom turned the communicator back on. "Harlene? We're, um, engaging."

"I see that," came her icy reply.

Jamison stood over Jake, pumping his shotgun. I wanted to look away, but I couldn't—a small part of me was curious. As much time as I'd spent around their handiwork, I'd never actually seen a zombie killed before.

Then, the girl was on Jamison, grabbing him around the neck from behind. She was in what my instructors called the "transitional" phase of her zombie transformation, which is actually when they're at their most dangerous, with the heightened abilities of zombies but with traces of human intelligence. Jamison's armor was the only thing that saved him from Amanda plunging her painted fingernails right through his throat.

They spun in circles, her hands still around his

neck–once, twice–until Jamison's feet were off the ground. With his armor on, Jamison had to outweigh her by at least two hundred pounds.

She let go and Jamison soared across the street, shattering a graffiti-covered phone booth. I wondered if we were responsible for destroying a historic landmark.

Tom frantically tapped my arm.

Beautiful Corpse Girl was looking in our direction.

The zombies are stronger and faster than us. After the necessity of head shots, that's the next thing they teach you at NCD training.

At the end of our first week of top-secret Washington zombie camp, our instructor hustled us dozen trainees into an elevator and brought us down to one of the building's classified subbasements.

The levels of the facility we'd been restricted to until then–where we sat in classrooms and listened to instructors drone on about zombie physiognomy and precognitive theory–were totally Dunder Mifflin, all cubicles and conference rooms and flickering fluorescent lighting.

But the subbasement? That was full-on *X-Files.*

Our instructor turned us over to a man in a bow tie and wire-rimmed glasses. I'd never seen him before, but by the way our instructor deferred to him and avoided direct eye contact, I could tell he was some kind of boss.

He was tall and thin, probably middle-aged but with one of those baby faces that made his age hard to peg, his jet-black hair combed into a severe side part. Mr. Bow Tie led us down a long, brightly lit corridor, through steel-reinforced doors accessible only by retinal scanners. He looked excited, like a little kid coming home to show Mom what he made in art class.

At the end of the hall, he ushered us into a dark little room. We crowded around in front of a wall of one-way glass that looked into a brightly lit padded cell.

And that's where I saw my first real, live zombie.

He was naked. That's what I noticed first, which I know is stupid, but I hadn't been expecting to see a nude middle-aged man that afternoon. He was hairy and dumpy and looked like he could've been a mechanic or, like, a really lazy construction worker.

"This," announced Mr. Bow Tie, "is Subject Number Eleven."

Number Eleven didn't look like a zombie. He looked like a nude guy huddled in the corner of an empty room. Of course, he *was* absently chewing on the twitching body of a live chicken, so that was kind of a giveaway. But other than the brown feathers stuck to the chicken blood in his chest hair, Number Eleven just looked like a regular guy.

Mr. Bow Tie began lecturing. "Similar to rabies, although it acts much faster, the zombie virus has an incubation period of about one month. After that, the infected will necrotize for the first time. The body shuts down—it dies—except for the functions that the virus needs to feed. Once enough living flesh has been consumed—human flesh is best, although as you can see Number Eleven here has been subsisting on chickens—the heart restarts and the subject will appear human. Until it needs to feed again."

One of the trainees raised his hand. Mr. Bow Tie glanced in his direction.

"What's it called?" the trainee asked. "The virus?"

Mr. Bow Tie cocked his head at the trainee.

"We don't name things that don't officially exist," he replied as if this was obvious. "Any other questions?"

"Is there a cure?" asked one of the others.

"If there was," answered Mr. Bow Tie, "we wouldn't be down here, would we?"

The group went silent, all of us just staring at Number Eleven. He'd finished off the chicken, tossed it aside, and was curling up in a ball to sleep.

Mr. Bow Tie yawned. "We'll come back tomorrow, when things get interesting."

As promised, Mr. Bow Tie brought us back to the subbasement late the next day. Number Eleven had changed. And he had company.

This time, Number Eleven was definitely dead. Or, undead, I guess. His skin was the color and texture of oatmeal left out to cool. A chunk of flesh had fallen off his chest, revealing a piece of his yellowed rib cage.

A pair of scientists stood in the room with him. They had Number Eleven shackled to a treadmill that had to be running at its highest speed, but Number Eleven sprinted along, no problem. He moved faster than a corpse had any right to.

They had his arms tethered to resistance bands and from time to time he'd reach forward, causing the bands to snap taut.

He was reaching for a severed human hand they'd hung at the end of the treadmill. It was still dripping.

"We stopped feeding him yesterday," explained Mr. Bow Tie. "He's been in this undead state for just under three hours."

He turned to us.

"It's adrenaline that makes them turn," he explained. "When they get hungry, a survival instinct kicks in, not unlike when we humans find ourselves in mortal danger. That, combined with their paradoxical rate of cell degeneration and reconstruction, makes them far stronger and faster than us."

Mr. Bow Tie clasped his hands behind his back and watched Number Eleven with an almost wistful look. "Eventually, he'll tire if he isn't fed. In the meantime, he's quite the formidable opponent. . . ."

The zombie was a bit of a mindblower, sure, but what

really weirded me out was the severed hand.

Where had NCD gotten a freshly severed hand?

Mr. Bow Tie was looking right at me. He fixed me with a thin and unpleasant smile, like a teacher that had caught a student texting in class.

"Any questions?" he asked, still staring at me.

I shook my head in unison with all the other trainees.

They took us down to the subbasement every day after that to check in on Number Eleven. By the second day of starving and nonstop sprinting, he had gone from Danny Boyle Olympic athlete zombie to full-on George Romero shambler.

On the fifth day, Number Eleven was gone.

The point is that at first, when they start getting hungry, the zombies are scary strong. Which is why the cheerleader was able to pitch our refrigerator-size Special Forces–trained badass across the street, no problem.

"Harlene?" Tom was trying to keep his voice steady, likely for my benefit, and doing an altogether crappy job. "We're in some trouble here."

Above us, the *whip-whip-whip* of the helicopter had grown fainter.

"We're looking for a place to put down," replied Harlene. "Just get out of there, you hear? Don't look back."

"But–Jamison–"

"He's a big boy, Tom." Harlene's voice was stern.

"Jamison can take care of himself. You need to keep my Sweet Pea safe."

Tom started to clamber into the driver's seat, but recoiled with a yelp.

Amanda was right outside the window.

She looked down at her clenched fist, as if considering what to do with it. Then she took a swing at us. It wasn't even good form, but the punch shattered the window, spraying Tom with broken glass.

It didn't seem fair. Even halfway zombied-out, this girl still looked drop-dead. Her skin was just starting to go that congealed milk color; a gash from the accident above her immaculately plucked eyebrow had turned a rotten shade of purple. But I bet boys would still go crazy for it.

She wasn't quite in full eat-'em-up mode yet. Even if I could've shoved my way into her mind—which is never an easy task in an intense situation like this—I was too freaked to make contact. Even so, I could feel her mind out there. She was still thinking. That was good. Maybe I could get through to her, try to talk our way out of this situation.

She made a grab for Tom's neck, but he flung himself backward, pinning himself against the passenger door.

"Hey," I said. "It's Amanda, right?"

Amanda cocked her head, noticing me for the first time. A girl her age in an NCD jumpsuit. She squinted at me, like my being there didn't make any sense.

Her words were sort of slurred, the zombification taking over. "You're a kid," she said, trying to make sense of my presence along with, you know, the whole undead thing. "What the hell?"

I didn't know what to say. I didn't exactly have a plan. I was just trying to keep her mouth moving in a non-devouring way.

That's when the pay phone receiver smacked Amanda in the temple.

Jamison stood behind her, swinging the receiver by its metal cord.

"Come on, you zombie whore," he said. "Try me again."

I felt Amanda's mind shut off. She screamed, a feral noise that turned my blood cold, and lunged for Jamison.

He let her. She buried her teeth in the shoulder of his armor, her fingers scratching at his face.

I smelled burning hair.

Jamison had triggered his armor's zombie-defense system. Only a few of the front-liners, the ones most likely to get bitten in action, have it hardwired into the mesh of their armor. It's a concentrated burst of electricity for when a zombie gets too close. Like, teeth-in-shoulder close. The current shot across the surface of Jamison's armor, into Amanda. She sizzled, the tips of her blonde hair smoking. Her left eye popped, spilling in liquid form down her cheek.

I remembered this stupid trick my ex-sort-of-boyfriend Jason used to do when he'd take me on dates to the diner. He'd palm one of those plastic things of coffee creamer, hold it up to his eye, and stab it with a fork. This was just like that. Except for real.

Amanda fell back against the side of the SUV with enough force to rock the car. Tom grabbed my hand.

Jamison stood over her, the pay phone receiver still clenched in his fist, and started to punch her.

It's probably a good thing I couldn't see it happening. Hearing the bones in Amanda's face crunch under Jamison's blows was bad enough. I felt that afternoon's cheesesteak starting to crawl up my throat.

"Police brutality!" someone shouted.

I hadn't seen them come out of the row houses, but the sidewalks were suddenly filled with people. Watching us. An old lady with curlers in her hair aimed a beat-up camcorder at Jamison. I could imagine what this looked like to them. A huge man in a government truck massacring a couple of innocent teenagers.

"You leave that girl alone!" shouted one of the bystanders.

"Real cops are on the way!" yelled another.

Jamison rounded on the woman with the camcorder, pointing at her with the bloody phone. "You turn that fucking thing off!"

He didn't see Jake coming.

Like a hero out of those corny kung fu movies, Jake came flying in, jump-kicking Jamison right in the ribs. The force sent Jamison skidding to the sidewalk where the emboldened good Samaritans immediately tried to hold him down.

"Oh dear," Tom said. "We are in so much trouble."

Jake looked inside our SUV. I could tell he wasn't as bad off as Amanda in the zombie department. Other than the gaping hole in his abdomen, he still looked human. He looked at me, then down at his midsection. He waved at it with shaky hands.

"Does this look bad?" he asked.

I didn't know what to say. I nodded.

"Shit," he said, and lifted Amanda into his arms.

As I watched him run down the block, I couldn't help but wish someone would come carry me out of this mess.

JAKE

I RAN TRACK IN THE EIGHTH GRADE. NO LIE.

That was back when my parents could still guilt me into doing shit. So I showed up at practice a couple of times and ran some laps. Whatever.

Mostly, me and Adam DeCarlo used it as an excuse to sneak into the equipment room and get high. Those big, poofy mats they keep around for the pole-vaulters? Absolute bliss when you're stoned.

(Ugh, Adam. I'm sorry I ate you, man. I'm metaphorically pouring out some Mad Dog for you right now.)

But the reason I bring up my brief stint as a track participant is that, back then? Eighth grade? Pretty much the best shape of my life.

Yet there I was, carrying Amanda in my arms while hauling ass at a full sprint down the block. And I was doing it with a gaping hole in my stomach courtesy of Roadblock-from-G.I.-Joe back there.

That dude was not cool.

Amanda didn't look so good. Her body was cold in my arms, and she was all gray and rotten again like in the cafeteria, but worse than that was the half of her face that was pretty much smashed in, and the eyeball-cord thingy that dangled down her cheek.

But even though she was cold as ice and beaten to shit, she was still alive. She gurgled into my chest, making a guttural noise that reminded me of the sound my stomach had been making all morning.

Which reminded me that it now had a gaping hole in it. A gaping hole that for some reason wasn't bothering me at all. There wasn't pain; it just felt unnatural, like the breeze blowing over parts of my body that should never have been exposed. There's no accurate way to describe the feeling of open air on your large intestine.

And somehow, even without a stomach, I could feel my hunger coming back. My vision was starting to go crimson at the edges. But something told me this would be a really inconvenient time to lose control. I tried to focus.

I didn't even see the old man until he was standing right in our way, his hands held out.

"Son, you're hurt," he said. He had a deep and soothing voice like Morgan Freeman. "An ambulance is coming."

"Mister–" I started to tell him to get the hell out of my way, but then Amanda leapt away from me and wrapped her arms and legs around the old man like a freaking capuchin attack monkey.

He never knew what bit him.

I guess it was sort of a dick move to just let Amanda tear that poor dude to shreds. He was only trying to help and if not for him and the fuck-the-police attitude of this whole neighborhood we'd probably never have gotten away from Roadblock and his band of surprisingly young fascists. But, as I watched her tear off one of the old man's ears and try to jam her sucking lips into the bloody hole to get at the brain, all I felt was jealousy.

Not for the ear action the old man was getting. Come on. I wanted Amanda Blake but not that bad.

I was jealous of her getting to eat. It looked so good.

I was really considering getting down on my knees and joining her when a shotgun blast exploded behind us.

I turned to see that Roadblock had somehow gotten his weapon back and fired a warning shot in the air. The people that had bailed us out were scattering. He'd be coming for us soon, and I wasn't sure I could go another round.

In the distance, I heard sirens.

I looked down at my wound. My guts had started to turn gray. One of them was leaking this dark yellow pus, and I'm no doctor but that totally didn't look normal. Also, as I poked at a hanging flap of intestine, I noticed that the skin under my fingernails had turned a purplish black.

I wasn't exactly checking my pulse or anything, but I'm pretty sure my heart had started to beat slower. It should've been pumping like thrash metal considering how keyed up I felt, yet it was stuck on slow-jam R & B.

Basically, I wasn't sure how long I could keep it together. I was starting to figure out that this heart-stopping, dying thing was when we went total zombie. We needed to lam it.

"Amanda!" I shouted. "Come on!"

She replied by tearing one of the old man's fingers off at the knuckle and popping it in her mouth. Come on, if you're going to put us in mortal danger by pigging out, at least go for the meaty parts.

I tried whistling, a trick that used to work on my dog, but she ignored that too.

Finally, I just grabbed her around the waist and took off down an alley.

She struggled at first, trying to pull out of my grasp and go back for seconds. I was a little surprised that she didn't try to bite *me*. Maybe that was a testament to, like, our blossoming friendship or something.

Or maybe I just wasn't appetizing. I tried not to let that thought hurt my feelings.

As I ran with Amanda under my arm, her feet dragging along on the cracked alley beneath us, she turned her face up to mine. I could swear she was smiling, but that might've just been because her upper lip had fallen off, exposing a full row of her perfect teeth.

It seemed like some color was coming back to her face. I mean, don't get me wrong, she still looked very much like something I had just stolen from the mausoleum of hot chicks. Relatively speaking, she looked better. The fucked-up side of her head had regained some of its definition too. Still no eyeball, though.

Her healing like that—it couldn't be possible, right? It was probably just wishful thinking.

Amanda's mouth and cheeks were smeared with the old man's blood. I couldn't help myself; it looked so good, I bent down and licked it off.

"Stop . . . licking me," she gurgled.

I booked it through backyards. I hopped chain-link fences like some kind of champion hurdler, all with Amanda still slung under my arm. We passed an empty kiddie pool filled with broken electronic equipment. In one yard, a pair of snarling pit bulls made a lunge for us, but shied away, whimpering when they caught our scent. We needed a place to hide. And I needed something to eat.

Amanda fumbled at the side of her face with one of her hands, tugging on the cord that should've been connected to her eyeball.

"Oh no . . . my . . . my face," she babbled.

I got why she was upset. The hottest girl in school had just gotten her face bashed in. I'd be a little freaked out too. In one day she'd gone from having the world at her fingertips, able to make any dude melt with a look, to being a fugitive that was going to spend the rest of her life wearing one of those *Phantom of the Opera* masks.

I didn't have a ton of experience dealing with the fairer sex, but I'm not a total idiot either. I knew that you're supposed to, like, compliment them on what they're wearing and try to notice if they've gotten a haircut. I figured that still held true in a situation like this.

"Shh," I said, trying to sound soothing. "You look good. You can hardly notice it."

I'm not sure how many yards we ran through. Far enough that the sirens were lost to the distance and far enough that I was sure Roadblock couldn't possibly still be chasing us. It seemed like I'd been running forever and we were no closer to finding a place to hide. My hunger pangs were turning into hunger gongs.

Finally, I noticed an open basement window. It was the first one I'd seen that wasn't protected by metal bars.

I shoved Amanda through the opening and climbed in after her.

The basement was huge and smelled like the science wing at school on fetal-pig-dissection day. As my eyes adjusted to the dimness, I realized why.

We were in the basement of a funeral home.

One wall was covered in shelves containing all kinds of chemicals for the bodies, as well as makeup and perfumes—shit I figured might come in handy if we needed to cover up Amanda's face later.

In the corner next to the shelves was an old record player. *That's pretty cool,* I thought. If I was down here playing dress-up with dead bodies all day I'd want to have something to jam to.

In the center of the room were two metal slabs. One was empty, and on the other lay a peaceful-looking old lady in a pale flower-print dress. Probably somebody's grandma. Someone had been working on her recently, but quit before finishing. Half her face was pancaked in fresh makeup, the other looked uncomfortably similar to the splotchy gray skin on the backs of my hands.

Of course, Grandma immediately caught Amanda's attention. Before I could even think to stop her she was crawling on top of the body, sniffing her. Cautiously, she nibbled at the dead lady's forearm.

Amanda spit out the dead-lady meat and rolled onto the tile floor of the basement, curled into a ball, clutching her stomach and moaning.

I didn't know what the fuck to do. She rolled away from me when I tried to pat her back.

"Okay, calm down," I said. "Just stay here."

I left Amanda there and crept upstairs.

The basement opened up into the actual funeral parlor, like where they showcase the bodies for the crying families. I guessed this place would be getting a lot of business soon on account of what Amanda and I had done earlier.

Lucky for me there wasn't a funeral scheduled for that day. The parlor was empty except for rows and rows of folding chairs and the big pedestal thing where they put the coffin. I bet it would've really freaked people out if I'd come stumbling upstairs during an actual service. Do funerals have a money-back guarantee if they're interrupted by a wandering corpse?

I could hear the sound of a television tuned to the news. I went toward it.

On the other side of the parlor was a musty little apartment where the owners lived. What went wrong with their lives, you know? I mean, I guess someone has to be the funeral director and the dead-body makeover artist. That's cool, it's noble—like all the jobs no one wants to do. It's just not the kind of work I would want to bring home with me, much less live right on top of. Like, oh man, my commute is such a pain in the ass, I'm going to just start spreading makeup on these dead people in my basement now.

I know I shouldn't judge. Life can take some pretty twisted turns.

I walked past a cramped kitchen that smelled worse than the basement, then down a hallway where the walls were covered in framed photographs of children that were probably taken in, like, the Great Depression. I glanced into a bedroom and saw nothing but stacks of yellowing newspapers surrounding a twin bed.

Finally, I emerged into the living room.

Two people sat rapt, staring at the small, rabbit ears–style TV. They didn't even notice me come in.

The first was just a little mummy lady, wrinkled as all get-out. She was sitting in what had to be the world's creakiest rocking chair, a wool blanket tossed over her lap. She had both her hands covering her mouth, like she was shocked at something, and in the blue glow of the TV I could see the definition of her bones through the backs of her veiny hands.

The second was a middle-aged guy, probably son-of-the-mummy. He was chubby, wearing a black rubber apron and latex gloves, and still holding a pair of weird tong-type things. He was obviously the one who had been in the basement dolling up the corpse. His face was flushed. It looked like he'd run upstairs in a hurry.

On the TV, the news was in we-interrupt-this-program mode. The on-scene reporter looked like she was barely holding back tears. Behind her, some paramedics were carrying a gurney out of a building I sort of recognized. Suddenly, one of them broke away from the gurney and puked into the grass.

Then, I noticed the headline: SCHOOL SHOOTING AT RONALD REAGAN HIGH.

"Uh, what the fuck?" I said out loud.

Both the mortician and his mom turned to me with a start. The old lady pointed a shaky hand at the rotten hole in my stomach. The mortician held out his tongs in front of him like they could actually do something.

I could hear their hearts start to beat faster. Just as mine totally, like, stopped.

I was so hungry.

Then all I saw was red.

I woke up back in the basement, lying on the slab next to the dead lady that Amanda had tasted. The first thing that I noticed was the stairs and the thick trail of blood that dripped down them, ending in a sizable puddle beneath the last step. The blood was running toward me, into a drain positioned under the tables, the whole basement built on an angle to account for any accidental corpse spillage.

There was a second stream of blood coming from the corner by the stairs. A tarp covered a pile of something pink and copper smelling—I figured that was what was left of the mortician and his mother. Had I dragged those bodies down here? Covered them up? And, oh shit, where was—

Amanda.

She was crouching with her back to me, thumbing through the mortician's record collection. She must have heard me sit up because she turned to look at me.

"Holy shit!" I exclaimed. I couldn't help myself.

"What?" She instinctively reached up to touch her face, a note of panic in her voice.

"You look amazing."

Amazing. Way to play it cool, dude. She did look amazing, though. For starters, her eye had grown back inside her skull. The rest of her face was back to normal too. Maybe her hair was a little mussed from not showering after all the people-eating we'd done but, overall, she had that glowing, just-woke-up look about her.

"I mean," I tried to clarify, "you look better."

Amanda smirked and looked away. I think she was blushing, but maybe I was overestimating the power of my charm.

"You look better too," she said.

I glanced down at my abdomen. My T-shirt was all torn to shreds, but beneath that was nothing but perfect pink skin, all of my guts modestly hidden.

"MOTHERFUCKING WOLVERINE!" I shouted.

Amanda glanced at me again. She was trying to look annoyed but I could see there was a spark of something in her eyes—not amusement, I wasn't that funny—but, like, shared excitement. We could heal!

"He's an X-Man," I explained lamely. "He can—"

"Yeah, I know who he is. Hugh Jackman."

I rubbed my belly, just happy to have it back.

"We made it."

"Uh-huh. We made it to the basement of a funeral parlor in Newark."

Well, it didn't sound so good when she said it like that. Still, I felt a deep sense of relief. We'd escaped those psychos in the black SUV and were whole again. I mean, don't get me wrong, we had some serious problems to figure out, but when you see a girl grow back her face, everything else seems way more workable.

"So, Jake," she said, awkwardly fingering a clump of dried blood in her hair. "You sort of saved me back there."

"You saved me too."

"Yeah." Amanda shrugged. "Thanks, though. You didn't have to do that."

I didn't know what to say. The way she thanked me, it seemed like Amanda Blake wasn't used to dudes sticking their necks out for her. I thought of Chazz Slade and what he might've done if he had been the one turned into a zombie with his girlfriend. Probably would've copped a quick feel while he was carrying Amanda down that alley, that's for sure.

I should've thought of that.

"My dad loves this old stuff," Amanda said, still looking through the mortician's records.

"Is there anything with, like, sixty guitars? Because I feel like rocking out."

"Uh, no," she said. "This is a good one."

She took the record out of its dust jacket carefully, as if the dead mortician would give a shit, and gently placed it on the record player.

It was a Frank Sinatra recording: "The Way You Look Tonight." Not really my thing, but something told me that after that night in the basement it'd be a song I committed to memory.

We listened to the beginning in silence—Sinatra doing that old-man crooning stuff over some horns. Amanda drummed her fingers on her thighs.

Before the second verse, she grabbed some weird metallic plunger from the mortician's toolbox. That thing had probably scooped so much goop out of so many corpses, but that didn't stop Amanda from lip-synching into it. She mouthed the words in perfect time with Sinatra, working an imaginary crowd of lounge-goers, even doffing an imaginary hat, all while barely containing her laughter.

I watched in amazement. Holy shit. Amanda Blake was kind of dorky.

We'd just turned into flesh-eating brain-sucking monsters and eaten a bunch of our friends. And some other people. We'd also narrowly escaped some gun-toting government hard case. Plus, if I remembered that fuzzy TV report I'd seen upstairs correctly, they were calling us "school shooters" on the news. That's a day of heavy transformative shit right there.

And yet, for some reason, I felt content. Almost normal.

Maybe it was the Sinatra, although honestly I thought he was kind of boring. Maybe it was just the fact that down in that basement, right then, we could take a deep breath and shut out all the craziness for a minute. Whatever it was, as random as the timing seemed, I'm pretty sure seeing Amanda lip-synch into that cadaver-spatula was the moment I fell in love for the first time.

CASS

"IT'S KILLING ME!"

I hummed a few bars of the song for Tom. It'd popped into my head out of nowhere and I couldn't shake it loose. In my experience, the only way to exterminate one of these earworms was to play the song in question. Before I could look it up on my government-provided off-brand MP3 player, I had to figure out what the name of the song was.

"No clue," Tom said distractedly. He wasn't really listening. He was still pretty shaken up from the fight earlier. Just like I had never actually seen an out-and-out blood-spattered zombie showdown, neither had my handler. Tom was an exploding-brains virgin too. We made quite a pair.

"You did a good job, hon," Harlene had told Tom when we'd returned to Ronald Reagan High School. "You kept my Sweet Pea safe." He looked relieved to hear it, although the color still hadn't totally returned to his face.

Then Harlene had rounded on Jamison, and for a second I thought she might grab him by the ear and drag him off for a serious scolding. He had it coming, disobeying a direct order, almost getting us killed. Harlene kept up the sugary southern belle sweetness, though, touching Jamison gently on the arm.

"How you feeling?" she asked.

Jamison looked down, sheepish. The top of his shaved head was covered in little nicks from where the girl—Amanda—had launched him through the telephone booth.

"I lost it," he muttered. "It won't happen again."

"It better not," replied Harlene, and that was that. Matter settled. Back when I actually went to school, the best teachers always had this way about them—they wouldn't yell or lecture or threaten bad grades—you just wanted to do well in their class because, if you didn't . . . That was unthinkable. They'd be so disappointed.

Harlene had that way about her. It's probably what made the pageant judges love her so much back in Georgia, and it's what made her such a good squad leader now.

"I want people to think of me as calm and cool like that," I told Tom as soon as Harlene and Jamison were out of earshot.

"Unflappable," offered Tom.

"Yeah," I agreed.

"I was far from that today."

"We were both pretty flapped."

Tom flashed me a guilty look. "But I'm supposed to be your guardian."

I waved my hands, demonstrating my aliveness. "You guarded."

"I've never seen one of them talk before," he said. "The girl one talked to us."

"Yeah, that was freaky," I said, although I hadn't really been thinking about my brief exchange with Amanda. I was more stuck on Jake—the gruesome wound on his abdomen, his wide-eyed look, the way he carried Amanda out of danger. *He* had seemed pretty unflappable. Were zombies supposed to be unflappable? It was all kind of confusing.

I had to remind myself—again—that he had eaten a bunch of kids and needed to be put down.

Anyway, Tom and I stood on the lawn back at RRHS as the chaos unfolded around us. NCD reinforcements had arrived: guys in jumpsuits like mine, other more important-looking ones with cheap suits and earpieces. The local cops had shown up too, manning a perimeter of yellow tape and flashing blue lights. They kept the journalists at bay and gently escorted the crying parents away. We never let the cops near the actual scene—they'd get fed the same cover story as the rest of the civilians, a cover story I'm sure Harlene and her boss back in Washington had already cooked up.

"School shooting," Tom said as if he'd read my mind.

"Seriously?"

Tom nodded.

"That's screwed up."

Containment—that's a nice way to describe killing a zombie—was only part of my unit's job. The other part, the one that wasn't nearly as cool as doing telepathic CSI on the freshly eaten, was called "Incident Management." A bunch of dead kids was an "Incident" and we were here to "Manage" it.

They handed out the color pamphlet during the second week of NCD training. The cover read AM I READY TO LEARN ABOUT ZOMBIES? and pictured an elderly man with a curious look on his face. Inside the pamphlet were a bunch of pictures of people with similar wondering looks, each of them helpfully labeled, like SMALL-TOWN SHERIFF, or KINDLY DOCTOR, or YOUR MOM.

In bright-red block letters above each picture was the word NO.

"The point is," our instructor intoned, "that our leaders in Washington don't think the general populace is ready to learn about the zombie outbreak."

Oh good, because the pamphlet didn't make that clear.

I'll be honest; this part kind of freaked me out. If I was just an ordinary civilian, I'd definitely want to know if there was a plague that might one day turn my neighbor into a superstrong, decomposing, human-eating machine. That's what they invented that annoying emergency-broadcasting thing for, right? *This is not a test, there are monsters coming to eat you. . . .* I'd want to know that. I'd want to know that big-time.

On the other hand, and this probably doesn't sound very mature, but it felt like I was *in* on something. The president himself trusted me with top-secret information. I was the first line of defense between America and the undead. Sort of. That was pretty freaking cool. So what if, in every disaster movie I'd ever seen, government secrecy led to even bigger disasters? This was real life. We were doing the right thing, keeping the public safe.

One of the other trainees raised his hand. "Is it true that we've completely lost Iowa?"

Our instructor glanced over his shoulder to where Mr. Bow Tie was sitting, hidden behind a newspaper.

He'd been observing this class from the start, making everyone including the instructor uneasy. Now, he lowered his paper, neatly folded it, and smiled indulgently at the question asker.

"Where did you hear that nonsense?" asked Mr. Bow Tie.

"There are rumors floating around campus," replied the guy nervously. "People, um, talk."

"Of course they do," said Mr. Bow Tie, motioning for the instructor to resume his lecture.

"Part of your job will be to make sure the public remains safe, comfortable, and unaware," the instructor said, ignoring the question. But I was paying more attention to Mr. Bow Tie now. He was still eyeing my too-curious classmate, typing something into his cell phone without looking down at the keys.

Come to think of it, after that day, I don't remember seeing the question asker again.

I'd done my fair share of Incident Management since joining the NCD, but never one as big as Ronald Reagan High School. There was that football game in Cleveland where a fan had transformed and eaten a couple of his pals before being subdued. We'd played that one like a couple of rival fans had got out of control and started a vicious brawl. Most other times, the attacks were isolated and the zombies easily tracked down. In those cases, there wasn't as much cover-up needed. We leaked stories to the papers about domestic violence, or home invasion, or grizzly bear attacks, or weird new drugs that made people go crazy. As for the people who weren't so easily convinced—for them, we had "special techniques." And just like that, our version of events became the truth.

But this time, there were so many bodies and killers still on the loose. Plus, the attack had taken place at a posh suburban high school. There were a lot of eyeballs on this one.

We were going to be here all night.

So, Tom and I sat on the RRHS lawn, waiting for our orders. We shared a Ziploc bag of mandarin oranges Tom had packed that morning, and I kept bothering him about my earworm.

It was past ten that night when another telepath named Linda came to find me. Tom was dozing in the grass and I was watching the stricken parents milling about the police barricade. There were a lot of kids still sequestered in the school, awaiting NCD questioning.

"Cass, they want you inside," said Linda, dabbing at her bloody nose with a crusty paper towel.

Linda and I had similar jobs, except she was in her thirties and nowhere near as good a telepath. Let's just say I'd never gotten any bloody noses from overexertion. If they'd flown Linda out from DC, they must've really needed all hands on deck.

"Me too?" asked Tom.

"Actually, Harlene wants you to go grab some coffees."

"At last, a job I am uniquely suited for," declared Tom before squeezing my arm. "Don't work too hard, Psychic Friend."

Linda led me into the school. We walked down a hallway where a line of students waited, some of them blood-spattered and wrapped in blankets, all of them exhausted. They leaned or sat against the lockers, under the guard of a Jumpsuit holding a submachine gun. I was picking up serious anxiety vibes. How could we make a traumatic day even more traumatic? Just like this.

I felt like maybe I should say something comforting because I was their age. Like, *It's cool, you guys, we don't mean you any harm, sorry your friends are dead.* But I doubted it would do any good. The kids not huddled together crying were fixing me with suspicious looks. I wasn't one of them; I was one of the Jumpsuits.

Harlene had set up shop in one of the classrooms. She sat behind the teacher's desk, attendance sheets and permanent records piled up before her. We needed to go through every student before they'd be allowed to leave.

I glanced around the room—there was a big anti-smoking poster on one wall, all yellowed teeth and cancer-speckled gum lines. Next to that was one of a couple kids in torn jeans and flannels—a total relic of the '90s—that explained why it was "boss" to wait to have sex.

"Health class," I observed. "Ironic choice."

Harlene gave me a tired smile. "You up for this, hon?"

I nodded and plopped down into a chair next to her. Jamison showed in the first kid. She looked like a freshman. She was shaking like a leaf as she slid into the mustard-colored desk-chair combo pulled closest to Harlene.

"Everything's okay now," said Harlene, her voice soothing.

"When can I go home?" asked the girl.

"Soon," replied Harlene.

The girl's name was Victoria. She hadn't been in the cafeteria when the incident took place; she'd been in math class, struggling with sine and cosine. She'd heard rumors, though, that Amanda Blake, the most popular girl in the school, had eaten a bunch of kids. Some other guy had been involved too. Some stoner dork whose name she didn't know.

Of course, Victoria didn't actually tell us any of that. I picked it up off the surface of her mind.

Every mind might be like a house, but that doesn't mean I can just go barging in. Well—I *could*, except it's unpleasant for me and even worse for the mind on the receiving end. You have to be subtle: peek in the windows, press your ear up to the door, and pick up whatever stray thoughts you can. It was a lot easier when a person was scared or tired, like Victoria. When you're that way—unfocused—thoughts have a way of just shooting off your brain like sparks.

It was just like the psychometric test they gave me back in school. I didn't know what shapes were printed on the military recruiters' cards, but the recruiters did, and they were thinking about them. Thoughts close to the surface like that are easy to pick up on.

Going deeper than that top layer of thoughts, or staying linked to someone like I was with Jake, that was harder. Physical contact helped, or an object like *The House of Mirth*. Something to focus on. And I couldn't keep up that contact for long. I could still feel Jake out there, in the back of my mind, but that link would grow fainter soon. It's why we tried to track down the zombies as quickly as possible.

But for now, we had to deal with Victoria and the rest. Incident Management was tonight's top priority.

"I'm sorry to keep you here so late on such a horrible day," Harlene said to Victoria, her voice gently authoritative. "We've just got to talk to every student about the shooting."

"Shooting?" asked Victoria, her eyes widening.

Harlene laid out the story. Frustrated popular girl and her secret, unpopular boy-toy hatch a plan to get revenge on a school that never took them seriously. Guns purchased on the internet, a cold-blooded killing spree, a cowardly escape. Honestly, it's not something that would pass the smell test. It sounded like the plot from a bad after-school special.

That's why I was there.

I closed my eyes and slipped up against Victoria's mind, being as gentle as possible. It was sort of like playing Operation on the astral plane. Don't push too hard or the alarm buzzes and everyone gets a migraine.

As Harlene laid out the details, I nudged Victoria toward believing them.

Imagine every piece of information you hear entering the labyrinth of your mind via one of two doors: "truth" and "bullshit." (It's actually a lot more complicated than that; there are doors for "things I want to believe" and "things I believe to make myself feel better"—hundreds of doors, really.) Anyway, my job was to make sure our cover story entered Victoria's mind the *right* way.

When I was satisfied that Victoria had accepted Harlene's version of events, I opened my eyes and gave Harlene a subtle nod. She smiled and dismissed Victoria.

I rubbed my temples. Even though I liked to think of myself as some kind of telepathic prodigy, massaging Victoria's psyche was harder than I expected after such a nutso day. Tracking Jake and now this . . . I was definitely going to need a fistful of Advil in the morning.

Harlene watched me. "You let me know when you're tired, hon. Linda's here and we've got the rest of the telepaths in from Washington too—you'll work in shifts."

"I'm cool," I said, not wanting to get shown up by any B-teamers. "Getting tired of telling that shooting story yet?"

Harlene looked mournfully at an empty paper coffee cup. "You've got no idea."

"Hey." I hummed a few bars of the song that was still stuck in my head. "That sound familiar?"

Harlene shook her head. "Not a good time for that, Sweet Pea."

The next kid Jamison showed in was nearly as big as him: he was the kind of guy who looked like he'd gotten his first gym membership sometime around kindergarten. Someone had thrown a blanket around his shoulders, probably to hide his blood-spattered white T-shirt.

"Chazz Slade," said Harlene. "Have a seat."

Chazz squeezed his bulk into the little desk, remaining slightly doubled over. He was holding his stomach and looked pale, with dark circles around his eyes. I really hoped he wouldn't vomit. That guy could probably hold gallons of gross cafeteria food.

"So," began Harlene, "I understand you were dating Amanda Blake."

Chazz nodded dumbly, keeping his eyes focused on

the scratched surface of the desk in front of him. I realized Harlene had said that more for my benefit; it would be harder to massage our lie into someone like Chazz who had a more intimate understanding of our runaway zombie bimbo. Also—not to sound catty or anything—but after seeing Amanda, it totally made sense that this guy would be her boyfriend.

"We're soul mates," Chazz mumbled.

I had to contain a snort at the way the big lug so casually played the soul-mate card. Chazz sure didn't look like the type to get all poetic.

"I see," replied Harlene. "So you weren't aware of her relationship with Jake Stephens?"

"Who? What the fuck, lady?" Chazz clutched himself tighter and, as he did, his stomach let loose a seismic rumble. A thick vein on his neck throbbed. "Ugh—I need to go, I'm gonna be sick."

Chazz wasn't taking this well; convincing him that his high school sweetheart had made a death pact with some *other* guy was going to be a tough sell.

Harlene glanced at me. "Just another moment, Mr. Slade. We need to discuss Amanda."

I probed Chazz's mind. I expected to find anger and confusion, maybe some stifled feelings of inadequacy or the urge to go punch a smaller person in the face—you know, typical emotions for a cheating-girlfriend situation. Instead, I found a cold place. A mind rapidly going numb.

While most minds are labyrinthine, Chazz's mind only had room for two thoughts just then: *fight it* and *eat them*.

Oh my god. He was one of them. Right on the verge of full undead mode.

"Harlene!" was all I managed to scream before Chazz lunged across the desk. Harlene was just quick enough to get her arm up, Chazz's teeth sinking into her forearm instead of her throat. He tore off a chunk of flesh, and Harlene fell backward in her chair.

Chazz tossed his head back, gulping down the bite he'd taken out of Harlene. The throbbing vein in his neck had turned black under his suddenly paper-white skin. He'd gone full zombie. His eyes were sunken in his head, dark and empty.

And staring right at me.

I heard Harlene shouting for Jamison, but even though he was just in the hallway outside, I knew he'd be too late. Chazz would tear me apart before Jamison had even unholstered his gun. Two zombie massacres in one school on the same day? At least I'd be part of some NCD record.

As Chazz lumbered toward me, I acted instinctively. I wasn't even sure what I was doing—probably like those moms you read about who lift cars off their babies. I reached into his mind as hard as I could, ignoring the cold and clammy feeling touching that dead organ sent shooting through me, and basically just thrashed around. Like groping for a light switch in a dark room. When my astral fingers came up against something, I yanked with all my mental might.

Chazz collapsed to the floor inches in front of me, unconscious, just as Jamison burst through the door with his gun drawn. Mere seconds had passed since Chazz had bitten Harlene.

I felt dizzy, like I'd gotten up too fast, and then white spots flashed across my vision and my head started aching like I was being stabbed repeatedly in the brain. I fell to the floor next to Harlene, who was clutching the wound on her arm, blood squeezing through her fingers.

"What did you do?" she wheezed. Her words sounded like they were coming from underground and I couldn't make my mouth form an answer, even though that answer would have been "not a freaking clue."

Jamison peered curiously down at Chazz's body, then cocked his pistol. He looked to Harlene. "Should I?"

"That won't be necessary."

The voice came from the doorway. At first, I thought I must be hallucinating, some weird side effect of whatever telepathic mojo I'd just worked on Chazz. But then I saw Tom, holding a tray of coffees and looking more nervous than he had facing certain death that afternoon, standing right next to Mr. Bow Tie. Whoa. I hadn't seen him since training, didn't think he was even the kind of NCD bigwig to leave Washington. If he was here, we must really be in crisis mode.

Mr. Bow Tie strode into the room, the heels of his fancy loafers sounding like thunder to me as they crossed the floor. He spared a brief glance for Harlene, then crouched over Chazz's body. He laid a hand on Chazz's head, as if trying to feel the brain beneath.

"Hm," he said, then turned and knelt in front of me. Everyone in the room was quiet, watching, as the big, scary boss from Washington handed me his handkerchief. "Your nose is bleeding."

Unlike Harlene's, Mr. Bow Tie's voice was totally clear, cutting precisely through the layers of fuzz suffocating my brain. I took the hanky and pressed it to my face. So much for never getting a nosebleed.

Mr. Bow Tie patted my shoulder. It was a gesture of approval, like you might pat a dog after it successfully rolls over. Come to think of it, I felt like rolling over right then and just sleeping for days. He started to stand up but then looked back at me, a thin smile on his lips.

"'The Way You Look Tonight,'" Mr. Bow Tie said. "That's the song."

I felt pretty out of it, but I can say with some certainty that I wasn't humming.

JAKE

I WOKE UP IN MY OWN BED. IT'D ALL BEEN A REALLY heinous dream. Everything was fine and I'd definitely never eaten a person. The end.

And then I realized that this wasn't my bed. My bed at home—my comfortable, amazing bed where I should have been waking up with a full agenda of video games and comic books to look forward to—did not smell like old-lady arthritis cream. My room didn't have a giant yellow water stain shaped like Abraham Lincoln spread across its ceiling. There wasn't a stern-looking, black-and-white picture of a turn-of-the-century dude holding a pitchfork hanging on my bedroom wall.

This was the mortician's mother's room.

So it all really happened.

Things got a little weird last night. I mean, socially weird. Not to be confused with the much weirder events of the afternoon.

After the whole rush of no longer being gut-shot (me) or hideously disfigured (Amanda) wore off, the reality set in that we didn't really know each other and, holy shit, we're fugitives holed up in a funeral home. One minute Amanda's playing records and the next minute it's too quiet, we've got nothing to say to each other, and there's a pile of recently gobbled body parts that we're both struggling to ignore.

Luckily, it turns out the undead still need to sleep. Which is all right with me because sleeping happens to be one of my favorite activities.

Also, eating. But that's sort of ruined for me now.

We explored the house in awkward silence, just talking to agree on sleeping arrangements and which one of us would get to shower first (her, of course). I'd offered Amanda the mom's bedroom, being all chivalrous and junk, but she said the idea of sleeping in someone else's bed grossed her out. We'd both decided the mortician's room was out of the question, neither of us wanting to sleep in the same bed as the guy who handled dead people. Kinda stupid when you consider our clothes were stiff and crusty with other people's gore.

When Amanda went off to shower, I picked out some clothes from the mortician's closet. He was wider and taller than me but they'd have to do: a musty white T-shirt, a faded brown flannel, and some bright blue jeans that looked like the kind my dad would buy.

I found a bottle of coconut air freshener and sprayed the shit out of my new outfit. There was a washing machine in the basement, but after the mess we'd made downstairs, neither of us was eager to go back.

While I was giving the mortician's clothes a coating of tropical scent, Amanda poked her head into the bedroom. Her blonde hair was still wet from the shower and she'd found a faded, flower-print dress in the old lady's stuff. It fit her better than the mortician's clothes would fit me. It would probably look like a polite little church dress on the mortician's withered mom, but on Amanda it became some retro-chic thing that a free-spirited college girl might wear. It still smelled funny, though. I could tell even surrounded in my own personal coconut fog. Everything in here smelled stale, and I hoped I didn't develop some kind of brain disorder where I forever associated hot chicks with the smell of mothballs.

I offered her the can of air freshener.

She wrinkled her nose. "I think that's actually making it worse."

I sniffed my new outfit. Whatever. I liked it. Coconut was definitely preferable to the lingering formaldehyde smell.

"So," continued Amanda, "about tomorrow."

"Yeah?"

"You're going to be here, right?"

"As opposed to . . ."

"Taking off in the middle of the night."

"Why would I do that?"

"Because they're looking for two of us," explained Amanda. "And you think it might be easier to get away on your own."

"I don't think that. I'm not even sure what we're getting away from." I held up my change of clothes. "I hadn't thought about much beyond the air freshener."

"Okay," said Amanda. "Good."

"Wait. Did you think that? About bailing?"

"I thought about it," she admitted, shrugging. "But I decided it'd be better if we stick together."

So Amanda had considered ditching me—crawling out the bathroom window, maybe hot-wiring another car and leaving me to figure this zombie thing out by myself. Not cool. Although, I guess those are the kind of self-preservation decisions popular girls make all the time.

A look of hurt must have shown on my face, because Amanda sheepishly looked elsewhere.

"Sorry. I didn't think about it for long," she insisted.

"It's okay."

"We'll figure it out in the morning." Amanda lingered in the doorway, like she was scrounging for something reassuring to say. I cleared my throat and busied myself with rummaging through the mortician's closet. I didn't really feel equipped to discuss the future with Amanda Blake and she must've felt something similar because she crept downstairs while my head was still buried in smelly clothes.

Now morning was here, and shit was just as confusing as yesterday.

Downstairs, I passed by the funeral parlor where the display model coffin was open, a blanket hanging out of it.

"Uh, did you sleep in the coffin?" I asked, walking into the living room where Amanda was sitting on the couch, watching the news.

"It was the only place in here that didn't smell funky," she replied. "I didn't close the lid."

"Oh, well, as long as you didn't close the lid, I guess that makes it totally normal."

"I think normal stopped applying to us around lunch period yesterday, Jake."

"Well, whatever. It does make me rethink my whole vampire theory. Did you feel particularly *drawn* to the coffin?"

But Amanda's face had gone pale. She shushed me and pointed to the TV. There we were, on-screen. Amanda's glamorous senior photo, taken next to a gentle waterfall, her blonde hair practically freaking glowing, next to my cheapie yearbook photo taken in front of those green screens with the neon laser background, looking sort of baked and like I'd just been forced to take off my winter hat. I awkwardly ran my fingers through my mop of hair, as if doing so could magically improve the me on the TV screen. The news guy was talking about the carnage at RRHS but I didn't pay much attention to that. I was more focused on the headline beneath our pictures.

SCHOOL SHOOTERS IN CUSTODY.

"Not a word of that's true," I said.

"No shit," said Amanda.

I thought about those psychos in the black SUV. How they didn't show us any badges or even try to arrest us before opening fire. How the squirrelly girl in the backseat didn't seem all that surprised to see me walking around with a hole in my stomach.

"They want people to think we're caught," I said.

"And to think we used guns," added Amanda. "Instead of, like, teeth."

"Conspiracy?"

"Total conspiracy."

I flopped down on the couch next to Amanda.

"Everyone thinks we're arrested. *My parents* think I'm arrested."

"My mom's probably trying to sell her story as we speak. She's always wanted me to be famous, now's her big chance."

I gave her a screwed-up look, because that was a seriously screwed-up thing to think.

"No way," I said. "I don't care how many cars you've stolen—which is an awesome skill, by the way, can you teach me?—there's no way your mom, or *anyone*, would try to cash in on her own daughter's murderous rampage."

"Yeah, well, you don't know my mom," she replied. "She's nice enough, I guess, but she's still a little mad I never became a child star."

We fell silent, the enormity of it all sinking in. Yesterday, my biggest problem had been an oral presentation. Today, I was an enemy of the state.

On the screen, our images were replaced by those of twenty or so of our classmates. Amanda quickly turned off the TV, and we both pretended we hadn't noticed the death toll of yesterday's rampage. I sort of never wanted to think about it. I wanted to pretend that it was something I hadn't done. It wasn't me—it was Zombie-Jake, and me and that guy weren't on speaking terms.

Amanda grabbed a plate of peanut butter toast off the coffee table, one piece missing a tiny bite. She held it out to me.

"Try this," she ordered.

I took a bite. It was cold, with a ton of peanut butter, probably to cover up that she'd burned the bread.

"Mmm," I said, not sure why Amanda was looking at me so expectantly. "You're really good at making toast?"

She rolled her eyes, shaking her head. "Do you feel anything?"

"Um. Grateful?"

"How about less hungry?"

I had to think about this. I looked down at the piece of toast and realized that I didn't have any urge to eat more. It's not that it was repulsive to me, it's just that I didn't feel the need to eat.

"You just slept like ten hours and you're not hungry," said Amanda. "Weird, right?"

I took another bite. A denial bite. I didn't feel anything. I ran my hand over my belly, checking for the thunderous tremors that had started my day yesterday. All quiet on the stomach front.

"I'm not the *other* kind of hungry either," I said. "So that's good, right?"

Amanda nodded. "Me neither. For now."

"How long do you think we have?"

"I don't know," she answered. "What're we going to do when it happens again?"

I didn't have an answer to that. I looked back to the TV where just moments ago the faces of our dead classmates had peered out at us. Amanda followed my gaze, hugging herself.

"Shit," I said. "More reasonable portions?"

We found some old pastel-blue suitcases in the back of the old lady's closet. Judging by the wrinkled yellow tags still attached to their handles, the last time they saw any use was in the early '70s for a trip to Hawaii.

We stuffed the choicest clothes into those suitcases, which meant they were mostly empty. It was like raiding a really bad thrift store. We tried to pick stuff that fit us, that wouldn't make us stand out, and that would keep us warm. Amanda insisted I pack sweaters in case we had to sleep in the car.

The car. We found the keys hanging by the back door. It was a beat-up old station wagon, brown, with that classic wood paneling down the sides. Amanda frowned at it, but I figured taking this car was better than her just stealing another random ride. No one would be missing the mortician for a few more days, hopefully. And at least it wasn't the hearse.

The mortician had thirty-five bucks in his wallet. We found another three hundred stuffed in a coffee can on top of the fridge. It would buy us more than enough gas to get out of New Jersey.

After I'd loaded our stuff into the car, I went back inside and found Amanda in the basement, standing in front of the tarp covering the mortician and his mom. It had started to smell a little down there, worse than just the chemical smell the room had started with. Like rotten meat.

"Should we say something?" asked Amanda, looking at me over her shoulder.

I thought about it. We'd eaten these people, slept in their house, and were stealing their stuff. "Sorry?" I ventured.

Amanda nodded. "We're sorry," she said to the tarp.

We headed west on the interstate. I drove and Amanda fiddled with the radio, scanning all the AM stations for that weird radio show her brother had talked about—*Coast-to-Coast AM*. It was the middle of the day, though, and she couldn't find any talk of undead plagues or government cover-ups, just a bunch of loud old dudes screaming about Canadian sleeper agents sneaking into our country to spread socialist propaganda, and old ladies reading passages from books I'd never heard of. Boring stuff.

"I think we should go see him," said Amanda, flipping over to some lame FM pop station.

"Your brother?"

"Kyle, yeah. He'll know what to do. He goes to school in Michigan."

"You want to drive to Michigan?"

"We've gotta drive somewhere."

"You don't think he'll be a little freaked out to have his baby sister, the alleged school shooter, show up at his dorm?"

She shrugged. "More or less freaked out than when I tell him I'm a zombie?"

"Good point," I admitted. "But don't you think he'll have, like, gone home? To be with your family?"

"My mom's probably already got the 'for sale' sign in the yard. She won't be hanging around New Jersey." Amanda paused, thinking. "Your folks won't either."

"Huh?"

"You think our families will still be welcome in town after what we did? Government cover-up or not, the result is the same, you know."

Jeez. I hadn't even thought about that. My dad worked at the same office as Mr. DeCarlo. My mom was a cochair on the PTA. And Kelly, she couldn't go back to school with kids whose brothers and sisters I'd eaten. They'd have to move or maybe go into hiding. For the rest of their lives, people would look at my mom and dad, wondering what they'd done to screw me up so bad.

The car shook as I hit the rumble strips on the side of the highway. I'd drifted off the road. Amanda stared at me.

"Jake?"

"This is so fucked," was all I could say. "We really messed up."

I groped for a pair of cheap plastic sunglasses the mortician had left on the dashboard and shoved them onto my face. I really, really did not want to cry in front of Amanda Blake.

"I've been thinking about it," said Amanda, looking out her window. "What we did was awful, but we couldn't control it. And if there are people out there trying to cover it up, then they *did* know. About all of this. They know about zombies and they're just, like, letting it happen and cleaning it up afterward."

"You're not making me feel better."

"Jake, if you want to pull over and go turn yourself in, that's cool, I get it. I'm sad that some dude with a shotgun will probably blow your head off, but that's your call. Me? I want to find out what the fuck happened to us and why."

The highway stretched out before us, all semis and station wagons. I kept an eye in my rearview for any ominous black cars. Was I going to have to do that for the rest of my life?

I felt bad about the people we ate, their families, our families—everyone, pretty much. It was just, like, sadness and guilt galore. But Amanda was right. I didn't want to turn myself in.

"You really think your brother can help?"

On the radio, a trio of gelled-hair pretty boys made heavy use of Auto-Tune, whining about some girl that'd blown off their advances at a nightclub. My sister, Kelly, had a crush on the redheaded one with the eyeliner. I remembered the poster on her wall that I'd mercilessly mocked. They used to have a show on the Disney Channel before they turned eighteen, sexed up their image, and learned some aggressive pelvic dance moves.

I changed the station, flipping until I reached one spinning a scratchy B-side from The Clash.

"What?" asked Amanda. "You don't like C'mere Eyes?"

"What are those?"

"The band I was listening to before you put on this junk."

"First, this is not junk and I should revoke your listening pass for saying that."

"Listening pass?"

"Second, I have a little sister. I'm more than familiar with the songs of C'mere Eyes. More like Khmer Rouge."

"Funny."

"Because their music is like genocide."

"I got it, thanks."

"My question was literally, What are c'mere eyes?"

"Like this," said Amanda.

I looked over at her. She was staring at me with half-lidded eyes, like a kitten stuck in a really smoky room, her lips in a come-hither sort of pout. It was a look that probably would've melted me yesterday afternoon, you know, before I saw Amanda with one of her eyeballs hanging halfway down her face. Actually, it was still pretty good.

"So, sex eyes," I said, turning back to the road in time to stop tailgating the truck she'd distracted me from.

"Those are *not* my sex eyes," she replied, acting offended.

"If you say so."

The Clash cut ended and I would've changed the station again if Amanda hadn't shoved my hand away from the dial. The mellow-sounding DJ was going to commercial—but first, an update from the newsroom.

"More strange and dark details emerging from eastern New Jersey today," intoned a stoic anchor lady, "as four bodies were recovered from a house just miles from the scene of yesterday's horrific massacre at Ronald Reagan High School. Authorities have identified the bodies as the parents and grandparents of RRHS senior Chazz Slade. Slade, eighteen, a survivor of yesterday's shooting, is now in custody while authorities investigate potential links to shooters Amanda Lynne Blake and Jacob Albert Stephens.

"Stay tuned for more of rock's classics on The Nerve 96.5," concluded the anchor.

I didn't want to stay tuned. I turned the volume all the way down, wanting to process this latest bit of information in silence. First, the news was using our full names now, like they always do with serial killers, which meant my great shame—well, my great shame until yesterday—*Albert* was going to be out there. Second, the same guy who'd almost beaten me up yesterday was accused of snuffing out his whole family.

I looked over at Amanda. She was sitting stiffly, a look I'd describe as confused disgust scrunching up her features.

"So, uh, you were going out with a serial killer," I said.

She blinked. "We were breaking up. I mean, we *were* broken up."

"Okay," I said, nodding slowly, not wanting to pry but also, like, really wanting to pry. "Did you know anything about—?"

"Did I know Chazz was going to kill his parents?" she asked sharply, shooting me an annoyed look. "Yeah, Jake, I just decided to keep that one to myself."

"Do you think it has anything to do with us, you know, eating people?"

"Could you just be quiet for, like, two minutes, please?" she snapped. "I need to think."

It took more like twenty minutes for Amanda to collect her thoughts. I tried to drive as quietly as possible, even though awkward silences made me nervous. No tapping on the steering wheel, no searching for something decent on the radio. I was still getting used to having Amanda around, and still a little concerned that she might toss herself out of the speeding car if I annoyed her too much. With our newfound healing abilities, that was a total possibility.

Finally, Amanda turned to me.

"Okay," she said, sort of hesitant. "I'm going to ask you a question that's gonna seem really weird, but you need to answer honestly."

I shrugged, just happy we were talking again. And anyway, that's what road trips are all about, right? Getting-to-know-you questions and profound spiritual experiences. I remember Adam DeCarlo—RIP—had loaned me a copy of this Jack Kerouac book when he was trying to convince me to take a road trip to some music festival with him. We'd even started planning everything, but then ended up just getting stoned in my basement instead.

"Is Sasha Tremens a zombie?" Amanda asked.

"Huh?"

Amanda was right; that was a weird question. Why would she ask about Sasha? My ex-girlfriend. We started going out junior year, but after the summer she decided to get a fresh start as a senior. We hardly talked anymore, but we'd always have that awkwardly fumbling first time on her stuffed animal–covered bed while her parents were away for the weekend.

"You hooked up with her, right?"

"How'd you know that?"

"It's high school, dude. Everyone knows about everyone."

I didn't think that was true, but then maybe part

of maintaining popular status was keeping tabs on the relationships of other kids.

"But why would you ask if she was a zombie?"

"Yeah, you're right," said Amanda, toying with her seat belt thoughtfully. "That was forever ago anyway, right? It couldn't be Sasha."

"What couldn't be Sasha? You're not making any sense."

Amanda sighed. "Okay, so listen. Chazz and I were broken up. We broke up like a month ago."

"I didn't know," I replied. It was kind of weird that I didn't know. Unlike *my* dating status, a newly single Amanda Blake would've been front-page news in the school paper.

"Yeah," continued Amanda, "it was sort of unofficial. Chazz didn't really accept the breakup."

"Wait, so you dumped him?"

"Yeah. Well, I tried to. Cindy said she saw him hooking up with some college skank at a party and I believed her, but Chazz denied it and, like, basically said he'd beat up anyone else I tried to date. You know, that possessive thing guys do."

"Uh, no, I don't know that move."

Amanda ignored me. "Anyway, then Chazz stopped coming to school and I figured, whatever, good riddance. He called me a bunch and left these weird rambling voice mails, but I never really listened to them.

I was just waiting for him to lose interest."

"Your romantic life is seriously fascinating to me," I said.

"Shut up," she countered, not missing a beat. "He finally showed up at school yesterday—remember, when you interrupted us with all your lame jokes?"

"That's not *exactly* how I remember it."

"So, at the time, I figured it was just, like, desperate guy-talk because he didn't want to break up. All this bullshit about being soul mates and blah blah blah. But he said one thing that seriously grossed me out at the time and now has, like, some heavy context to it."

"Please tell me he quoted you poetry."

"No," she answered. "He told me I was the only girl in school he didn't want to eat."

I laughed. "Is that a pickup line?"

"It is if you're a zombie."

I blinked.

"Wait. What?"

"The reason for that huge relationship over-share is that I have a theory," Amanda continued patiently, "but it relies on you having gotten some action since Sasha. So, spill it, Jacob Albert."

"Uh, hypothetically," I stammered, feeling my face start to flush like it always did when the sex talk started up, smooth operator that I am, "let's say I have. What does that prove?"

"Well, yesterday you pointed out that when we bite people, they don't turn into other zombies like in the movies. Which makes sense because nobody bit me either. But I've done, um, *other stuff.* With my sort-of ex-boyfriend who probably ate his parents. So, Jake . . . how do you think we caught zombie?"

"Oh," I said, Amanda's theory finally clicking. "Oh gross."

"Yeah. Way worse than anything they told us about in health class."

"So you've got like herpes of the undead?"

"You do too, buddy. Which is why I asked about Sasha. Because I know *we* didn't hook up, and I seriously doubt you hooked up with Chazz."

"It wasn't Sasha."

"Oh. Who was it then?"

Janine. That night in Princeton, which at the time had seemed like my rite of passage into the world of getting down with hot bohemian college chicks. Now it turns out that was, like, the biggest mistake of my life.

"You wouldn't know her," I said. "She's from out of town."

Amanda laughed. "First time I've ever believed that line."

We eventually dropped the whole undead sex topic and fell into a mellow silence, just listening to the radio. Still, all those revelations about Chazz and Amanda, their relationship . . . Not to mention, her being single totally changed the dynamic of this road trip. I just had to ask.

"What did you see in Chazz Slade anyway?" I blurted.

Amanda tilted her head at me, half smiling. I could tell she was trying to figure out how honestly to answer me.

"Well," she said, "have you seen his abs?"

Oh yeah, I'd seen them. Chazz made sure *everyone* saw them. He'd strut around in the locker room after gym class daring people to break their hands on his six-pack. I shook my head.

"That's it? Seriously?"

I sounded more disappointed than I'd meant to. Amanda sighed and shook her head.

"No, Jake, that's not it." She paused, thinking. "I don't know. You won't get this, but it's like it was *expected*. He was good-looking, and cool, and could buy beer—I sort of *had* to date him, you know?"

"You're right," I said. "I don't get it. You really wanted to lock up prom queen, huh?"

Amanda shrugged. "I'm not saying it didn't get old sometimes, but high school doesn't last forever. Might as well make the most of it."

"Yeah, getting cheated on and catching a top-secret zombie plague is really living life to its fullest."

Amanda crossed her arms and leaned back, the

better to study me. I glanced over at her—she was smiling coolly, pulling a version of those c'mere eyes she'd shown me before.

"Why, Jake, are you sniffing around because I'm stuck in a car with you and you just realized I'm on the rebound? Free advice—talking shit about a girl's ex is not a good way to woo her."

"I'm not, uh, wooing . . ." I stammered, then reached forward and turned up the radio. "Oh man, love this song."

I'd never even heard it before.

The sun was setting when my stomach started to quake. We hadn't even crossed all the way through Pennsylvania. Amanda looked over at me, concerned.

"That can't be good."

A few miles later, I lay down in the backseat, and Amanda took over driving. It was a matter of necessity; the people in the other cars had started to look seriously appetizing and unbidden thoughts of ramming those other cars, breaking them open, and sucking out their delicious human filling flooded my mind.

"I'm going to need to eat," I told her, covering my eyes with my forearm.

"We need to figure that out," she said. "I mean, we can't just go around killing people. Right?"

"Right," I agreed, and my stomach did a loop as if to

tell me that I didn't have much choice in the matter. "I don't know if I can help it."

"Maybe—I don't know—take some deep breaths. Fight it off."

That sounded stupid but I tried it anyway. While the car sped along, I focused on breathing slow. In, then out. In, then out. I focused on my heartbeat. It was chugging along way too slow, just like yesterday at the mortician's, right before I lost control.

Keep beating, you bloody little thing, keep beating.

"Aw shit," I mumbled, because it was suddenly really hard to talk.

Amanda looked into the backseat, her eyes widening. Her face was starting to get a little pale too, her own hunger not far off.

"Oh gross," she said.

"Shut up," I groaned, looking at my hands. They'd turned gray, the veins beneath my suddenly paper-thin skin sludgy and thick. I shook my hands, trying to work feeling back into them, to get the circulation flowing. The fingernail on my index finger came loose and flew right off my hand midshake and into Amanda's hair. She made a disgusted face and gingerly flicked it out.

Amanda pulled off into the nearest exit. It was dark, hardly any streetlights. We were in some rural part of western Pennsylvania.

"Talk to me, Jake," said Amanda.

"This sucks," I replied, my words slurring.

Amanda pulled into a gas station, the only lit building in sight. There weren't any other cars there. She turned around and gave me a stern look, like she was explaining something to a bad dog.

"I'm going to check it out," she said. "You stay here."

"Check it out for *what*?"

"I don't know," she said, sounding panicked. "Maybe they sell raw hamburger?"

"You think that will work?" I exclaimed.

She didn't answer. I heard her own stomach growl as she got out of the car and jogged toward the gas station, and as soon as she was gone, I forgot what she'd told me. Couldn't hold on to the thought. It wasn't about eating, so it didn't matter. The world around me was going red again.

I'm pretty sure that's when my heart stopped.

I sat up and tried to open the door but she'd locked it and though I fumbled with the power locks I suddenly couldn't figure out how they were supposed to work. So I just slammed my head through the window. I spit out a piece of glass along with a rotten brown tooth, climbed through the window, and moved toward the gas station.

I made a real effort to keep my arms at my sides, not wanting to alarm anyone by doing the grasping zombie-arm thing. I was more conscious this time than back at school. More aware. But I *really* wanted to charge, to dive through the gas station window and bite the kid I could see checking out Amanda from behind the cash register. Even though my limbs felt cold in the places where I could feel them at all, I felt like I could run, could hunt, could kill.

Everything went red.

Next thing I remember, Amanda had her arms around my waist and was dragging me back toward the car. She was surprisingly strong.

"No, Jake," she was saying. "No. He's just a kid."

I screamed. Or howled. Dark phlegm spilled down my chin.

So hungry.

I broke Amanda's grip easily enough and sent her falling to the pavement. The gas station attendant came outside then—probably trying to play knight in shining armor. When he got a look at me, though, he ran back inside.

I sprinted after him. I could smell him. It was delicious.

And that's when the headlights washed over me, and the Prius with the devil-horns hood ornament ran me over.

CASS

I WOKE UP FEELING LIKE MY BRAIN HAD GAINED FIVE pounds overnight. Not five pounds of intelligence . . . It felt as if my brain had literally swollen up to the point where my skull was no longer big enough to contain it. A few months ago, Tom had shown me part of this nutso '80s sci-fi movie called *Scanners* without thinking about the fact that the sight of telepaths exploding one another's heads with watermelon-style special effects was maybe not the most comforting viewing material for a teenage telepath. He'd turned it off after he'd come to his senses, but I'd seen enough of it to know that, right now, I felt like the Scanners probably felt right before, you know, *splat*.

Tom was standing in the middle of our dingy New Jersey motel room, ironing a pair of pleated gray slacks. I'd gotten used to waking up in places like this; our tracking missions sometimes kept us away from Washington for a few days, and the government wasn't exactly known for splurging on four-star hotels.

Tom was keeping an eye on me. When I leaned up on my elbows and groaned, he grinned in relief.

"There you are," he said. "Did you have a nice nap?"

I tried to reply, but a weak *ugh* was all I could manage. My mouth tasted like it'd been dusted with sock-flavored flour. Tom nodded to the bedside table, and I greedily grabbed the bottle of OJ and bag of donuts he'd picked up for me. My head immediately cleared when I started to eat—ah, vitamin C and whatever magical ingredients create strawberry jelly filling.

"So, I don't want to alarm you," began Tom, "but you've been asleep for sixteen hours."

"Jeez," I replied. "How much of that time did you spend ironing?"

Tom guiltily looked down at his aggressively flattened pair of pants. "About four hours."

I've never been a late sleeper, even back when the government wasn't making my schedule. In fact, the summer when my big sister, Carrie, came home from college a victim of the "freshman fifteen," she made me promise to wake her up every day and force her to go running. I didn't even need to set an alarm; I woke every day an hour after sunrise and dragged Carrie down to the track behind the school. So it was kind of worrisome that I'd been passed out for more than half a day.

"What happened?" I asked Tom. "Am I okay?"

"They said you knocked that zombie out with your mind," Tom answered. "What's okay after that?"

"I don't know *what* I did, really."

"Well, whatever it was, you probably saved Harlene's life. You deserved a good sleep." He said it casually, but I could tell Tom was a little freaked out too. Whether by my Sleeping Beauty routine or by my telepathic knock-out punch, I couldn't tell.

"I screwed up," I replied quietly, studying my half-eaten donut. "I read that scene and only saw two zombies, not three."

Tom shook his head. "Slade didn't change at the school with the other two. We sent a team to his house last night. Found his parents eaten along with a bunch of dogs from the neighborhood. The prevailing theory is that he necrotized weeks back and had been hiding out."

I thought of the big map in Washington with its little red lights for zombie incidents. There hadn't been any other blinking alerts in the area. "How is that possible?"

"If nothing gets reported, I guess it's possible for a zombie to slip through the cracks," answered Tom.

I'd never thought of the NCD as anything but this infallible zombie-hunting agency. If a guy like Chazz Slade could go unnoticed, though, I wondered how many other zombies could be out there undetected. The thought made me shudder.

Tom set his ironing aside and sat down next to me on the edge of the bed. "How are you feeling?" he asked. When I sat up to answer him, I noticed a rust-colored stain on my pillow. I picked at it curiously with my thumbnail.

"Your nose bled a little during the night," he explained.

"Again? I never get nosebleeds."

He shrugged. "I wouldn't worry about it, Psychic Friend."

My head felt a million times better after a hot shower. Before I'd even finished getting dressed, there was a knock on the motel room door. I padded out of the steamy bathroom in my jellies—I thought they were dorky, but Tom insisted I never let my bare feet touch the floor of a rented bathroom—to find Jamison waiting in the doorway. Tom was giving him a dirty look, yesterday's bad judgment still not forgiven, but Jamison wasn't paying him any attention.

"Boss wants to see you," Jamison said to me.

"Harlene?" I asked, glad to hear she was up and giving orders. "How's she doing?"

Jamison shook his head. "The *other* boss."

At first, I didn't know who he meant. Then, I remembered last night's weirdly convenient appearance of the man from Washington.

"Mr. Bow Tie?"

Now Jamison and Tom exchanged a look, their animosity momentarily forgotten.

"I wouldn't call him that," muttered Jamison.

"His name is Alastaire," Tom offered helpfully.

"Is that his first name or last name?"

"You know," said Tom, "I'm not really sure."

"Just stick with 'sir,'" said Jamison.

It was cold and dark, the sky spitting sporadic bursts of rain. I pulled a thick wool hat on over my wet hair, shivering. I suddenly really wanted to get out of New Jersey. The barracks in Washington where Tom and I lived in between missions may have had terrible food and a seriously limited DVD collection, but right now they seemed like the coziest place in the world.

Tom and I crossed the motel parking lot to where Alastaire was waiting, leaning against the side of a black sedan, furiously typing on his phone. A blank-faced, burly G-man in a drab gray suit was standing next to him, holding an umbrella so not a drop of rain dampened his bow tie. As we approached, Alastaire slipped his phone into one of those lame leather hip holsters.

"Ah, there you are," he said.

"Good evening, sir," I replied, sticking to the governmental tone Tom and Jamison recommended.

The guy in the gray suit promptly folded up the umbrella and opened the back door of the car.

"Shall we go for a ride?" Alastaire asked.

I climbed into the car, trying not to show how nervous I felt being around this guy. Tom tried to climb into the car behind me, but Alastaire put a hand gently on his shoulder.

"We'll be okay without you, Thomas," he said.

"But I'm her guardian," replied Tom meekly.

"I know that," said Alastaire, and his patient smile was a tight thing that seemed almost painful for him to use. "I hired you. Don't worry, I'll bring her back safe."

Alastaire slid into the seat beside me, and the driver slammed the door shut. I watched Tom through the tinted window and had to resist the urge to put my palm up to the glass, like a kid in some movie being taken away from her parents and sent to a sinister orphanage.

The town was quiet as we drove through it. I figured most people were spending their Saturday inside after what had happened yesterday. You know, being close to family, being quietly reflective, all that typical grief stuff. We drove past the school, which was surrounded by yellow police tape. Flowers, candles, and framed photographs had begun to pile up on the sidewalk.

It was a depressing scene. We were usually too busy tracking down the undead to stick around the site of the crime after an incident played out, so this was the first time I'd ever seen the sadness that follows. The mourning. Just like yesterday was the first time I'd ever seen a zombie talk. Right when I thought that I'd gotten used to the NCD lifestyle, or at least gotten accustomed to the grind of reading death imprints and telling my team where to start their hunt. All this–well, it was a lot to think about.

But something told me that now wasn't the time to get reflective. The car was warm and mellow classical music was on the radio. Still, Mr. Bow Tie–Alastaire–made me uneasy. He wasn't staring at me–he was too busy typing into his phone–but somehow I felt like he was *observing* me.

"I'm glad we have this chance to talk," he said, his voice smooth as silk.

"Um, yeah. Me too," I replied reflexively.

"What you did last night was rather impressive."

I didn't even know how I'd managed to knock out Chazz Slade, and I sure didn't want to give Alastaire any inkling that I didn't know what I was doing. I just let the compliment hang there, hoping that would be the end of the discussion.

“Do you think you could do it again?”

I touched my nose. “It was kind of painful.”

He smirked. “It gets easier. Trust me. Most telepaths wouldn’t be capable of such a feat, much less at your age.”

“Is he dead?” I asked. “Chazz, er, the zombie?”

Alastaire laughed, shaking his head. “Well, dead is relative,” he said. “But he’s as alive as his kind ever gets. Your action allowed us to preserve him for study. Thanks to you, we’ll be able to better understand what we’re up against.”

An image popped into my head of Chazz strapped to a metal gurney, a man in a blood-spattered white lab coat standing over him with an electric bone saw. Chazz looked terrified. I squeezed my eyes shut and pushed the vision away. Was that just my imagination, or something else?

I’m not a big hospital person. The pungent antiseptic smell, the harsh lighting: it all just reminded me of my daily after-school visits with my dad as he was dying of pancreatic cancer. He was hooked up to all these machines and tried to joke and smile like he used to, but every day there was less and less of him until he was gone.

Alastaire put a hand on my shoulder as we crossed through the hospital lobby. I got the feeling that he was trying to comfort me, and that just creeped me out more, so I sped up my walk, his hand falling back to his side.

It was weird—as we passed the front desk, the nurse on duty didn't even look at us. I expected Alastaire to check in or something, but he seemed to know right where he was going. Of course, I didn't have a clue.

"What're we doing here?" I finally asked as we continued down a hallway in intensive care.

A doctor filling out paperwork jumped at the sound of my voice. It's like he hadn't noticed us until I'd spoken.

My head was still achy, but I forced my mind to focus. Alastaire was radiating something. . . . It's hard to explain, sort of like when you see a pan on a stove and can tell it's hot without touching it. Whatever he was doing, it caused the people walking by not to notice us. Their eyes just passed right over us, like we were slippery. It reminded me of the way we handled Incident Management—guiding our cover story into the minds of civilians—except now it was as if Alastaire was directing the way people perceived our very presence.

Wait—Alastaire was doing *what*?

My breath caught. Oh my god. He was a telepath too. What kind of nasty things had I been thinking about him?

"We're here to visit a particularly stubborn patient," he explained, either not noticing that I'd just had a major revelation about his mutant status, or choosing to ignore it. "Up to this point, she's resisted our cover story."

The patient's room we entered was completely dark except for the glow of the machines she was hooked up to. Alastaire closed the door behind us and I felt like I'd been locked in a room where some kind of séance was about to happen, the ghostly electric greens of the heart monitor floating like evil spirits around the bed of this shriveled, old gypsy woman.

This lady was little. Like, really little. Her feet poked up under the sheet about halfway down the bed. Yet even lying down and barely conscious, she had this air of authority about her. She had a tangled mop of frizzy gray hair, a big gold crucifix around her neck, and a giant bandage on her clavicle where one of our runaway zombies had taken a bite out of her.

"Ms. Hardwick," Alastaire said softly, "we're here to talk to you about yesterday's shooting."

"Pah," the woman spat, and when her eyes snapped open I actually jumped back from the bed. They were bloodshot but laser focused, swinging imperiously between me and Alastaire. "That was no school shooting, young man."

"Oh no?" Alastaire looked mildly amused. I didn't think there was anything funny about Hardwick. The way she looked at us—at me, in particular—was like she knew our every secret, had judged them, and was totally disgusted. I couldn't imagine what it must have been like to walk the halls of RRHS with that old wackadoo stalking around. It must have been impossible to get away with anything.

"I saw the devil in those children," said Hardwick with grave certainty. "He has risen."

Alastaire gave me a subtle nod, telling me that I should get on with bending Hardwick's mind to our version of events. I widened my eyes at him, mouthing, *Me?* He nodded again and turned back to Hardwick.

"My dear," he said to Ms. Hardwick. "What you're suffering from is post-traumatic stress."

Why would Alastaire make me do this when he was a perfectly good telepath himself, one obviously more powerful than me and without a psychic hangover? Was this some kind of test? It felt like it—like he'd been evaluating me, *watching* me, from the moment I got into his car.

I reached my mind out toward Hardwick's. It felt like my brain had just run a marathon and now I was asking it to bang out a few more laps. I immediately started sweating, something that had never happened before when I used my psychic powers. I leaned against the railing on the side of Hardwick's hospital bed, feeling dizzy. All I knew was if this was some kind of test, it was probably a good idea to pass.

As Alastaire went through the now familiar school-shooting narrative, I watched the words enter Hardwick's mind. Or try to enter. If all minds have doors where information enters, Hardwick's were locked, barred, and sealed over with bricks. Alastaire's words just bounced off her mind.

I probed the cracks in her mental walls, looking for a place to slip in. She really believed that Jake and Amanda had been some devil-sent sign of the apocalypse. To change that in Hardwick would mean altering her most firmly held beliefs. I saw a vision of Earth bathed in white, holy light and a giant, stern-faced bearded man reaching down, collecting her, and pulling her up to heaven where together the two of them shot lightning bolts down at the unlucky scum who remained. These beliefs went deep. If I did manage to get her to believe our story, I'm not sure what would've been left of her personality. Would she be a vegetable? I had no idea.

I didn't think I had the strength to full-on brainwash this old lady. More than that, I'm not sure I *wanted* to. Yeah, she was totally twisted, but I wasn't cool with just wiping away a person's deepest convictions—even if those convictions were about the Rapture and how most teenagers were walking devil enablers.

I felt pressure building in my sinuses and broke off contact. I snuffed my nose clear and tasted blood. It was just a trickle, but it'd happened again. Another bloody nose.

"Save your stories for the man at the pearly gates," Hardwick was telling Alastaire. "See how far they get you."

When we left Hardwick's room, another dark-suited NCD agent was waiting outside. This one was a member of Alastaire's personal team.

"Don't let anyone speak with her," Alastaire ordered as we walked out. He had his hand on my shoulder again but this time I didn't shake it off. It was the only thing keeping me steady.

Alastaire led me to the hospital waiting room and sat me down. He handed me a paper cup full of water and I drank greedily. I'd failed his test, and although I wasn't sure what that meant or why I'd even want to impress this creep and his bow tie, I was still pretty disappointed. I'd always prided myself on this whole telepath thing.

I thought of the story of Fred Hardy, this valedictorian that'd graduated the year before the government pulled me out of high school. Rumor was that he'd turned into a total burnout. My sister said he'd gotten to college and suddenly found that he wasn't the smartest kid in the room anymore, so he'd switched his major from engineering to keg stands, flunked out in his second semester, and now worked at some fast-food restaurant in the mall. I felt like Fred Hardy must have.

"You get people like that from time to time," Alastaire said, sounding more sympathetic than disappointed that I'd failed. "Sometimes they've got mental walls that you just can't get through. I didn't expect that you'd be able to change her mind, so to speak."

"So why have me try?"

Alastaire shrugged. "I wanted to see what you could do. You remind me a little bit of myself."

I could tell he'd meant that as a compliment, but it made me feel worse than when I thought I'd failed some test. So I was just another guinea pig.

"In Harlene's report, she mentioned you'd made telepathic contact with the male zombie fugitive. Is that true?"

I nodded, not sure why he'd suddenly changed the subject to Jake Stephens.

"Can you still feel him out there?"

"A little," I answered. "I need an object or something that he's touched to really focus in."

Alastaire waved this off. "The physical connection is just a crutch. Once you've made contact, you should be able to maintain it."

As soon as he said that, my mind came alive, as if it was suddenly eager to stretch its legs again. I swept across the astral plane, out of New Jersey, across Pennsylvania and—

What the fuck is on me? Is this a net? Did these bitches have a net?

I'm so hungry. They do not want to mess with me right now. Hitting me with their car was bad enough, but a freaking net?

Where's Amanda? Oh shit, are those crazy girls seriously shoving her into their car? I should help. I should do something. But I'm so hungry.

If I could just get this fucking net off me, I could still totally eat that stupid clerk before he calls the cops and *save Amanda.*

I gasped, coming back to myself. I'd just been in Jake Stephens's mind. Or what was left of it—it was a colder, more necrotized version of Jake than I'd peeked in on before, more like the zombies I usually tracked. For a moment, what he'd been feeling lingered: the heavy weight of the net he was covered in, the cold feeling of a wound in his side, an unnatural hunger that I hoped I'd never feel personally. Then it was gone, and Alastaire was looking at me expectantly.

"Well?" he asked.

"Nope," I replied too quickly. "Nothing."

I'm not even sure why I lied. Maybe after he'd forced me to play his little game, I wanted to rebel against Alastaire. If it were Harlene or Tom asking, I probably would've told them the truth. I trusted them, but not Alastaire. There was something wrong with him, like maybe he took a little too much pleasure in all this zombie hunting and mind screwing. Also, I really didn't want him to start thinking of me as some kind of protégé. And part of me, well, part of me didn't want to sell out Jake, even a gross version of Jake that was way too focused on stuffing his face. He was still just a kid like me, and if a zombie like Chazz Slade could slip through the cracks . . .

I shouldn't think things like that. Jake would have to be tracked. Killed. I just didn't want Alastaire to be the one to do it. I imagined Jake ending up like Subject Number Eleven, strapped to a treadmill for study. It wasn't right.

Alastaire frowned at me. *Now* he was disappointed. A weird feeling came over me then. It was like a strange hand was slipping underneath my shirt, slippery fingers sliding up my spine. Except, it was happening in my mind. I flinched and pushed that hand off with all the force my mind could muster.

"Unh," grunted Alastaire. He was watching me, his expression suddenly cold. He wetted his lips in this gross way that took too long and I had to look away. If they made hot telepathic showers, I'd have curled up in one right about then.

Alastaire stood up. I still didn't want to look at him.

"You're tired," he said. "I hope you'll feel differently tomorrow."

I said nothing and he walked away without another word. I had to call Tom from a pay phone to get a ride back to the motel.

JAKE

I WOKE UP FLAT ON MY BACK WITH THE REMAINS OF A dead raccoon on my face. The carcass was still warm and from the bristles of raccoon fur stuck between my teeth and the sticky, dried blood on my cheeks and mouth, it seemed like a pretty solid bet that I'd eaten that thing and then dozed off. *So, that's my life now. Eating vermin and napping. Great.*

Although part of me was glad that I'd apparently de-zombified this time by eating a friendly woodland critter. It was better than snacking on people. I guess.

My memory was all messed up. I remembered chasing that gas station attendant and getting hit by a car, and then I remembered getting attacked by a couple of teenage girls and winding up under some net. As for how I came to be lying on the concrete floor of a strange basement? That was the big mystery.

I sat up, squinting into the near darkness and spitting fur. Something moved next to me and I flinched.

"Relax," whispered Amanda, who was kneeling beside me. "It's just me."

"Shit," I whispered back, gulping a deep breath. "Where are we?"

"Basement of some house," she replied, sounding a little uncertain herself. "Weird freaking place."

"Weirder than the funeral home?"

"You tell me," said Amanda, helping me to my feet. There was a scratching sound when we started to move, followed by a couple high-pitched keens and snarls.

Something was down here with us, and it wasn't cool with company.

I looked around, my eyes now fully adjusted to the lack of light. The basement was unfinished and pretty much empty; some bricks and plastic tarps collected dust in one corner, a hot-water heater still in the box next to them. The place had an under-construction vibe.

Except I doubt the contractors had lined the far wall with locked pet carriers. A dozen sets of nocturnal green eyes peered out at me—possums, raccoons, a couple mangy stray cats. Some of them scratched at the cage walls, others sat huddled in the backs of their cages, hissing whenever Amanda or I moved. There was one cage just filled up with rats, the dark shapes climbing all over one another, searching for escape.

"Whoa," I said. "This is some serious serial-killer shit right here."

Amanda shook her head. "I think they eat them."

I noticed a possum carcass next to my raccoon left-overs. So, they'd fed us. Part of me was glad I didn't remember Amanda chewing through possum belly.

"Who are they?"

"As far as I can tell? A couple of crazy zombie lesbians."

"Oh."

The ceiling creaked above us. I could hear two hushed voices having an argument upstairs.

"What do they want with us?" I asked.

"The mean one seemed disappointed she couldn't eat us," said Amanda. "The other one insisted they bring us back here."

The arguing above us stopped, and the basement door was flung open. Someone turned on a light—just a single bulb dangling from the ceiling, which really added to the whole mass-murderer ambience.

I started looking around for something big enough

to knock out a lesbian. One of those loose bricks would do nicely.

Sensing me tense for action next to her, Amanda touched my arm.

"Whatever you're thinking about doing, don't."

"Seriously?" I whispered back. "Isn't this a fight-for-our-lives situation?"

"If they wanted to hurt us, they could've done it already."

Combat boots clomped heavily down the wooden basement steps. They belonged to a burly girl with spiky black hair. She was maybe nineteen and looked like she belonged to some militant punk rock band's vicious mosher hall of fame. She was dressed in an old army surplus jacket, a nostril piercing connected by a chain to a gauge in her ear. And she was holding a crossbow—seriously. I was definitely reconsidering my whole hit-her-with-a-brick strategy.

"I take it this is the mean one," I whispered to Amanda.

She nodded, her eyes on the girl who didn't look at all pleased to find us standing upright and communicating.

"No talking," she snarled, gesturing with the crossbow as she came down the steps. "Stand with your backs against the cages."

We did as she ordered, most of the animals shrinking away as we came near. A particularly bold raccoon pawed at Amanda's hair, but she gritted her teeth and pretended not to notice, keeping her eyes on the crossbow.

"If either of you fucking newbs tries anything shady, I will not hesitate to put an arrow through your brain. And believe me, you won't get up from that."

"That's like Zombie 101," I said, more to Amanda than the girl with the crossbow. I wasn't trying to be sarcastic, it was like a genuine moment of clarity. Like, of course, head-shots! That's how it would work. The girl with the crossbow glared at me, then turned to stare at Amanda.

"Is your boyfriend retarded, cheerleader?"

"We're not dating," said Amanda.

"You correct her about that, but not the retarded thing?"

"Shut up!" snarled the girl, shaking the crossbow in a way that made me worry a bolt might fly loose. "What are you doing in our territory?"

Neither of us answered. I made a big charades-style gesture with my open hands, hoping to convey confusion. She did tell us to shut up, after all.

"Ugh," said the girl. "You can talk."

"There are territories? Like, zombie territories?" asked Amanda.

The girl sighed. "Unofficially. Too many asshole undead in the same place acting stupid like you were in the gas station, and you'd fuck it up for all of us."

"Oh, well, we didn't know," I said. "We're new at this."

"No shit."

I noticed that one side of the girl's head was shaved. There, stenciled into the buzzed hair with barber precision, was the lightning-bolt logo of the greatest rock band in existence, Severed Lung.

"Cool," I said, pointing at her head. "I love those guys."

The girl narrowed her eyes at me. "Don't even try it," she said.

"Oh, come on, Grace," chimed an exasperated voice from the top of the stairs. "Would you just bring them up already?"

The girl with the crossbow—Grace—seemed to deflate a little at the sound of the other girl's voice, like all the scary had been sucked out of her. Well, most if it anyway. She lowered the crossbow and waved us toward the stairs.

"For the record," said Grace, "I probably would've killed you."

At the top of the stairs, our other captor was waiting.

"I'm Summer," she said, greeting first Amanda and then me with a warm hug. Summer was willowy, maybe an inch taller than me, and had a crazy mane of auburn hair that hung halfway down her back.

After she'd hugged us, she took Grace by the arms, pulling her close.

"You were *so* scary, baby," she said quietly, and pressed a little kiss onto her mouth. Grace was still trying to look tough, keeping one eye on me and Amanda, but I could tell Summer's approval had melted her a little.

I glanced over at Amanda. She was watching the couple with that "aww" look girls get when they see something totally adorable. I guess we were just going to move past that whole crossbow death-threat thing.

"Come on," said Summer. "I'll make you guys some tea and we'll talk."

Grace and Summer were shacked up in an empty, half-built house, part of a planned community that was abandoned when all the shiny suburbanites that wanted fancy, new houses went bankrupt a couple years ago. The water wasn't working, but Summer made tea by heating up a pot of bottled water over an electric grill. It was like a new kind of camping: roughing it in the suburbs.

"They never got around to finishing the roof," Summer said. "So we stay in the living room." Their few possessions were spread out around a space heater: sleeping bags, a couple lawn chairs, and a laptop. It looked like they'd been squatting here for a while.

In one corner of the room was a door with a heavy board nailed across it and a padlock bolted over the door handle. What were they keeping locked in there? With the way Grace was still giving me the stink-eye, I decided not to ask.

Summer settled us all around the space heater, Amanda and me on one of the sleeping bags and Summer in a lawn chair while Grace paced around behind her. Summer handed out cups of bitter-tasting tea. It was almost like being huddled around a campfire.

"So," Summer began, "when did you guys first turn?"

"Yesterday," Amanda answered.

"I knew it," said Grace. "They're like babies."

Summer nodded, giving us an understanding look. "The first days are the hardest. The hunger is bad while your body adjusts to the changes. It'll get easier to manage. Eventually, you won't need to eat as often to avoid going all—" She made a zombie face, mouth hanging open, eyes rolled back in her head. "You know."

"You're lucky we found you and stopped you from doing anything crazy," grumbled Grace, a hint of resentment in her voice. "We didn't have anyone to explain the rules to us."

"Yeah," I replied, glancing at the crossbow that now leaned against the wall. "Thanks for the hospitality."

"Hey! We fed you some of our animals," said Grace, staring me down. "You know how hard those fuckers are to catch?"

"So you can eat animals to control your hunger, as long as they're still alive," Summer chimed in, obviously trying to keep things mellow. "It's not like eating people, but it will keep you from changing for a while. The more you exert yourself, the sooner you'll need to eat. I find that meditation helps keep the hunger in check."

Grace snorted, rolling her eyes. Finally, we were in agreement about something. I couldn't picture myself sitting cross-legged, going *ohm ohm ohm* until the hungries went away.

"What about yoga?" asked Amanda.

"What *about* yoga?" replied Grace.

Summer smiled thoughtfully. "Never tried it. We could give it a shot, I guess. The meditating just helps to keep your mind off the hunger. It's important to keep the mind working, to stay in control, especially when the body starts to die."

Grace was staring daggers at Amanda, probably imagining exactly what I was—Summer and Amanda in those tight sweatpants doing all kinds of sexy stretches. Of course, my mind working the way it does, these thoughts led me to a natural question.

"So, how did you guys zombify each other?"

Grace's expression darkened even more, which I hadn't thought was possible. "What are you asking?"

"Uh," I stammered, glancing at Amanda for backup. It was her theory I was trying to verify after all, but she was just staring at me like she couldn't wait to see how I got myself out of this one. "Well, uh, you get it through sex, right? So, um, how did you . . . ?"

"Lesbians have sex too, genius." Amanda had finally decided to cut in now that it was already way too late. "Don't be such a heterosexist pig."

I scowled at her and saw her glancing over at Grace for approval, but Grace was just squeezing the bridge of her nose, like all this ignorance was giving her a migraine.

Luckily, Summer seemed ready to hold off on stringing me up by the balls. At least for now. "Yes, it's sexually transmitted," she explained patiently. "We didn't give it to each other. How we turned . . . Those aren't good stories. Eventually, we found each other."

"How?" asked Amanda.

"Zombie Facebook?" I added unhelpfully. Amanda shot me a look.

"We met on the Iowa border," answered Summer.

"What's in Iowa?" asked Amanda.

"A bunch of bullshit," replied Grace.

"It was six months ago. We'd heard rumors of a place for people like us there," said Summer. "A safe place. Some people even talked about a cure there. But the rumors were only half-right. There *was* a place for us. It just wasn't safe at all."

"And the cure . . . ?" asked Amanda, her eyes widening hopefully.

"It's bullshit," said Grace.

"I'm sorry, but I think I would've heard if there was a zombie city in Iowa," I said.

"Oh really?" Grace sneered. "Are you like Zombie-Anderson Cooper? Are your fingers on the pulse of the undead in America?"

"Technically, do the undead even have pulses?"

Amanda elbowed me. "Come on, Jake," she sighed. "We're all on the same side here, right?"

Grace ignored her. "Did you even know zombies existed before yesterday?" she asked me. "Maybe if you had, you wouldn't have eaten all your buddies."

Amanda and I stared at Grace, both of us dumbfounded.

"You know about that?" Amanda finally murmured.

Summer sighed. "We recognized you from the internet. The 'school shooting' is big news."

"It's why I said we should kill you," Grace went on. "Stupid assholes went and ate a bunch of innocents. You're going to fuck everything up for the rest of us."

"It wasn't our fault," said Amanda, her voice shaking. "Like you said, nobody told us the rules."

"It's okay," said Summer, reaching out to take Amanda's hand. "It *wasn't* your fault. It's a sickness. Even so, I can't imagine the guilt you're feeling."

For a second, I felt like I should put my arm around Amanda, but then she slipped her hand out of Summer's and sat up straighter, sticking out her chest a little (or maybe that was just my imagination). It was queen-bee Amanda summoning the powers that made kids like me scurry away from her in the halls.

"You said you hunt around here," said Amanda. "Just for animals?"

Grace and Summer exchanged a look.

"Well, *sometimes* animals," Summer said, sounding less than perfectly composed and sure of herself for the first time. "Animals help tide us over but . . ." she trailed off.

"Then what? Who is it okay to eat?"

Grace took a ring of keys out of her pocket.

"Come on," she said. "I'll show you."

They led us to the padlocked door. Summer held a candle while Grace unlocked the door and lifted the wooden bar.

Inside, huddled on the floor, was a middle-aged man. He was dressed in a suit, his hands and feet wrapped in duct tape, a strip also slapped across his mouth. A trickle of dried blood wormed its way down from his nose, across the tape. He looked like any other boring corporate dude: receding hairline, kinda pudgy, horrified to see teenagers.

"Perverts," announced Grace. "We eat perverts."

CASS

TOM STOOD NEXT TO MY BED HOLDING A BOTTLE OF OJ and a stale blueberry muffin from the motel's weak continental breakfast. He was already dressed in a silk tie and sleek charcoal suit. That would definitely help him stand out from the other boxy-looking G-men still hovering around the motel. I wondered how many suits he'd brought with him. We'd already been in New Jersey longer than I expected, and I'd been wearing the same clothes since we got here. "Maybe one of these days you could bring *me* breakfast in bed," he joked, handing me the muffin.

"Sorry," I said, taking a small bite. "Are we getting out of here today?"

"Not yet," he said, chewing his lip. "They've got something else they want you to do."

"Ugh," I replied, setting the muffin on the nightstand and burying my face in a pillow. "I'm not sure I'm up for it."

"Your head still bothering you, Psychic Friend?"

"Um, yeah. It's killing me."

"Luckily, I don't think today's task is too intense," he said. "Well, hopefully not."

I lifted the pillow up a bit to squint at Tom. "What is it?"

"I think I should let Harlene explain it."

I tossed the pillow aside and sat up straight. It wasn't like Tom to keep things from me. He'd seemed really uncomfortable when I filled him in on the details of my visit to the hospital with that skeev Alastaire, and he was still acting spooked. I didn't like to see Tom like this. He was supposed to be the one reassuring me and making things seem almost normal.

"What's going on, Tom?"

"I ran and got a change of clothes for you," he replied, holding up a shopping bag. "We'll be downstairs when you're ready."

"Secret Agent Tom is kinda freaking me out right now."

Tom sighed. "I'm sorry, it's just—things are a little heavy with this one. We need to be on our best behavior."

"You mean *I* need to be on *my* best behavior."

Had Alastaire said something to Tom about last night? Did he complain that I'd psychically rebuffed him when he tried to worm his way into my mind? Because I was pretty sure being my boss's boss didn't give him the right to go molesting my thoughts.

Tom stopped just in front of the door and turned to look at me, really considering his words.

"You were talking in your sleep last night," he said.

"What?"

"You said his name," Tom continued. "Jake. You said it a lot."

I felt my face getting hot. "Just a weird dream. Stop watching me in my sleep, psycho."

"Okay," Tom said, rolling his eyes. "Just remember: best behavior."

Tom closed the door and I immediately sank back into bed, letting my mind drift out of my body.

So I wasn't totally honest with Tom. My head wasn't really killing me; my brain was sore, just not in the same way it had been after I'd knocked out Chazz. Now it was like a pleasant ache, like that feeling after you have a good workout and can just tell your body's gotten stronger.

Also, I hadn't really been having weird dreams. It's

just that . . . I couldn't stop thinking about Jake.

It was like Alastaire said. I could still feel Jake out there. After that first time at the hospital last night, it became easier and easier to push myself across the astral plane and slip right into his thoughts. When I'd gotten back to the motel I'd wanted to see if I could do it again and it was easier than I thought it would be: I slipped into Jake's mind right as some scary girl was putting a crossbow in his face.

I only stuck around for a second before I jumped back out quickly, feeling nervous and giddy. I was getting more powerful. I had to resist kicking my feet in celebration, worried I'd wake up Tom, who was already asleep in the bed next to mine.

Of course, I couldn't sleep after that. I told myself I'd just take one more peek. A quick one, to make sure that girl didn't shoot an arrow in my new favorite zombie fugitive.

I ended up psychic eavesdropping on an entire zombie-orientation class, right up until Jake and the others started to eat some accountant-looking dude that was tied up in a closet. I broke contact for that part. I wasn't ready to share Jake's feelings of satisfaction as he burrowed his face into warm human guts. That was a little intimate, even for mind reading.

But the rest of it had all seemed so normal, just kids sitting around talking. I mean, sure, they were talking about undeath, but I'd had so little contact with people my own age lately that I'd take what I could get.

My mom used to tell me that I had an obsessive personality. She said when I was a kid she never needed to buy me a lot of toys because I'd always get hooked on one. I remember having this toy animal hospital where all the animals had those big Japanese-style googly eyes. It was like the only thing I played with for a year.

It was the same way when I got older. I never downloaded just a single track, always the whole album, and if the music was any good I would wear that album out, listening to it straight through until I was sick of it. I watched my favorite movies over and over too. I'm pretty sure I could do all the Gwyneth Paltrow scenes from *The Royal Tenenbaums* from memory.

So now that I knew how to do it, I couldn't help popping back into Jake's mind . . . over and over. It was like watching a movie that never ended. Yes, he was a zombie. But also? Sort of a cool guy. He reminded me of someone I might have liked before I went all governmental.

But I couldn't really explain that to Tom. Or anyone else. Spying on Jake's mind would have to be my secret, which made it seem kind of stalkerish and also more alluring.

Now, as soon as Tom left me to change, I found myself wanting to check in just one more time. So I did. I've never been one for self-control.

This sucks. How are we supposed to dig a hole when the

ground is almost frozen? It's way harder to dig a grave in real life than they make it seem on TV. Those mafia dudes must be out there for hours whenever they have a body to bury. Stupid Grace and her stupid rules. At least she's out here digging too. So . . . ha.

There isn't even that much left of that dude from last night to bury, just gristle and bones and stuff. Gristle. That reminds me.

"Okay, take my mind off this manual labor. Top five Severed Lung tracks."

Grace has to think about it. Any true fan would have a Top Five ready to go in an instant. Or maybe she just doesn't want to talk to me. "Number five: 'Ejaculate Gristle at Sunset.'"

"Oh, no way. That's my number one."

I let go of Jake's mind, feeling guilty. What was wrong with me? I needed to get this telepathic addiction under control. Tom said they were waiting on me, I couldn't just stay in bed all day being a fly on the wall of Jake's brain. And maybe it wasn't the best idea to get to know a zombie that it was my job to track and help kill.

Even as I thought that, I knew I'd check back in on Jake later.

I got out of bed and opened up the shopping bag Tom left for me. A modest-looking black dress waited for me along with a gray cardigan sweater. It wasn't really my style, and it was definitely a far cry from my usual NCD jumpsuit.

Me wearing a dress, and Jake burying a body. I wondered which of us would have the weirder day.

• • •

The gang was assembled in the motel's shabby conference room. Some suited-up NCD agents milled around one side of the room, picking over a box of donuts and waiting for someone to give them an order. Tom and Jamison stood talking quietly with Harlene, who I hadn't seen since Chazz attacked her. Her arm was in a sling, the place where Chazz had taken a piece out of her wrapped in bandages, but otherwise she looked like her usual peppy self. Her makeup was done with the usual beauty queen flourishes, maybe a little heavy on the rouge to make up for lingering blood loss.

Harlene's grin was a thousand watts when I entered, but from the guilty look the others all had on their faces, I could tell they'd just been talking about me.

"There's my heroic Sweet Pea," bubbled Harlene as she wrapped me in a one-armed hug. "You really pulled my bacon out of the fire the other night."

"I'm just glad you're okay," I said, careful of her arm as I squeezed her back. "You are okay, right?"

"This?" said Harlene, raising her sling. "Pff, believe me I've had worse, baby doll."

I'm not really sure what could've been worse than a zombie bite, so I just smiled and nodded, letting Harlene do her fearless leader thing. It was nice to have her back. I hoped it meant Alastaire was on his way home to Washington.

"And look at you, all gussied up," she said, looking over the clothes Tom bought for me. "Your handler sure knows how to pick out a dress."

"I feel like I'm going to a funeral," I replied, feeling a little uncomfortable.

Harlene frowned at me. "Oh. Tom didn't tell you?"

It was standing room only in the town's big mega-church for the RRHS dedicated Day of Prayer and Remembrance. Kids and their parents crowded into the pews, all of them dressed in black, a lot of them crying. A big screen at the front of the church displayed a montage of photographs, smiling high school kids blissfully unaware that one day they'd be zombie food. Morbid imagery, I know, but thinking like that helped me stay detached from all the grieving; I needed to treat this place like just another crime scene. The dead bodies I'd encountered I could deal with. The live ones, on the other hand . . .

A lady from the PTA stood by the door handing out armbands in the red and gold RRHS school colors, each with a black 27, memorializing the final victim tally from Jake and Amanda's rampage. I took an armband but didn't put it on—it felt phony to do that. It was bad enough I was here spying on these people while they were mourning. I stood in the back with some other latecomers. No one noticed me.

My mission was to take the town's psychic

temperature. As far as I knew, the NCD had never had to create a cover story this huge before, and I was here to make sure it had taken root. I opened up my mind and let the thoughts cluttering the room drift in, scanning for any stray memory of flesh-eating zombies.

During NCD training, they told us that some telepaths have problems functioning in crowds, that they find the crush of other people's thoughts overwhelming, but I'd never had that issue. Letting all those grieving minds into my own was rough, though. Sampling the sadness of, like, three hundred people all at once definitely isn't something I'd recommend.

There was Keith DeCarlo's mind—father of the late Adam DeCarlo. He'd come alone, his wife unable to get out of bed. He'd known Jake since childhood and couldn't believe the same boy they'd had over for hundreds of sleepovers would do something like this. He hated him for it.

There was Eliza Brady's mind. She'd been in the same clique as Amanda Blake but was sort of a hanger-on. Her lesser position at the lunch table had probably saved her life. She accepted that it had been a shooting: she remembered the blood and guts, but she couldn't remember actually seeing Amanda shoot anyone. It had all happened so fast.

It was like that in all the kids' memories. There were fuzzy gaps that any good telepath would notice as psychic screwing around, but I doubted whatever grief counselor the school hired would be trained in the brainwashing arts. As for the parents, they hadn't been there, so they believed the official story. No one was thinking about zombies. Most of them were totally focused on their grief.

It was becoming overwhelming, that sadness, seeping in with every mind I scanned. I felt tears well up in my own eyes; my breath got short; my legs started to tremble.

It was too much. I needed to get out of there. I staggered to the door, wiped my eyes on my sleeve, and burst out into the cold air. I could still feel echoes of sorrow bouncing off the walls of my brain even as I walked quickly away from the church, swearing to myself that I'd examine a thousand of the nastiest zombie crime scenes before I'd go back to a funeral like that again.

The street was empty outside the church.

And then I saw someone, a lone girl sitting astride a bicycle across the street. She watched the church apprehensively, a knit hat with a brim pulled down almost over her eyes. There was something familiar about her. Her mind radiated something different from the people's inside the church—it was sadness, but also guilt and anger.

Maybe I was still feeling all emotional after the buffet of human suffering I'd binged on in the church, or maybe part of my subconscious recognized this girl before I even realized it, but I found myself crossing the street to talk to her.

She saw me coming and immediately hopped on her bike, starting to pedal away. I realized then who she was and, not really thinking that this was probably a major violation of NCD conduct, I waved and shouted her name.

"Kelly!" I yelled at Jake's sister, jogging after her. "Hey! Hold on!"

Kelly stopped reluctantly, eyeing me. She looked nervous. I'd never considered what the whole school-shooter narrative might mean to Jake's little sister. She definitely wouldn't be a popular person in town.

"Do I know you?" she asked.

I answered without thinking. "I know your brother."

"My brother, the school shooter," she spit, looking away.

"Um, yeah." I realized this was probably a really bad idea. What was I doing talking to Jake's sister? I mean, I did kinda feel like I knew her brother, but that was literally all in my head.

"Were you there Friday?" Kelly timidly asked. "During the whole . . ." she trailed off.

"No." I shook my head. "I was home, sick."

"Lucky you," Kelly replied. "Look, I'm, uh, sorry, if my brother killed any of your friends or anything."

"It's okay," I replied, because apparently my immediate reaction in these situations is to say the dumbest thing possible. Kelly looked relieved, though. I wondered if she'd talked to anyone since the incident.

"I just . . ." She hesitated. "This is gonna sound dumb,

but he drove me to school that day. He didn't have, like, a backpack full of guns or whatever. I mean, he was worried about some stupid presentation."

Ah, crap. A skeptic. Still, I figured I could just let this one go. It was natural that Kelly wouldn't want to believe that her brother was a school shooter. And she was just a middle schooler–it's not like anyone would listen or care if she started spouting off doubts. It wouldn't be in violation of NCD protocol to let her go on thinking of her brother as not-a-murderer.

"You knew him, right?" she continued. "He's, like, a lazy idiot. What they're saying he did doesn't make any sense."

"It's what happened, though," I replied, the words sounding weak when I said them. This conversation was a huge mistake. I needed to bail.

No sooner had I thought that than a black sedan rolled up to the curb next to us. The passenger window rolled down and Alastaire peered out at us. I had the sudden urge to steal Kelly's bike and pedal away as fast as I could.

"Brrr," said Alastaire. "Sure is cold out. Would you girls like a ride?"

Such a creep. I was about to turn him down, but then Kelly dropped her bike on the sidewalk and climbed robotically into Alastaire's backseat. He'd done something to her–given her a psychic shove. Alastaire adjusted his stupid bow tie, watching me closely.

"Coming?" he asked.

JAKE

"SO, WHAT DID YOU HAVE PLANNED THIS WEEKEND?" I asked Amanda.

"Definitely not this," she answered.

We watched through the living room window as Grace tackled a short, hairy little man, driving her shoulder into his gut and pinning him to the ground. Right away she mounted him like one of those professional cage-fighters and just started punching the crap out of him. Outside of Roadblock teeing off on Amanda the other day, this was easily the worst beating I'd ever seen.

Amanda looked away. I didn't blame her, really—this was intense. Not zombie-feeding intense, but still.

Apparently, it was all routine for our hosts.

The hairy guy's name was SkiChamp69. That was his screen name anyway, and that's all Grace and Summer knew. They'd lured him here via some chat room. I didn't really want to know the details, but they assured us that he deserved to get locked in the closet and served for dinner.

Outside, Summer crossed the lawn and tapped Grace on the shoulder. She immediately stopped punching SkiChamp69, who looked knocked out. They each grabbed a wrist and started dragging him toward the house.

A thought had occurred to me when I was burying last night's dinner in the backyard, and it hit me again now: *Is this what zombie life is going to be like?*

Yesterday, Amanda had gotten me all inspired to be a fugitive and fight the government or whatever the plan was. It was one thing when it was just the two of us, driving cross-country—hell, I would've been down for that experience prior to turning undead. Having Amanda around, even with her shitty taste in music, was pretty much the only good thing that'd happened to me since Friday. But now, watching Grace and Summer shove SkiChamp69 into the closet, it was like . . . maybe this was life now? Maybe the whole road-trip thing was a crappy idea, like we were in zombie denial or something, just trying to outrun our problems.

I mean, it seemed like Grace and Summer had a good thing going here, in a way—a nice, low-key place to live, no government hit squads, food showing up on their doorstep.

But was this it?

"Thanks for your help out there," Grace said to us as she slammed the closet padlock back into place.

"It looked like you had it under control," Amanda replied.

"Yeah," snorted Grace. "Well, eventually, you'll have to start working for your food if you want to keep hanging out here."

She tossed me a set of car keys.

"At least go see if he's got anything useful in his car before we ditch it."

I saluted. "Yes, ma'am."

Amanda and I marched outside to SkiChamp69's car. It felt like Mom sending the kids out to get the groceries, except in this case Mom was a bitter zombie that could probably moonlight as a bare-knuckle boxer. I could tell Amanda was starting to get tired of this whole scene, particularly of Grace. She was carrying herself like the regal ice queen all the time now, not showing any signs of the secret dorkiness I'd been digging that night at the mortician's.

"How long do you want to stick around here?" she asked as we started rifling through the fast-food wrappers and road maps in SkiChamp69's car. There was a bottle of whiskey hidden in the glove compartment. I tossed it into the yard—maybe our hosts would want to raise a toast with tonight's feast.

"I don't know," I replied, shrugging. "What if this is, like, the best we can hope for?"

"Seriously?" She sounded offended by the very idea. "Personally, I don't want to spend my undeath re-creating *Dateline* specials."

"There's free food here," I countered.

"For now. You heard Grace." Amanda slid out of SkiChamp69's backseat, disgustedly brushing her hands off on the backs of her jeans. "You think they'll keep feeding us forever?"

"Summer might," I said, shrugging. "She's a hippie. They're nice like that."

"And Grace still looks at us like she might put an arrow in us at any time."

"Bolt."

"That's what I'm suggesting."

"No, I mean, they're called crossbow *bolts*. Not crossbow *arrows*."

"Who gives a shit, Jake?" Amanda sighed. "Stay on topic."

There wasn't anything exciting in the car. I sat down

on the trunk, looking out over the half-finished houses. Amanda sat next to me.

"You still want to go to Michigan?" I asked.

"Yeah," she replied. "First there, and then I want to check out Iowa."

"What? They made it sound like a total shit-show," I said, thinking back to the evasive way Grace and Summer had talked about the Midwest last night.

"They mentioned a cure."

"Psshh—haven't you seen *any* zombie movies? There's never a freaking cure." I waved back toward the house where Grace and Summer were waiting. "They even said it was bullshit."

Amanda looked unconvinced. "I'll take bullshit over the alternative. Staying here in our little zombie commune of four, finding people to eat over email. You don't think someone's going to come looking for these guys? Like gross-ass pedophiles don't have families? We'd be safer on the road."

She made some good points. But then, she always seemed to make good points. I would've put it down to just the hotness factor—like, I'm sure it was easy for girls like Amanda to win arguments and get their way—but I think I'd started to build up an immunity to her good looks. She really had done all the thinking so far. And meanwhile, all I could think about was how much I didn't want to think about being a zombie.

Amanda had it all figured out and maybe I was slowing her down. Like, if she'd ditched me back in Jersey she would've already unraveled a government conspiracy and turned Iowa into a zombie utopia. Or maybe cured the plague. I wouldn't put it past her.

It's just . . . I didn't share that can-do attitude. I wanted my basement, my bowl, my Xbox. I wanted normal.

"You know what I had planned this weekend?" I asked her, totally changing the subject, thus avoiding any big zombie-plan decision. "*Nothing.* I was just going to hang out in my basement and do nothing. And I was so, so, so cool with that."

Amanda studied me for a second, trying to figure out where the hell my mind had gone. Then she shrugged and decided to play along.

"I didn't have any big plans."

"Seriously?" I asked, stunned. "No big party at Cindy St. Clair's house?"

"I was kinda off those parties since Chazz started being all stalkerish. I probably would've stayed in, worked on my college applications, hung out with my mom . . ." she trailed off, her voice a little shaky.

"Wow," I said. "I never knew popular girls were so boring."

Amanda elbowed me. "Says Mr. Cool over here, chilling in his basement. Were you just going to do that for the rest of your life?"

"Huh," I replied, actually thinking about it. "Yeah, I guess that sort of was my plan."

"Sad plan, Jacob Albert. Time for a new one."

"If it's because of Grace, I promise she's not always like this," Summer said. "I think she feels a little threatened. It's been just the two of us for a while. Well, the two of us and our houseguests."

I'd told Summer that Amanda and I planned to leave as we picked our way through the woods behind the housing development, looking for snacks. We took a zigzag route through the trees, stopping every twenty yards so Summer could bend down to check the snares and traps they'd set. So far, we hadn't come across any squirming wildlife to add to their basement stockpile.

"We don't think staying in one place is a good idea for us, that's all," I replied. I'd only met Summer yesterday, but I still felt weirdly guilty telling her we were bailing. I guess bonds form quickly when you devour people together. Also, it felt comforting to know there were other zombies out there, making a go of it.

"I never asked, how long have you guys been zombies?"

"I don't know about Grace," answered Summer, examining an empty loop of rope and then burying it beneath a blanket of leaves. "She doesn't like to talk about it. Nine months for me."

"That's it? You guys have such a system, I figured it'd be longer."

"Nine months is long for our kind," she replied. "You know, you guys aren't the first other zombies we've met."

I didn't want to ask what happened; I had a feeling that it involved men in black SUVs with heavy artillery. Summer's mind was off someplace, though, not even paying me much attention as we wandered through the woods.

"Grace and I were part of a couple larger groups that made it to Iowa about the same time. The place was crawling with ghouls so bad it's all you could smell."

"Ghouls?"

Summer shrugged. "My name for what happens when we don't eat for too long. Just dead bodies walking around aimlessly, trying to bite anything warm. When you reach that point, I'm not even sure feeding will bring you back."

"Did you go to Iowa because of the whole cure thing?"

"At that point—I don't know—we were just going. Just to keep moving. The others talked about some doctor there, but it was just talk. Something to keep our spirits up. I guess even zombies need to believe in something."

"Oh," I said, sounding disappointed.

"If you're thinking of going there—don't," Summer said, her eyes wide with fear as she remembered. "The government—I guess that's what they were—they'd set up, like, a blockade and were shooting the ghouls from up there. When they saw us, realized what we were, they shot at us too. Killed everyone except Grace and me."

"That sucks," I replied, and even though I totally meant it sincerely, it was the exact same half-ass condolence I gave Henry Robinson when his pet lizard crawled under the dryer and cooked itself. Heavy situations were sort of difficult for me.

"Yeah," said Summer, turning away. "But the group I was with, they'd feed on anyone. Like you with the gas station attendant. They weren't the best crowd to be hanging around with, anyway."

"Right," I said, guiltily kicking a tree branch.

"Grace went a little over the top beating up that guy today," continued Summer, "but he's bad. He deserves to be eaten. We have to eat or our minds shut down, our instinct takes over, and then who knows how many people we hurt. Animals don't always sate the hunger. But the way Grace and I go after humans, we figure we do the world a favor with every meal, and we keep ourselves in control."

I scratched my head, not totally sure how to respond to that outpouring of zombie philosophy. It was like Summer had been practicing that speech—maybe using it on herself a lot.

"You know what's funny?" she asked. "I used to be a vegetarian. Now I'm a flesh-eating monster."

"'Monster' is harsh," I said, but Summer immediately waved this off. She started back toward the house and I followed a few steps behind.

"My folks were Buddhists," she said. "They raised me to think of everyone as inherently kind and generous. But now I know that's not true. We're all bad, selfish people. You know how I know?"

I didn't really want to know. This conversation had taken a serious turn for the depressing. But Summer answered without waiting for my reply.

"Because if I wasn't so selfish, I would've killed myself nine months ago. Instead, I just keep eating people."

Amanda and I drove out of western Pennsylvania after nightfall. Amanda was in the passenger seat, studying a road map in the yellow glow of the dome light.

"This thing is nuts," she said, shaking her head.

As soon as we told her we were leaving, Grace had become a lot more helpful. She'd found the road atlas under SkiChamp69's passenger seat and had spent a couple hours marking locations and addresses on it, filling the map with enough potential zombie pit stops to keep Amanda and me fed all the way to Michigan. It's like she'd already had the information ready, a list of bad people to eat if she ever found herself crossing the country. Meanwhile, Summer had peeled about three hundred bucks off a roll of bills they kept squirreled away, money

I assumed they'd taken off the perverts before burying them in the backyard. She'd also donated a spare blanket and a pet carrier filled with rats. I turned up the car radio loud enough so I didn't hear the little things squeaking in the trunk every time we went over a bump.

"They aren't even all pedophiles," Amanda said, squinting at the map. "Like this guy in Ohio—Grace wrote that he stole money from his employees' pensions and ended up retiring in a mansion after six months in jail."

I didn't feel like talking about Grace's road atlas of victims. I was feeling pretty bummed out; something about the way Grace and Summer had stood on the front steps of their house and watched us go made me feel like we were now really heading for somewhere unknown. It was like a couple of pedophile-murdering parents watching their kids go off to their first day at zombie school. Grace waved good-bye, maybe half sarcastically, while Summer just smiled sadly, her arms clasped around herself. I wondered if we'd see them again. Probably not, right? Summer made it sound like the life expectancy of a zombie wasn't long—you either get killed by the government or go full-on starving ghoul. Not a lot to look forward to.

"Gotta eat someone," I replied absently.

"Yeah, okay, but where do we draw the line?" she asked. "Do you know how I knew how to hot-wire that car back in Jersey? Because my dad taught me."

"Seriously?"

"Yep. It's what he used to do, before he got caught. Now he's in jail. So would he be on Grace's list?"

I looked over at Amanda to see if she was screwing with me. She wasn't.

For some reason, I'd always assumed all the popular kids at RRHS were born to some secret society of rich yacht-club parents, explaining their seemingly natural ability to rise to the top of the social food chain. My head was starting to hurt.

"What about your mom?" I asked. "Is she a car thief too?"

"No," answered Amanda, looking out the window. "Lucky for me and Kyle, she has her shit together."

I felt compelled to share something back. "My dad is an accountant. My mom manages a kids' clothing store."

"Cool," said Amanda. "So, we won't be eating your parents."

"Uh, no, I hope not."

"My point is," she continued, "the vigilante zombie stuff feels like a slippery slope, you know? I'm not sure I want to be making those decisions."

I sighed. All this zombie talk was getting to be a real drag.

The highway zoomed past, mostly empty with a few headlights headed in the opposite direction. I was trying hard to maintain a positive outlook on all this undead bullshit, but it was tough when talk kept going back to the ethics of eating people.

"Dude. This is making me hungry. Or something. Let's just have a normal conversation, okay?"

Amanda snorted, but closed the road atlas and looked over at me. "Okay. Topic?"

I thought about it. "You remember that career test the guidance counselor gave us? What did you get?"

"Theoretical physicist," said Amanda.

"Shut up!" I was so surprised that I swerved into the next lane. The car behind me blared its horn.

"No." She smiled. "I'm screwing with you. I don't even remember what I got. Something insulting, like secretary. Tests like that are basically a high school version of those what-celebrity-are-you Facebook quizzes. It's, like, who cares?"

"I didn't get anything," I admitted. "I didn't score high enough to get *anything.*"

"You failed a career test?" Amanda laughed, then covered her mouth. "Oh, Jake, that's so *sad.*"

"Well, think of it this way. I'm really good at flunking tests. It's a talent."

"I would've wanted to be a lawyer, I think," said Amanda, tapping her lip thoughtfully. "Or a psychologist. Something to help people, I guess."

"You'd have made a badass lawyer."

"Thanks."

We fell silent, probably both thinking about what we would've done if cannibalism hadn't chosen us. The road less traveled, right?

"Hey," said Amanda, "pull over."

"What for?"

"Just do it."

We were just over the Ohio border. It was a densely wooded and dark section of road, no streetlights for this backcountry stretch. I pulled us off to the shoulder and killed the engine. The car was dark except when a passing vehicle rumbled by, shaking us, headlights briefly lighting up Amanda's face. She rummaged for something underneath her seat.

"I swiped this before we left," she said, and held up SkiChamp69's bottle of whiskey. "Want to see if zombies can still get drunk?"

CASS

I EXPECTED ALASTAIRE TO HAVE HIS DRIVER TAKE us back to the motel where the rest of my NCD division waited. Instead, we drove toward the outskirts of town, the peaceful suburbs giving way to eerily quiet blocks filled with shuttered factories and crumbling buildings. It was like the textbook definition of "wrong side of the tracks." We were near the spot where just a couple days ago my team had let Jake and Amanda get away.

"Ah, the real New Jersey," mused Alastaire. "So charming."

I couldn't figure out where we were going, but I didn't

feel like it was anywhere good. What would a polished suit like Alastaire want in a place like this unless he was up to something dastardly? Like mustache-twirling, petting-a-cat-with-an-iron-glove dastardly.

I told myself I had no reason to feel paranoid—that I worked for the US Government, that the president himself had called my mom. Still, I couldn't help it. What if Alastaire knew that I'd spent most of the last day secretly hanging out in the psyche of a priority target? What was the NCD penalty for insubordination? Treason? They hadn't gone over that in orientation.

It certainly didn't help that Jake's sister, Kelly, was sitting next to me basically catatonic. She had her hands folded in her lap, eyes straight ahead. I tried to get a feel for her mind, psychically probing as gently as I could, but her brain was like a brick wall.

"Any luck locating the Stephens boy?" asked Alastaire casually. I glanced at Kelly, but she didn't react at all to the mention of her brother.

"It's hard—" I began, trying to phrase my answer in a way that wouldn't necessarily be a lie. "I'm still having trouble focusing."

"Mhm," was the extent of his reply. Pretty much impossible to tell whether he believed me or if I was in trouble or what. I assumed trouble.

"Where are we going?" I asked, trying to sound equally casual.

"Oh," said Alastaire as if the minor detail of our

destination had just slipped his mind. "I want to show you a little project I've been working on."

A few minutes later, our car pulled up to an abandoned factory that looked like it had once hosted a riot, been set on fire, and then been struck by lightning. There were a bunch of NCD guys waiting for us, but not anyone that I recognized from previous missions. They were Alastaire's private team and they looked different somehow—angrier, more grizzled, with perpetual Clint Eastwood stares. It's like Alastaire had assembled himself a crew of only Jamisons.

A pair of agents met us at the huge, iron double doors of the factory. One of them escorted Kelly away from us and she followed with wordless, brainwashed obedience. The other one opened up an umbrella, shielding Alastaire from the rivulets of rust-colored water that leaked down from the factory's ceiling.

"Where's he taking her?" I asked, watching the agent disappear around a corner with Kelly.

"Interrogation," answered Alastaire, looking me over. "You're going to ruin that nice sweater."

I glanced down at myself. The leaky ceiling had already dribbled a couple light brown stains on my new outfit. Alastaire gestured for me to stand under the umbrella with him, even offered me his arm. My whole being recoiled—it was like he'd flopped a slimy tentacle at me—but I remembered Tom's advice to be on my best behavior and decided to try to heed it. For now.

Cringing inwardly, I slipped my hand through the crook of Alastaire's elbow and we made our way across the factory floor like a lord and lady on the worst stroll in recorded history.

"They used to process meat here," said Alastaire. "Isn't that interesting?"

"Very," I said dryly, my eyes following moldy conveyor belts to stripped-down machines that looked like big blenders.

"The conditions aren't ideal, I'll admit," continued Alastaire, sounding like a tour guide. "But I've been looking for an opportunity to field-test some of my work, and this is the best we could come up with here in New Jersey."

It didn't look like Alastaire's skeleton crew of NCD goons was doing much work. They stood around under the sections of ceiling that leaked the least, polishing weapons and glowering. Alastaire led me past them without a word.

"I've thought long and hard about this country's zombie problem," Alastaire lectured. "On the one hand, they're monstrous beasts that present an imminent threat to our quality of life. On the other hand, they have certain qualities that I find appealing."

"Like all the brain-eating?" I asked, the words out before I could bite my tongue like a good little psychic trouper. Alastaire smirked.

"They're just animals," he said. "Animals with heightened strength and speed, animals with miraculous healing abilities. I want you to remember that, Cassandra."

They're sick people, I wanted to say, but I managed to hold my tongue this time. I felt like my view of zombies was starting to move away from the official NCD doctrine, like maybe they hadn't given us all the facts in training, but I definitely didn't want to have that discussion with Alastaire. I especially didn't want to let on that last night I'd been in Jake Stephens's mind and had found it very un-animallike. Except for the part where he and his friends ate that guy. But everyone had their flaws, right?

"Like all animals," continued Alastaire, "I believe they can be trained."

We approached a heavy steel door at the back of the factory. A meat locker. The NCD guards manning the door stepped away discreetly as Alastaire approached.

"There's a line of red tape on the floor of this room," he said. "Don't step over the red tape."

The door squealed on its rusty hinges when Alastaire pushed it open. As we walked through, the guy with the umbrella peeled off. Now it was just me and Alastaire. The room was lit by halogen bulbs that flickered and dimmed constantly; freestanding metal shelves made two rows down the center of the room, broken in places with jagged edges. I itched for a tetanus shot just looking at them. Between the shelving hung metal hooks on chains. The whole place still had a rotten-meat smell to it.

I looked down at my feet to check out this red line Alastaire had put down. My toes were right against it.

When I looked up, a zombie was charging at me.

I'm a little embarrassed to admit that I screamed. I'm less embarrassed to admit that I immediately jumped behind Alastaire, using him as a human shield.

There was a *clang* of metal snapping taut, and the zombie jerked to the ground, falling just inches short of the red line. I breathed a sigh of relief. He was tethered to the far wall by a chain that was attached to a collar around his neck. The chain was shiny, new steel—it was probably the only shiny thing in this whole factory.

The zombie scrambled to his feet, snarling at us and snapping his teeth at the air. His skin was gray and saggy, his eyes yellowed and sunken. He was so corpselike that it took me a minute to recognize him.

It was Chazz Slade.

I stayed a half step behind Alastaire, just in case that chain wasn't bolted into the wall properly. Alastaire didn't seem at all concerned, standing with his toes on the line, watching the muscles in Chazz's neck strain as he tried to bull toward us. When Chazz reached out, his grasping fingers nearly brushed Alastaire's bow tie. It was sort of thrilling to be this close to a creature that wanted to eat you alive but couldn't, like getting right up against the glass of a lion's cage at the zoo. I had to force myself to look away from Chazz and his thoughtless stare of hungry rage.

"Why is he here?" I asked.

"I told you, it's very difficult to take them alive," said Alastaire. "Back in Washington, I was running out of test subjects. The procedure I've been developing is dangerous, you see. At least for them. Aneurysms mostly, but sometimes a persistent vegetative state. Sometimes the procedure just doesn't take, and the subject has to be terminated."

"Um, what procedure? What are you talking about?"

Alastaire shrugged out of his suit jacket. I noticed for the first time that he carried a gun—a silver thing holstered under his armpit, big enough to impress even Jamison. Alastaire draped his jacket neatly over his arm and held it out to me.

"Would you mind holding this?" he asked.

I took his coat, too frazzled by the scene in front of me to do anything but comply.

"It has taken some years of trial and error," explained Alastaire, "but I believe I've finally perfected it. A procedure that will let us control the zombies."

My mouth hung open, eyebrows raised. Alastaire smiled at me, amused.

"I'm sorry," I said. "What do you mean, 'control' them?"

"They're savage beasts that think of nothing but their hunger," answered Alastaire, "but that doesn't mean they can't learn some very basic concepts. That food comes when they behave. That they shouldn't bite the hand that feeds them."

I was considering upgrading Alastaire from creepy bureaucratic overlord to full-fledged mad-scientist psychopath. His whole spiel was out-there, even for the NCD. I wondered if Harlene and Jamison knew about his experiments.

He rolled up the sleeves of his dress shirt. On the underside of his forearm I saw a plastic implant, like a nozzle, surrounded by fading pink scar tissue. It reminded me of the long-term chemo tube the hospital had put in my father. Just looking at it made me queasy.

"Observe," Alastaire said.

He picked up a piece of translucent silver tubing from one of the nearby shelves. I hadn't even noticed it draped there. The tube was about six feet long, the width of a dime, and screwed perfectly into the nozzle on Alastaire's forearm.

I noticed that Chazz had stopped snarling and biting. He watched Alastaire with the zombie equivalent of fascination—only one eye rolled back in his head.

"You see the way he looks at me?" asked Alastaire, glancing from Chazz to me. "He knows me."

Alastaire stepped over the red line. I put out a hand

to stop him, my instinct to avoid seeing anybody turned into zombie lunch overriding my revulsion for him, but he was out of reach.

Chazz watched Alastaire approach with his head cocked, a low growl rumbling in his throat. That he didn't just attack right away was already mind-blowing enough. Then Alastaire spoke.

"Kneel," he said.

Chazz swayed back and forth for a moment, made a plaintive groaning sound that ended with a string of black phlegm spilling down his chin, and fell on his knees. I covered my mouth to keep something stupid and horrified from tumbling out.

Alastaire circled behind Chazz. He put his hand on Chazz's head and shoved Chazz's chin down into his chest. I could see it then, a node drilled into the back of Chazz's head just like the one on Alastaire's wrist. Of course, the doctors hadn't taken nearly the care with Chazz's surgery as they had with Alastaire; the flesh was blackened and swollen around the node, rotten even for a zombie.

"I've been working on this for some time," said Alastaire, tapping the node on Chazz's skull. "I call it 'The Pavlov.'"

I nodded dumbly, vaguely remembering the guy with the dog and the bell, still stunned to see someone walking around a zombie so casually, touching it, commanding it.

Attaching himself to it.

Alastaire screwed the other end of the hose attached to his wrist to the back of Chazz's head. My skin crawled.

"The Pavlov gives our boy Chazz his reward," continued Alastaire. "It lets him know he's been a good boy. After he's been fed a few times this way, he begins to bond with me."

Alastaire pressed a small button on his wrist. He grimaced briefly, though he hid it well. I watched—stomach roiling—as a dark substance flowed down the tube, out of Alastaire and into Chazz. Was that blood? It seemed to please Chazz, the zombie letting out a happy gurgle.

"It isn't just The Pavlov that keeps Chazz from attacking me," said Alastaire as the blood continued to pump. This whole thing was more like a lecture to him than a freaking horror show. "There's a great deal of psychic manipulation at work. You've seen what zombie minds look like—it's not the most pleasant place. I've made some mental tweaks with Chazz to make our bonding possible. Of course, my work doesn't leave much of the original Chazz behind. But that was mostly gone anyway, of course. The feeding is just enough to keep him in the state we prefer—strong, fast, and pliable. And because it's my blood that he's bonded with, he's inclined to follow my instructions quite easily."

Alastaire unhooked the feeding tube, placed it back

in its spot on the shelf, and grabbed Chazz by the chin, his fingers tantalizingly close to his mouth. He lifted his face.

"You're perfect, aren't you, boy?" Alastaire asked Chazz, like he would a dog. The affection in his voice made my skin crawl. Then he let Chazz's chin drop and stepped back over the red line.

I managed to croak out a question. "What're you going to use him for?"

"Right now, Chazz is still in beta testing. I'm not yet sure of the limits of my control. Shall we test them out?"

"Um, that's okay."

Alastaire ignored me. He waved to a camera mounted in the corner of the room and, seconds later, the meat-locker door swung open for an NCD agent escorting Kelly Stephens.

"Whoa, whoa," I said. "What's she doing here?"

"I told you," replied Alastaire. "Interrogation."

Kelly still moved like a sleepwalker, not even registering the copious amounts of macabre all around her. The NCD agent marched her right up to the red line. Chazz watched, sizing her up, a strand of drool dangling from his chin. Alastaire unclipped his tube from the back of Chazz's skull and smiled at Kelly.

"Hi, Kelly," said Alastaire.

"Hi," she replied dreamily, like she was hypnotized.

"Where is your brother?" he asked.

"I dunno."

"Hm," said Alastaire, then dispassionately, "Chazz. Attack."

Chazz lunged forward, straining against the chain that still held him to the wall. His teeth snapped at Kelly, fingers clawing just inches from her face. I could hear the wall creaking as Chazz frantically jerked. My instincts took over and, even though I knew Chazz couldn't actually get at Kelly, I grabbed her around the waist and yanked her back from the red line.

"What are you doing?" I shouted at Alastaire, angry tears filling my eyes. "She doesn't know anything!"

"No," said Alastaire, his voice raised to be heard over Chazz's feral growls. "But someone in this room does. Chazz, heel."

Chazz snapped once more at Kelly, who I was still holding on to, then slunk back to Alastaire's side.

"This—this isn't what we do," I stammered.

Alastaire turned his gaze to Kelly, ignoring me. I could feel his psychic fingers curling around her mind. She slipped my grasp and walked forward, shaking me off as I snatched at the back of her shirt, and crossed the red line.

She stopped just a few feet short of Chazz. The zombie was shaking, eyes wide and ravenous. He wanted to feed.

"Shh," said Alastaire. "Stay, Chazz." Alastaire looked at me, eyes reflecting a morbid curiosity. "I wonder how long he'll listen, don't you?"

I didn't want to find out. I needed to get Kelly out of here, away from this psycho in a bow tie. It wasn't her fault that her brother was a zombie. This whole demonstration didn't have anything to do with her. It was for my benefit, meant to put me in my place. It did the trick.

"Western Pennsylvania," I practically shouted. "They're hiding in an abandoned housing development."

"Good," said Alastaire, then pointed at the floor. "You dropped my coat."

I stood outside the factory, holding myself, trying to push back tears and failing. I'd seen dozens of horrific post-zombie crime scenes since joining NCD, but today, in that meat locker, that was easily the worst thing I'd ever witnessed. The Pavlov, the way Chazz almost adoringly looked at Alastaire, seeing an NCD agent I basically worked for callously endanger a girl to prove a point. It was all too much.

I was dumbly waiting around for someone to drive me back to the motel when I had the urge to run. Just flee through this desolate part of New Jersey and hope for the best. It had worked out for Jake, so far. I wondered how far I could make it. Would they come after me? Fugitive status seemed appealing at that moment, but that'd mean bailing on my team—they were good people, totally not zombie-controlling maniacs. I needed time to think this through, to measure what I'd just seen against the good I was doing. Or the good I'd *thought* I was doing.

"Ah, the idealism of youth," Alastaire said from behind me.

I jumped. I hadn't heard him come out of the factory and now he was standing right next to me, like nothing was wrong. I hurriedly wiped my hands across my face and stood up straighter.

"You think I'm a monster," he stated.

"Are you reading my mind?"

"I don't need to," he said, his voice all low and understanding, disingenuous, like I was just some confused kid that needed some fatherly empathy. "We *are* monsters, in a way."

"We?" I spat, staring at him.

"Do you know why they administer those psychometric tests in every high school across the country?" he asked.

I was getting pretty sick of the whole Socratic-method thing, so I decided to stay silent. I wouldn't play along.

"To find the ones like us," Alastaire continued. "Because before there were zombies to hunt, there was *us*."

"What are you talking about? We don't hurt people," I replied. "At least, I don't."

"No, but we scare them. And when the zombies are gone, who do you think they'll hunt then?"

I shook my head. I didn't want to hear this, his screwed-up worldview. Just minutes ago, I'd still been convinced I was helping people, and now it felt like I was just a cog in something big and ugly.

"We'll never be like them, Cassandra. The normal ones. At best, we're something they use to solve a problem. At worst, we're something frightening to hunt." He paused. "Unless we make ourselves indispensable. Powerful."

Alastaire touched his forearm where The Pavlov's nozzle was hidden underneath his coat.

"This is the way we do that," he concluded. "You might not like it now. It might offend your childish ideas of right and wrong. But when you grow up, you'll thank me."

Alastaire walked to the car, leaving me standing on the sidewalk staring after him.

I tried to play it cool when I got back to the motel, but Tom saw right through that façade, probably because I was shaking like a leaf. I took a long, hot shower, thinking I'd never be able to scrub off the stench of the abandoned meat factory, my skin turning pink under the generic hotel soap. I thought about curling up into a little ball next to the drain like I'd seen freaked-out people do in the movies.

I thought about Kelly Stephens. We'd dropped her off at her house with no recollection of how she spent the afternoon or of how close she'd come to being zombie food just so my twisted boss could teach me a lesson. Sometimes it must be nice to be brainwashed—Kelly was lucky that she didn't have to remember anything that had happened.

I had to remember.

When I finally emerged from the shower, Tom was waiting with milk shakes at our little motel table. Oreo for me, banana-coconut for him.

"Okay," he said, "tell me what's been happening, Cass. I know something's up."

I took a long slurp from my milk shake to delay answering him.

"Do you think brain freeze could hurt my powers?" I asked Tom. "Like, an Olympic sprinter wouldn't smoke cigarettes, right? So, should I avoid quickly ingesting supercold liquids?"

"That's a new one," he said, watching me patiently. "I'll ask some of the scientists."

"Don't," I replied too quickly. "I'm sure they'd love to run the experiments on me."

Tom leaned forward, trying to look in my eyes. "Don't change the subject on me. Seriously. Tell me what's going on."

I wanted to talk to him, tell him everything, but I couldn't. I trusted Tom—it wasn't that. Even though he was getting paid to do it, he was still my closest friend. But, ultimately, he was doing a job. Working for Alastaire. How much of what I'd seen at that warehouse—of what

Alastaire had told me—did Tom already know?

Or let's say he was as in the dark as I was, convinced he was saving the world from a zombie epidemic while also babysitting. So then if I did tell him, would I just be putting him in danger?

"I'm sorry we sent you to that funeral," he said, still searching me with his eyes. "That was a little much."

I laughed bitterly. "The funeral was like the best part of my day."

"Whatever happened, you can tell me," Tom said, reaching across the table to squeeze my hand. "I promise it won't leave this room."

I could've touched his mind if I wanted to, checked to see if he was telling the truth. But that wasn't me. I didn't just go around invading people's privacy. That was an Alastaire thing to do. And who was I to worry about trust if I was just going to be scanning people's minds all the time?

No. *I trusted Tom.* And we were real friends, not just weird, secret-agent work friends. I was sure of it.

It all came spilling out of me. I'm not sure what Tom was expecting—maybe something about how it had been uncomfortable for me to deal with all those grieving families at the funeral. When I brought up Alastaire cruising by like some creep searching for his lost puppy, Tom's expression darkened. By the time I got to the part about Alastaire controlling zombies, Tom had pushed his untouched milk shake aside, the cup sweating a ring onto the table. I left out Alastaire's little speech about us telepaths sticking together; for some reason, I thought hearing about that might make Tom scared of *me*.

"Okay," Tom said, taking a deep, cleansing breath, trying to calm down. "I know I promised that what you said wouldn't leave this room, but you seriously need to let me report that son of a bitch. Harlene needs to hear about this. Tonight."

I felt drained after telling my story. I could only breathe a sigh of relief and nod as Tom got all righteous avenger in front of me. I'd made the right choice believing in him.

Tom strode out of the room with purpose, and seconds later I could hear him pounding on Harlene's door down the hall. She didn't answer, but I heard another door open and Jamison gruffly ask Tom what had his designer undies bunched. I couldn't make out Tom's reply, it was a harsh whisper, but it went on for a while and you didn't need to be psychic to know that he was pissed off.

Tom was red-faced and agitated when he brought Jamison back to our room. He forced a smile when I tried to hand him his milk shake, but didn't take the cup. He paced the room, and Jamison sat down next to me, looking stoic as ever but studying me closely.

"Controlling zombies," Jamison said, prompting me, and I could tell he didn't want to believe whatever abridged version of my story Tom had told him.

"Yeah," I said. "Like sit, roll over, eat this person." And then I launched into the whole tale again, this time for Jamison. When it was over, he leaned back in his chair, arms crossed over his muscular chest in thought. Tom stopped pacing, waiting to see what Jamison's reaction would be.

"That is some motherfucking bullshit," he said. Jamison always had a way with words.

Tom shook his head, like Jamison wasn't outraged enough.

"I need to find Harlene," Tom said. He glanced from me to Jamison. "Will you stay with her?"

Jamison and I shared a look of surprise. We'd done dozens of missions together, but I couldn't think of a time we'd been alone. I kind of felt like Tom was going a little overboard with the protectiveness. On the other hand, after what I'd been through today, having a big hulk like Jamison around didn't seem like such an awful idea.

"Yeah," Jamison grunted. "Just hurry up."

Tom practically flew out of the room, leaving Jamison and me sitting in awkward silence at the little motel table. After a moment, I pushed Tom's unfinished milk shake toward him.

He shook his head. "No thank you."

I shrugged and started in on milk shake number two. After a few seconds of my slurping, Jamison cleared his throat.

"Look," he began, trying to lower his usual gruff

quotient by half, "I never apologized to you for the other day. I shouldn't have put you out there, in danger."

"It's cool," I replied. Friday's encounter with Jake and Amanda seemed rosy in comparison to my day with Alastaire.

"No, it wasn't," Jamison rumbled. "I lost my head. Those things, what they did, it got to me. But if you'd gotten hurt . . ."

He trailed off, knuckling his forehead with one of his meaty hands. Then, he reached for the milk shake, pulling a big gulp through the straw.

"I had a daughter," he said bluntly.

"Oh, I didn't know that. What's—?" I stopped myself from asking his daughter's name, realizing he'd used the past tense.

"Yeah," he grunted. "The things got her. Doesn't make it right, what I did. Just wanted you to know."

I nodded, not really sure what to say next. *I'm sorry your daughter got eaten, but some zombies might not be so bad if you spent some time in their heads?* Probably not what the big guy wanted to hear. Anyway, it seemed like the conversation was over.

"We can watch TV if you want," Jamison said. "You like sitcoms?"

Tom came back an hour later. He never did find Harlene, but we'd see her at the briefing tomorrow. A unified front of really unhappy NCD campers.

JAKE

I WOKE UP IN THE BACKSEAT OF OUR STOLEN CAR wrapped in Grace and Summer's blanket, with Amanda still asleep, her face wedged against my chest. My back was sore and my eyes were crusty, but I couldn't help grinning. No matter what else is going on, waking up next to a hot girl always makes the world feel a lot less bleak.

I looked onto the floor of the car and saw the empty bottle of whiskey lying there. *Seriously, thanks for everything, whiskey.*

I now knew that zombies could get drunk with the

best of them. Based on the headache pounding in my skull, we were also still capable of a wicked hangover.

The night before, with our car parked on the side of the highway, Amanda and I had passed the bottle of whiskey back and forth between the two of us, just talking—not about being undead, or the heaping piles of crazy that we'd gone through in the last three days, but just shooting the shit, chattering aimlessly about whatever stupid thing popped into our booze-addled minds.

Amanda told me about the time her brother, Kyle, had convinced her to climb the water tower with him to look for UFOs. She told me about the time her dad had showed her how to hot-wire her fifth-grade teacher's car after she'd sent her home from school in tears.

My stories seemed sort of boring by comparison. Neither of my parents were criminals and the only conspiracies that interested my little sister were the ones between contestants on *Top Model.* I had a lot of stories about getting stoned and waking up in strange places. Like that time I'd woken up surrounded by what I thought were lawn gnomes but had turned out to be plastic statues of sword-waving archangels and crucified Christs. I'd stumbled into a backyard dedicated to bringing all the scary parts of the Bible to life, fallen asleep with my arm around some bearded dude holding a naked baby up to God for smiting. I'd figured out later that it was Assistant Principal Hardwick's backyard.

Amanda cracked up at that one.

At some point, when the bottle had been empty for ages, we'd crawled into the backseat and curled up together until we were asleep. I guess we'd spent the whole night that way, because now Amanda was snoring into my armpit. It was pretty sweet.

Without thinking about it, I pressed my face to her skull and took a deep whiff. I don't know how her hair smelled so good after everything we'd been through but it did; it smelled like ocean and flowers, with no trace of formaldehyde or musty basements or corpses. I guess a girl like Amanda Blake has her hair-care secrets.

But that was nothing new. Amanda Blake had always been hot. She had always smelled good. But now I was realizing that there was so much more to her too. I never would have guessed that she would be strong enough to survive something like this. Come to think of it, I never would have guessed that about myself either. Had turning into zombies made us into something more than we'd been? Or had we just been waiting for something to come along and force us to prove ourselves?

I was still wondering about that when my stomach rumbled. It wasn't the hide-the-children rumble that came moments before going full, out-of-control eating machine, just a modest growl that announced my system would sure like an injection of living meat. Summer had been right; the hunger was becoming easier to manage.

Amanda stirred, shielding her eyes with the back of her hand.

"Ugh," she mumbled. "Does your belly have a snooze alarm?"

"Sorry," I answered.

Amanda sat up, rubbing her face. She yawned and stretched her arms.

"Was I dreaming or were you *smelling my head*?"

"What? No. Definitely a dream."

She gave me a look but I just slid myself out from under her and hopped out the back door, where I stood by the highway and stretched my legs. A truck rumbled by, honking its horn, and I found myself waving back, smiling.

I was happy in a way that made no sense. But it was sunny out, the air was crisp, and I'd spent the night with Amanda Blake—even if all we'd been doing was sleeping. If little cartoon birds had come fluttering out of the woods to merrily chirp around my head, it wouldn't have surprised me.

I walked around to the back of the car, popped the trunk, and reached my hand into the pet carrier filled with rats. I closed my hands around one, feeling his little claws digging into my palms. I brought him up to my face and looked him in the eye. His little head was poking out between my thumbs.

"Sorry, Templeton," I said. Then I bit his head off.

It wasn't so bad really, no better or worse than eating a banana. A crunchy banana.

As my teeth crunched through bone, I looked down at my hands and saw the little cuts from the rat's claws turn from zombie-gray to blood red and then miraculously close up and disappear.

Amanda was sitting with her legs out of the open back door, rubbing her calves.

"Rat?" I asked, and reached into the trunk.

"Yes, please," she said, holding out her hands.

"Think of it as breakfast in bed."

Amanda raised the rat toward her mouth and as she did her lips turned a bloodless shade of gray, corpse lines spreading from her mouth and along her jaw. It was the zombie coming out again. I wasn't shocked by it anymore. It was still her. This is just how we looked now.

"Don't watch," she said with girly self-consciousness.

Amanda drove us west on I-90 through Ohio, singing along to some terrible Auto-Tuned country crap. If I wasn't already undead, I'm sure a cross-country road trip listening to nothing but FM radio would've eroded my life span. Out of the corner of my eye, I watched Amanda bob her head and couldn't help shaking my head.

"Don't judge me," she said, catching me. "This is great driving music."

I'd been perusing the zombie atlas Grace had given

us, running my fingers from location to location, trying to decide on the least unappealing option for lunch. Sometimes you'd do anything for a damn Cracker Barrel, right?

"Hey, we're going right through Cleveland," I said. "Let's stop at the Rock and Roll Hall of Fame. I always wanted to go there."

"Really?" asked Amanda. "Seems a little touristy for Jake Stephens, all-knowing music critic and Severed Lung superfan. Would Pitchfork approve?"

"I'm surprised you even know what Pitchfork is," I snarked back, though I was kind of flattered that she remembered my love of Severed Lung.

"Cool people have the internet too, you know."

"Anyway," I said, "I won't totally respect the Hall's legitimacy until Iron Maiden gets inducted, but whatever. It'd still be kinda cool."

"So let's go."

"Seriously?"

"Why not?" she asked, shooting me a carefree smile. "My afternoon is open. What about yours?"

Since it was a Monday afternoon, we had the whole Hall of Fame pretty much to ourselves, and didn't have to be paranoid that anyone would recognize us as the notorious Jersey Shooters. It was nice to be normal again for a few hours, just two kids checking out John's badass Sgt. Pepper jacket.

"If I was going to steal one thing from the Hall of Fame, it would be that," I told Amanda.

"What? That dumb coat thing?"

"If you mean that awesome coat, then yes," I said. "I'd wear it proudly from the back of my trained elephant, leading my army of rock zombies into battle against the forces of evil."

"I don't think I'd eat any of the Beatles," Amanda mused.

"Me neither, no way," I replied, then reconsidered. "Well, maybe Ringo. They could get by without Ringo, right?"

"I guess," she answered. "But there's gotta be a more delicious drummer out there."

"Good point," I said.

We stopped by Madonna's display, pictures of her evolution through the years from skanky Catholic schoolgirl to sort-of-buff New Age chick. Amanda shook her head, a vehement no.

"No way," she said. "Lifetime no-eating pass."

"I don't think we can eat other zombies, so it doesn't matter."

"Madonna is *not* a zombie," replied Amanda, then squinted at one of the more recent pictures. "Although it would explain a lot, actually."

There was a life-size statue of Elvis wearing his

sequined white leather suit, doing that splayed-leg thing where he stuck out his junk, his hair swept into a huge, black wave at the front of his head.

"Too handsome to eat," declared Amanda.

I tried to emulate the king's pose, curling my lips into an about-to-barf sneer, even windmilling an air guitar. Amanda laughed at me.

"Not even close," she said.

"I'd eat Fat Elvis."

"I'm not sure you could *finish* Fat Elvis."

"I bet he'd taste like waffles."

"Peanut butter waffles," added Amanda, nodding enthusiastically. "*Fried* peanut butter waffles. Okay, you changed my mind."

We wandered through the rest of the Hall like that, riffing on who we'd eat, joking around. It was the kind of day that made the brain-eating seem bearable.

"I needed that," I told Amanda a couple hours later as we headed back to the car. She squeezed my hand in response, and I realized that Amanda was probably having the same things-are-looking-up feeling that I was and—whoa, hold on, when did we start holding hands? It'd just sort of happened, maybe back when we'd been debating the global ramifications of devouring Bono. Had she gone for it or had I? Did that even matter? It felt perfect, and I didn't want to get all twisted up thinking about what it meant.

Just let it happen, Jake, I thought. *Be cool. Don't acknowledge it.*

"I guess there's more to being a zombie than running from the law and eating people," said Amanda.

It was still a lot of eating people.

Just as we were about to walk out the door, I had a thought. "We should buy something from the gift shop. You know. Just to have a souvenir or whatever."

Amanda smirked. "Yeah, I can't wait to look back fondly on our time as zombie fugitives."

Way to dork it up, Jake. I'd had such a nice time with Amanda that I'd almost forgotten the predicament we were in. Just because Mom always insisted on buying the whole Stephens clan cheesy T-shirts commemorating every family trip didn't mean I should be keeping that tradition alive and nerdy.

"I don't know," I said, sounding more disappointed than I wanted to let on. "I guess it's stupid. Anyway, we should save our money."

Amanda gave me a thoughtful look. "No," she said. "I do want to remember today. No matter what happens. And I think now that we're zombies we can forget about paying," she added slyly. "What are they going to do? Arrest us?"

CASS

"TODAY, WE ARE ENGAGING TWO HIGH-PRIORITY necrotic targets. The incident at Ronald Reagan High School was our most high profile to date and, with Stephens and Blake still at large, we run the continued risk of public exposure," intoned Alastaire, standing at the front of the motel's small conference room. "Going forward, there will be some changes to how this unit operates."

I sat next to Tom in the afternoon briefing, his arm slung protectively over the back of my chair. He'd been staring daggers at Alastaire since he glided into the room, but I don't think Alastaire even noticed. Jamison sat in the row in front of us next to two NCD operatives whose names I didn't know but I recognized from Alastaire's personal squad. Harlene stood at the front of the room with Alastaire, although she hadn't said a word, deferring control of the meeting to her boss. She'd definitely noticed Tom's sourpuss face, though, and kept looking over at him with her plucked eyebrows arched curiously.

"First," continued Alastaire, "psychic support will now be on-site for all combat engagements."

"What?" interrupted Tom, almost lifting out of his seat in disbelief.

Alastaire finally looked at him, fixing Tom with that unfriendly smile. "Which part didn't you understand, Thomas?"

"The part where you said you were putting noncombat personnel who may happen to be under the voting age in mortal danger."

"I think we've seen over the last few days that there's no shortage of danger on the sidelines either," answered Alastaire coolly. "Your Psychic Friend has acquitted herself quite well, wouldn't you agree?"

Tom bristled at the use of our nickname, his mouth working hard to form a response. Harlene stepped forward, cutting him off.

"Tom, these operational changes have been cleared by Washington."

Tom sank back in his chair, breathing deep. I patted his knee, willing him to mellow out. I'd had the bad fortune of getting an idea of how Alastaire's mind worked. Wouldn't it just be perfect for him to replace Tom as my guardian with one of his own people? Outbursts like that and I could look forward to traveling around with one of the craggy-faced militia rejects that Alastaire was buddied up with.

"Keep cool," I whispered. "We'll talk to Harlene."

"Second," Alastaire resumed his spiel, "this unit's primary objective will now be to take all our targets alive. So to speak."

Now it was Jamison who spoke out of turn.

"All due respect, sir, but why the hell would we want to do that?"

I caught Alastaire's handpicked agents exchange a look and then size up Jamison. He was bigger than both of them, and way scarier. It was kind of juvenile, but I couldn't help feeling some pride that our ass-kicker could take down Alastaire's ass-kickers if push came to shove.

"Washington believes—and Harlene and I agree—that the undead are an asset better preserved than slaughtered."

Preserved to turn into weapons. So Alastaire's project was moving beyond beta testing. Wonderful.

"You're only to terminate if under the threat of mortal danger," concluded Alastaire.

"Sir, I signed up to kill zombies, not wrangle them," Jamison snarled.

"'Wrangle.' That's a fun word." Alastaire glanced at Harlene, who'd remained pretty much expressionless. "It's so nice that you foster an atmosphere of open dialogue with your subordinates," he said dryly.

Harlene swept her gaze across the room, scolding us with her eyes. I felt sort of bad for putting her in this position. She'd never been anything but kind to me and I doubted she even had an inkling of the scary juju her boss was up to. It was like she was the school's one good teacher, and Alastaire was the principal that'd just reinstituted lashings for wrong answers.

"Now," said Alastaire, "if I may continue. New operational standards mean . . ."

I couldn't help it. Even though I knew I shouldn't. Even though I was in the middle of a Very Important NCD Meeting. Actually, maybe it was *because* I was in the middle of a Very Important Meeting. I went looking for Jake.

When I found him, I was totally jealous.

It figured. Here I was spending my day learning how I'd be on the frontline of the zombie war while *they* were playing hooky at the Rock and Roll Hall of Fame. It didn't seem fair that the zombies should be having more fun than me.

Forget *fun*. It was impossible to ignore the fact that something was really happening between the two of them. *Something* as in, you know, they were obviously about two steps away from jumping each other's bones.

I was a little surprised at Jake. Amanda didn't seem like his type. But I guess you put two functioning boobs in front of a boy and the whole concept of a "type" goes out the window. So, whatever.

It was Amanda who was the real surprise, though. I couldn't see in her mind the way I could his, so maybe I was wrong about what she was thinking. But you don't have to be psychic to read body language. And hers was starting to get seriously cozy.

When they'd waltzed into the gift shop, and Amanda had stolen him a Rolling Stones T-shirt right off the rack—a mischievous glint in her eyes as she told him, "Hey, it'll look great on you!"—it was pretty easy to see what was up. She had stopped thinking of him as the loser from English class. Now he was the loser from English class who would look pretty sexy in a Rolling Stones T-shirt.

And maybe he wasn't such a loser after all.

I jumped out of Jake's mind just in time to hear Alastaire dismiss the meeting. My face was hot—analyzing zombie romance via the astral plane had made me start blushing. Great. I looked around; no one had noticed that I'd been spaced out.

"Off to Pennsylvania," sighed Tom, standing up. "Let's get this over with."

Oh yeah. And the location I'd given for Jake and Amanda? Totally outdated as of yesterday. Our team plus Alastaire's reinforcements were expecting to find a pair of high-priority targets.

Instead, while those annoying lovebirds were off making eyes in Cleveland, I was serving the NCD two lesbians with a penchant for pedophiles.

An hour later, we were back in our SUV. Tom had barely said a word since the meeting, and I could tell that he was still fuming.

Harlene turned around in the passenger seat.

"You all good, Sweet Pea?"

I nodded. Tom turned away from me, glaring at Harlene.

"She shouldn't even be on this mission," he snapped.

"Agreed," said Jamison from the driver's seat. It was the first word he'd said since the briefing. He kept his eyes on the road, looking more grim than usual as he followed the other black SUV driven by a couple bulked-up NCD guys Alastaire had loaned us for the operation.

"She'll do just fine," Harlene answered. She had a sympathetic smile for me, but her words had a heavy edge of authority. "You'll make sure of that, won't you, Tom?"

Tom glanced down at his lap where the pistol they'd outfitted him with rested awkwardly. They'd given him a holster, he just chose not to wear it because it bulged uncomfortably inside his suit. The piece made it official; he was combat personnel.

"Yeah, of course," said Tom, not exactly sounding like the pillar of confidence I'd hope for in a guardian.

He'd pulled Harlene aside after the meeting, but wouldn't tell me what she'd said. I could tell by his face that it hadn't gone well. She hadn't come and asked me about any of Alastaire's crazy plans, which could mean only one of two things: either she didn't believe my story, or she already knew.

We drove on in silence. Harlene absently rubbed the bandage on her forearm, probably trying to figure out how to get us acting like a team again.

A few hours later, our SUV rolled to a stop in front of the unfinished house in this neglected corner of suburbia. The place looked like a dollhouse that some deadbeat dad had gotten too drunk to finish assembling. The neighborhood was empty, with not so much as a squirrel moving. Of course I knew why that was; the rodent population around here was greatly diminished. Harlene turned around to face me.

"Hon, could you confirm our targets are inside?"

I already knew Jake and Amanda had lit out the

night before. Still, I unfocused my eyes, trying to put on the faraway look that I'd seen other telepaths get when they were tracking.

"There are two inside," I said, then added somewhat quietly, "just not the two we're looking for."

"What?" asked Tom, giving me one of those oh-no-you-didn't looks. I think he knew that I'd kinda sort of let Jake and Amanda slip away.

"Other zombies," I said, ignoring Tom, trying to play it off like I'd just accidentally led our team to a minor victory. Grace and Summer *were* zombies, after all. "Two girls."

"Huh," said Harlene, frowning. "Some luck."

"Zombies are zombies," grunted Jamison, then pointed to where Alastaire's two agents were already out of their SUV and approaching the house. "Look at these overzealous idiots."

That was a serious insult coming from run-and-gun Jamison. One of Alastaire's guys carried a standard-issue long-range stun gun, the other this big contraption that looked like it should be used to kill a whale but that Alastaire had explained was a high-powered net-chucker. He had a more technical military term for it, but whatever, it was a net-chucker. He'd given the same set of zombie-capture toys to Harlene and Jamison, yet I couldn't help noticing that when Jamison climbed out of our car he was toting his usual big-ass shotgun. Harlene didn't say anything about his choice of weapon.

"You stay put, okay?" Harlene said to me and Tom as she followed Jamison.

"Obviously," replied Tom.

"Oh crap—!" I yelled, remembering the vision of Grace I'd picked up from Jake's psyche. "Crossbow! I forgot to mention the crossbow!"

Harlene and Jamison were just a few steps away from the car when one of Alastaire's agents kicked down the house's front door. He staggered backward immediately, soundlessly, and flopped down on his butt.

There was a crossbow bolt sticking out of his eye socket.

I clasped both my hands over my mouth to stop from screaming. Sure, I didn't know that agent and, by the looks of him, Alastaire had probably found him burning villages in a Third World country, but he was still a person. A person shot in the face with an arrow. "Uh, maybe you shouldn't watch this," Tom said, and I could tell he was considering just covering my eyes.

I shook my head. I'd brought us here. Basically, I'd decided to swap Grace and Summer for Jake and Amanda. Whatever happened was on me. I was NCD combat personnel now and I was going to have to see what our missions really looked like.

The agent with the net-chucker didn't have time to fire before Grace was driving her shoulder into him, sending him flying backward down the steps. Their path clear now, Grace ran, holding Summer's hand as she sprinted behind her, the two of them making a break for the woods at the end of the cul-de-sac.

I watched as Jamison lifted his shotgun, took careful aim, and fired.

One second, Summer's mane of hair was flowing behind her in the wind like streamers off a maypole. The next, it was gone. A pinkish mist lingered in the air where Summer's head used to be. Grace skidded to a stop, still holding Summer's hand as her girlfriend's body collapsed to the ground. She screamed.

"Alive!" Harlene was screaming at Jamison. "We're taking them alive!"

"I was in mortal danger," he replied curtly.

Grace had reversed course, now sprinting right for Harlene and Jamison. Escape was off her mind; she was consumed by pure animal rage now and the adrenaline was starting to turn her: her skin had taken on that fetid gray pallor, and her lips were curled back over her teeth in an inhuman rictus.

Harlene let loose with her net-chucker. It was like seeing a spiderweb slung through the air at incredible velocity. It reached Grace, flipped her over at an impossible angle, and pinned her on the ground. I could see a jagged edge of bone sticking out of her collar.

Still, she kept coming. Or trying to, at least. The net

had to be almost fifty pounds; even firing the gun had nearly knocked Harlene down. Grace clawed her way across the ground, inch by inch, all gnashing teeth and zombie rage now, still trying to reach Jamison. I wondered if she even knew what had just happened. I was too afraid to try touching her mind.

Jamison walked over to her. Grace's fingers squeezed through the netting, digging fruitlessly at the toe of his boot. She sputtered and gnashed, trying to bite his ankle through the netting.

For a moment, I thought Jamison might just shoot her, but then he turned away in disgust.

"Does this look like an asset to you?" he snarled at Harlene.

I decided not to watch anymore.

JAKE

WE STOPPED AT A TRUCK STOP PAST CLEVELAND. I went inside to pay for the gas and ended up grabbing some other essentials. I could have stolen them, I guess, but after our "shopping spree" at the Rock and Roll Hall of Fame, I felt like it might be a good idea to avoid attention for a while. We had enough money left from what Grace and Summer had given us, and I figured when we needed more we could always just rob a bank or something.

There were cheap CLEVELAND ROCKS hoodies for sale, thick white socks, and discounted tighty-whitey underwear. I'd never seen underwear for sale at a gas station before. I didn't want to think about why it was necessary.

Back outside, a potbellied trucker that looked like he spent his cross-country journeys squishing moist towelettes into his swampy armpits stood a few feet from where Amanda was pumping gas, looking her up and down wolfishly, his thumbs hooked through his belt loops. He chomped on a hand-rolled cigarette.

"That offer's only good if you're eighteen," the trucker was saying. I was sort of glad that I hadn't heard what the offer was. Amanda ignored him as she hung up the gas nozzle, and he glanced over at me as I tossed my newly purchased wardrobe and some disinfectant wipes—to help clean off the rat guts, of course—into the backseat.

"This your faggy little boyfriend?" he asked Amanda. "That's cool. He can hang out."

I opened up the passenger door but didn't get in.

"Are you smoking a cigarette at a gas station?" I asked the trucker.

"Living dangerous, son," he said, winking at me.

"More than you know," I told him, glancing over at Amanda. She was studying the trucker. I heard her stomach growl.

"God damn, girl." The trucker grinned. "You hungry? I'll fill ya up."

"Does your wife know you pick up teenage girls at rest stops?" Amanda asked.

The trucker wiggled his thick fingers in the air, showing there was no ring. "You think a stallion like me could ever be tied down?"

Amanda nodded, as if that's what she expected to hear, and got into the car. I followed, slamming the door on the last heartfelt propositions of the trucker. He wandered away, toward the store.

"I'd eat him," announced Amanda.

"Really?" I asked, watching the trucker go. "He's just a gross idiot."

"Exactly. No one will miss him," Amanda countered.

I picked up the road atlas. "We've got this if you're hungry. We can go find one of Grace's handpicked perverts. Maybe tide yourself over with a rat on the way."

"I'm hungry now," said Amanda, and I could tell by the way her lips had started to turn a grayish blue that it was coming on fast. "What if we go to one of those addresses and the guy has turned his life around, has a blind puppy he takes care of or something?"

"Then we'd pick someone else," I said.

"What if I start to lose control?"

I thought back to the way Amanda had thrown herself at the old man that tried to help us back in New Jersey. Sure, the hunger was getting easier to control, but we didn't know our own limitations yet. If we let ourselves get that hungry again, who knows who we might end up eating?

"We should just eat this guy," she said. "He's probably in the road atlas anyway for torturing hitchhikers."

"Jeez, what did he say to you?"

"Nothing I haven't heard before," she replied. "He's just super convenient."

The trucker *was* convenient. A jerk that nobody would miss. I tried to think of a downside.

"What if he's transporting valuable medical supplies and when he doesn't show up a bunch of orphans die?"

Amanda glanced at the truck. "I think it's beef jerky."

The trucker emerged from the store then, but didn't head back to his ride. He had a magazine tucked under his arm and was headed for the bathroom around the corner. A lot of disturbing things had probably happened in that dimly lit truck-stop toilet. What was one more, right?

"Look," said Amanda gently, "we won't do it if you don't want to. It has to be unanimous. That'll be our rule."

"Okay." I nodded, coming to a decision. "Let's eat him."

Amanda glanced into the backseat. "Bring the baby wipes."

Afterward, with full stomachs, we stood back-to-back in the truck-stop bathroom and changed out of our bloody clothes. We did it in front of the sink where there was an island of clean floor—well, clean in that it wasn't smeared with the trucker's viscera. Most of what was left of him stayed in the handicapped stall where we'd found him, his dismembered hand still clutching the latest issue of *Hustler.* All class until the end, dude.

"We really need to stockpile some more freaking clothes," said Amanda as she pulled the ugly pink Cleveland hoodie I'd bought over her head. I tried not to watch her reflection in the smudged mirror over the sink because that wouldn't be at all gentlemanly, but, come on.

She caught my eyes in the mirror as she pushed her fingers through her hair, flipping it free of the sweatshirt's hood. "What?"

"Nothing," I said quickly. We'd just eaten a guy in what had to be America's grossest gas-station bathroom. And yet, despite the less-than-ideal ambiance, I still found myself checking her out. Not one-track-mind-horndog checking out either (okay, maybe a little of that). This was like poetic-appreciation checking out, like thine beauty doth shine even whence thou cheweth yonder intestines. What was wrong with me?

"Come here," she said, opening the tube of baby wipes. Amanda made me lift my chin and she wiped specks of blood off the underside of my jaw. "You did a really shitty job cleaning up."

I looked over at the bloodstained sink and the pitiful bar of soap. "These, uh, amenities aren't up to my usual standards."

"Uh-huh," she said, finishing up with my neck. "How am I?" She tilted her face back and forth so I could see all the angles.

"You're good."

"I feel like I've just been on the weirdest first date ever," she said casually.

I made an exaggerated look around. "This is your idea of a date?"

"We did an activity. We had dinner. Kind of a date." She thought about it. "Haven't had a good one of those in a while, actually."

"So it was good?" I asked, trying not to sound eager and failing miserably.

"Eh, not bad," she said with heartbreaking nonchalance. "You were kind of a messy eater. And you didn't even pay." She patted her back pocket, where she'd stuck the trucker's wallet after we'd eaten the rest of him. He'd been traveling with cash—there was five hundred bucks in there. Not a bad score, when you got right down to it.

"Yeah, well, you, uh, chew loud—" I stammered, waving my hands around because I didn't know what the hell else to do with them. We were standing really close together.

"Good one," she said. "Ready to go?"

"Sure," I replied.

But she didn't move. And I didn't move. We just stood there, looking at each other, and I'm pretty sure she was giving me a version of those c'mere eyes from the car, so screw it–trucker breath and all–I went for it.

I kissed Amanda. She kissed me back.

My first lame thought was: *Oh man, the guys will never believe this happened.*

But then I remembered I'd eaten all my friends, that I had no one to tell about this, and that just made me want to kiss her more. The kiss went from soft and tentative like every first kiss in recorded history to something else, like hungry and desperate, both her hands on the sides of my face, my arms reaching around her hips.

I suddenly felt hot. Not like a good make-out hot, but a weird sizzling sensation that started in my head and shot down through my body like an electric shock. I shuddered and jerked back, had time to utter a highly romantic "ugh," and then barfed chunks of barely digested trucker down the front of Amanda's new sweatshirt.

CASS

THAT NIGHT, WE STAYED IN A MOTEL OUTSIDE Cleveland. Nobody talked much on the way. We checked in. We went to bed.

I found myself lying awake, feeling weirdly alone even with Tom sleeping in a bed a few feet away. I reached across the astral plane, searching for Jake's mind. It may have been a strange place to go looking for comfort, but I needed to escape. To be out of my own body for a while.

I jumped into his mind just as he was kissing Amanda Blake in a dingy bathroom.

Something welled up in me. The stress of the last few days, the horrible things I'd seen, and now this admittedly totally inappropriate feeling of jealousy because the zombie I'd been spying on was kissing someone else. It was like an involuntary spasm of the brain. A psychic shock wave of icky feelings rolled through me and into Jake.

I gasped and severed our connection, sitting up straight in bed. Ugh, what was I doing?

More important: Had I just made Jake puke?

"Cass?" whispered Tom from his bed after a few minutes. "Are you okay?" Sometimes I wondered if he was a little psychic too.

I took a few deep breaths, thinking about my answer. A thin trickle of blood wormed its way out of my nose and I wiped it away. Not again. I turned my head, trying to find Tom's eyes in the darkness.

"I want to go home," I told him.

JAKE

WHAT DO YOU SAY TO A GIRL AFTER YOU THROW UP while kissing her? That's not an easy thing to come back from, even when the site of your make-out is a gas-station bathroom that could double as the winning image in a World's Most Heinous Crime Scene photography contest. I'm pretty sure even a girl as confident as Amanda would interpret the smallest amount of kiss-induced barfing as a damning criticism of her technique.

And the shitty thing was, I'd totally been into that kiss. I didn't know why I'd gotten sick. It was like a sudden surge of gut-bursting panic that was gone as quickly as it came on. Maybe there was some zombie rule that Grace and Summer hadn't filled us in on; like wait thirty minutes after eating before engaging in any kissing.

"So," I stammered as we drove across the Michigan border. "I'm really sorry about that."

"It's okay," said Amanda, obviously not wanting to talk about it.

"That's never happened to me before."

"You don't say."

"It wasn't, like, your fault," I said, sounding unbelievably lame.

"Whew," replied Amanda. "I was worried."

"It was weird—"

"Yeah," she interrupted. "Look, the whole thing was weird. We were just caught up in the moment, okay? Like, a last-two-people-on-Earth scenario. Let's just forget about it."

Well, that was a bummer of a way to look at our magical moment of ferocious post-cannibalism making out. I drummed my fingers on the steering wheel, mulling over a response.

"So, you wouldn't want to try again? Like after I've digested?"

Amanda looked at me like I had just puked all over again and then, without a word, unbuckled her seat belt and crawled into the backseat to stretch out.

"I don't know," she said. "I'm tired. Let's just not talk for a while."

"Because I'd try it again," I persisted. "It wasn't a last-people-on-Earth thing for me."

I looked at Amanda in the rearview mirror. She had one arm draped over her eyes and was chewing her lip nervously.

"It's like we're stuck on a zombie blind date," said Amanda. "I mean, we've been together four days and it's been pretty intense. How do we know it's *real feelings* and not Stockholm syndrome or something?"

"For starters, because I didn't kidnap you."

"You know what I mean," she said.

"Yeah," I muttered. "Real feelings. Okay."

"Look," Amanda said. "It's okay that you vommed on me. There's still a lot about this zombie stuff that we don't know. Maybe puking is part of the zombie-mating ritual."

"Yeah," I said uncertainly. "Maybe."

"Jake. I just need some time to process. Okay?"

I nodded. *Process.* That didn't sound so good. I felt like we were suddenly on one of those relationship-counseling shows where the dude is all incapable of understanding his emotions. But . . . I was "processing." At least I thought I was. My mind was consumed by what it meant to be a zombie, who it was okay to eat, what the hell my life was going to be like now—and really digging

Amanda Blake. That last part was the only thing that really made sense to me, the only feeling that seemed normal and good.

Maybe I should've told her all that. Then again, even if I thought Amanda sort of liked me, she'd still once gone for the macho Chazz type. *That* dude definitely wasn't wasting his time being introspective about his emotional voyage. So maybe I shouldn't either.

Ugh . . . feelings. Why couldn't turning into a zombie have cured me of those?

Then again, maybe I didn't want to be cured. Because just as I was swearing off human emotion forever, Amanda turned to me. "Look," she said. "I like you, okay? Don't make me get all sappy and gross on you. We've had more than enough grossness for today, don't you think?"

We got into Ann Arbor late that night. It was definitely a college town, the kind of place where I would've hoped to find myself in the fall if things had gone differently—not just undeath, but, you know, my grades. Even this late, students cluttered the sidewalks, lurching home from bars. We drove past a house where a bunch of bros were playing a game of beer pong right in the front yard. *Now that's freedom,* I thought, then reminded myself that I had nothing in my future but the open road. These suckers with their carefree school-night drinking and lack of parental supervision, they didn't know shit about the real world.

"My brother's house is on the next block," said Amanda.

"Just one pass," I said, and Amanda nodded, already peering out her window. We'd agreed it probably wouldn't be smart to just knock on her brother's door—those guys that had chased us back in New Jersey could be watching him. The plan was to swing by, check for his car or see if his light was on—get some sign that he was even still in Michigan—and then skedaddle.

Kyle lived in a house off campus with a bunch of "other nerds," according to Amanda. I slowed down, cruising my way down the block trying not to look too conspicuous. *Ho-hum, just another college kid looking for a parking spot after a tough night in the old lecture hall.* Really, I was keeping an eye out for any ominous black SUVs or dudes reading newspapers while talking into spy earpieces. Roof snipers, the whole nine yards.

"He's there," said Amanda, pointing at a tall guy smoking a cigarette in the darkness of his front porch. "Yuck, smoking again."

I shoved her hand down.

"No pointing," I said. "They're here too."

At least, I assumed it was *them*. A pair of guys parked a few car-lengths down the street in a boring beige sedan, one of them reading a newspaper just like I'd imagined, the other tipping back a huge Styrofoam cup of coffee. Amanda and I both sat rigid until we were down the block. When the beige sedan didn't pull out and start chasing us, we breathed a synchronized sigh of relief.

We drove through Ann Arbor, neither of us sure what the plan should be now. Amanda had gotten really quiet since catching a glimpse of Kyle, and stared out the window, watching the tree-lined Michigan streets glide by.

I cleared my throat. "So, I'm sorry that was a bust."

"What do you mean?" she asked, looking at me.

"Well, we can't exactly go see your brother now. They're watching him. Those government dudes probably have his phone tapped, his email hacked. There's some total Patriot Act shit going on, I bet."

Amanda shook her head in denial. "We have to find a way to talk to him. He can help us, I know it."

"Seriously? We met other *real-life* zombies, Amanda. And what did we learn? To stay calm and eat furry things. Do you really think your brother will know more than Grace and Summer did? Just because he listens to some radio show?"

Maybe all that came out a little harsher than I'd intended; it was late and I was feeling on edge. I steeled myself for a gust of icy boss-lady Amanda, but she just made a little snuffing sound and looked down at her lap.

"You're right," she said quietly. "The thing is, it's more than me just thinking he can help us. It's . . . If you had a chance to see your family, to set the record straight, wouldn't you want to take it? Seeing him back there . . . I mean, what must he be thinking? I can't stand it."

I thought about that. Obviously, I missed my parents; I even missed dumb-ass Kelly, and I would've killed to see them . . . which I realize is maybe not a figure of speech I should use casually. It wasn't the family part of what Amanda said that stuck in my head, though. It was the bit about setting the record straight.

Some government goon squad wanted to shoot at us, keep us a secret, and stalk our families, and we're just supposed to take that?

"People should know about us," I said, thinking out loud. "People should know about zombies. You're right! They shouldn't be allowed to just keep us secret."

"Exactly."

"He could get the word out," I went on. "Tell all his conspiracy buddies to, like, sound the cover-up alarm."

Amanda nodded. "Yup. It'd be like a dream come true for him. His big moment. *Finally*, I do something nice for my big brother."

"Okay, so now we just need to get to him. That's not going to be easy."

Amanda looked over at me. She looked rejuvenated, excited even. We were doing something besides running. We were being proactive! I wished really hard some Rage Against The Machine would come on the radio.

"I have an idea," she said.

• • •

Half an hour later we were huddled around a computer at an all-night internet café in downtown Ann Arbor. The bored dude at the counter barely looked up from his textbook as we paid for an hour of internet. Besides us, the only customers were two guys engrossed in a marathon session of *World of Warcraft*, and a college girl typing up a paper while randomly breaking into panicked sobs. Basically, no one in there was paying us any attention.

Amanda logged on to a message board called The Crop Circle. It was a whole online community for people who were into alien shit. There were different sub-forums for different kinds of aliens: Grays; Pod People; Lizard Invaders who were trying to take over the government.

Amanda's username was UFOphelia.

"Uh, why are you a member of this?" I asked as she scanned the screen.

"I made this account to screw with Kyle," Amanda admitted. "I pretended that I was an open-minded Swedish supermodel that was really into some of the theories he was posting about our extraterrestrial visitors."

"That's really mean," I said. "Great joke, but totally mean."

"Yeah, he wouldn't talk to me for, like, a month," said Amanda. "Anyway, if those government jerks are checking his phone and email, this is our best way to contact him. It'll look like just a message from one of his weirdo conspiracy friends, but Kyle will know the truth."

Amanda opened up a direct message to Kyle's username, BelieverNJ. She typed in a one-line message: LUNCH TOMORROW IN STUDENT UNION? 2 P.M.

"Good?" she asked, mouse hovering over the SEND button.

"If by good you mean vague and ominous, then yes. Are we seriously going to the student union, though?"

"We want someplace public, right? I don't think they'll shoot us in public. That'd be bad for their whole secrecy thing."

I thought about the guy with the shotgun that nearly killed us in New Jersey, even in front of a whole bunch of bystanders. I wasn't so sure.

"Also," continued Amanda, "we want someplace it's normal for him to go so it doesn't look suspicious. And we can come up with disguises."

"Disguises," I repeated. "Cool."

Of course, the disguises I pictured only would've made us stand out more. Me in a badass trench coat with the collar flipped up, a steaming manhole cover behind me for added coolness, and Amanda dressed in formfitting black leather—because inconspicuous leather is a thing—like a blonde version of the Black Widow.

Amanda was watching my face. "Whatever disguises you're thinking of, I veto."

She hit SEND on the direct message. Part of me—the increasingly paranoid part—expected a helicopter to suddenly appear outside, bathing the street in a spotlight as government spooks surrounded the building. Of course, nothing actually happened. The only sound was the furious typing of the other night-owl net junkies.

Amanda started to stand up. "Ready?"

"Hold on," I said, sliding over to take control of the mouse. "While we're here, we might as well research."

"This board is for alien lovers. Zombies aren't aliens."

I navigated over to the SEARCH button and typed in ZOMBIE, CURE, and IOWA.

"Worth a shot anyway," I said, glancing over at Amanda. She nodded, but stifled a yawn. "Isn't it all basically the same in the end?"

I resisted the urge to say "I told you so" when a post came up. It was dated three weeks ago from a user named Scully88. It read:

> Keep hearing rumors that Iowa is completely closed down. No way in and no way out. Rumor is it's because of a quarantine. I don't want to throw around the z-word but . . . can you say zombie outbreak? I'm in Denver and am thinking of driving up. Anyone else made the trip? Is it a hoax? Or something boring like small pox?

The thread was closed after only one response. It came from a moderator with the user name LordDM00:

> Rumors are true!
>
> If you're bold of spirit and hungry for a paradigm shift, we've got the cure for what ails you. Take the drive up!
>
> —The Lord of Des Moines
>
> PS: Here's a fascinating message from one of our honored guests! ;-)

There was a video embedded at the bottom of the post. I looked over at Amanda. "Should we?"

"It's probably just that Rick Roll guy," she said skeptically, but gestured that I should play it.

I turned the volume way down on the computer. We both leaned in toward the speakers, our heads close together as I pressed PLAY.

The video wasn't much to look at, grainy and shaky even for home-video standards. It took place in a dark room, maybe a basement, an eerie green glow lighting the shot from the edges. I couldn't make out anything else about the room because pretty much the entire frame was filled with the craggy face of a silver-haired old man. He was probably in his late fifties and had that haunted look of a dude that's seen some heavy stuff.

"This is the Grandfather," the silver-haired oldster introduced himself, his voice hard to hear over the weird hydraulic sounds behind him, "and this may be my last transmission. I remain stranded in Des Moines with no possibility of escape. If this is truly the end, there are two things you must know: First, the undead of Iowa grow bold and restless. It won't be long until they do something . . . unfortunate. Second, and more important, my work is finally completed. I have done what you said was impossible, Alastaire.

"I have cured the undead."

At that point, the camera shook and an inhuman bellow sounded from off-screen. It was totally a noise I was unlucky enough to recognize. That was a zombie scream; the feral noise that signified dinnertime.

The video cut off there.

"Iowa," I whispered, feeling an odd mixture of hope and fear.

"That kind of freaked me out," said Amanda, eyes still locked on the screen.

"It makes sense, though," I explained, suddenly inspired. "This is how it always goes in video games. All the NPCs keep telling you about a seriously scary screwed-up dungeon that no one's ever come back from, and you just know the one item you need to complete your quest is going to be down there. So you finally go down into that dungeon–and boom–not only do you make it, you come out with, like, a glowing sword."

Amanda slowly turned to me. "That has to be the nerdiest pep talk I've ever heard."

We drove out of the wealthy college part of Ann Arbor and into the part where the motels weren't in the habit of checking IDs.

The leering innkeeper at the All Nighter Lodge was surprised we wanted the room for the night and not just for a couple hours. I asked sarcastically about the continental breakfast, and he let loose a wheezing laugh that smelled like wood varnish. On our way in, we'd covered the pet carrier full of rats with an extra T-shirt to hide its contents, but I doubt our esteemed bellhop would've even raised an eyebrow if we hadn't.

Our day ended in a room that probably had a stain-to-square-inch ratio of 1:5. It was about an hour until sunrise.

I went to hit the room's light switch, but Amanda slapped my hand away.

"Better not to know," she said.

I went over to the bed and shoved my hands under the sheets, reaching around the bed carefully. Amanda watched me, an eyebrow raised.

"I saw this thing on the news," I told her, "where this lady got stuck with a syringe when she got into a hotel bed. Freaked me out."

"My zombie companion has OCD," announced Amanda. "Great."

When I was done inspecting the bed, the two of us stood on opposite sides, staring at each other. I was waiting for her to make the first move, but was it possible she was waiting to take her cue from *me*? It'd been a hellaciously long day, we were both way beyond worn out, and yet the awkwardness of *us* kept us from crashing. I didn't want to just climb into bed and presume that'd be cool, and Amanda—well, she was probably nervously waiting for me to barf again.

Finally, I sighed, pulled a pillow and a blanket off the bed, and started to lie down on the floor.

"Are you nuts?" Amanda practically shouted. "You don't know what's down there. There's probably herpes all over that floor!"

"So . . ." I nodded toward the bed. "We're going to . . . ?"

"Sleep in the same bed, yeah," she said, and resolutely climbed in, as if to demonstrate. Then her face softened. "Don't make it weird, Jake."

"Sorry," I said. "I was just worried this might be too *real* for you."

I climbed into bed next to her and we lay there in the dark, shoulder to shoulder.

"We can make a blanket wall if you can't control yourself," suggested Amanda. "Or if you feel like you're going to hurl."

"I think I'll be okay," I said.

I stared at the ceiling. A cockroach skittered across

the cracked plaster, disappearing into the rickety wooden ceiling fan.

Amanda saw it too but she didn't scream or anything, the way I would have expected her to. "Did you see that?" she asked, pointing. "It's like a shooting star."

"Uh," I said.

"I mean, kind of. If you think about it in a certain way. It's like the equivalent. Given our situation."

"Should we make a wish?" I asked.

Instead of answering, Amanda reached over and tentatively grabbed my hand.

I wasn't expecting that at all. *Be cool,* I told myself, even as I felt my heart beginning to race. I tried to think of something really suave to say, but nothing was coming immediately to mind. So we just lay there for a few minutes until I finally remembered how to speak English.

"What's the first thing you're going to do when you get cured?" I asked. Maybe not exactly the definition of suave, but it was something.

"I don't know," she answered. "I'm not sure I want to think about it. I don't want to get my hopes up."

"That's boring," I replied.

"Fine. What're you going to do?"

"I'm going to find the best vegetarian restaurant in the world," I told her. "And then I'm going to take you out to dinner there."

Amanda laughed. She rolled over onto her side, facing me.

"You think we're still going to hang out, post-zombie?"

"I hope so," I said.

"Me too," she whispered. "It's a date."

That night, I had this totally random dream about Vintage Vinyl, the used-record store in New Jersey I used to stop by on afternoons when I was skipping class. It was me and Henry Robinson and we were just rambling up and down the aisles, browsing, looking for bands we could go home and torrent.

The thing is, Henry and I weren't alone. There was this brown-haired girl with us and even though I didn't really recognize her, in the dream I felt like I knew her. I was sure she'd come with us for some reason, riding along in Henry's hand-me-down station wagon. She followed us up and down the aisles, not saying anything, but laughing and smiling at most of our stupid jokes.

Eventually, we had enough of Vintage Vinyl, so we moseyed out to the parking lot. When we reached Henry's car, the girl kept walking. She glanced over her shoulder at me and I thought about following her, but then I noticed she was headed for a black SUV parked in the next row over.

That's where I recognized her from! She was that teenage storm trooper that'd been riding around with the shotgun-toting maniac. This was one of those dreams where you're, like, aware that it's a dream, but are just going along with the flow. So I thought: *Wow, brain, what an obscure choice for a dream cameo.* I'd totally forgotten about her.

Secret-agent girl got into the back of the SUV, looking almost sad about it. The driver-side window rolled down and some middle-aged dude wearing glasses and a bow tie peered out at me. I didn't recognize him, but he looked like the mild-mannered type that secretly spends his weekends stabbing homeless people for the thrill of it. His bow tie started to spin, like a clown's would, and that made me laugh because I'm an easy mark for physical comedy. Inappropriate things spinning? Usually funny.

When I looked away from the bow tie, I noticed the man had pulled a big chrome-plated gun. He aimed it right at my face.

Whoa, wait a second.

The gun fired with one of those jagged flame-colored bursts you see in comics. It was a thunderous gunshot, and I had time to think about the ringing in my ears as the huge silver bullet spun toward me.

I woke up when the bullet hit me right between the eyes.

CASS

WHEN I TOLD TOM THAT I WANTED TO GO HOME, I hadn't meant back to Washington and the cold NCD barracks, though that's where I ended up. I'd meant *real* home, with my mom and sister. I wanted to be in my old room with the retro movie posters on the walls and the stacks of secondhand books I still hadn't read. It used to seem like a small and boring place to me, but now I felt like I could just hide there forever.

Instead, we'd been ordered back to DC while the NCD higher-ups figured out our next move. Our team had never allowed any zombies to stay on the loose this long; I guess that was sort of my fault. Now that we were back at base, I let myself hope that we'd just chalk up Jake and Amanda as lost and move on to the next case.

Here in DC, I shared a room with another telepath named Tara. She was in her twenties, and kept to herself, or at least it seemed that way because I hardly ever saw her. If I wasn't out on a mission, then she was.

Our room looked pretty much like a dorm, so at least I was sort of getting a college experience. Who knew if real college would be in the cards for me, though after my NCD service was over I'd end up with a government-issued high school equivalency diploma to go with what was shaping up to be a serious case of post-traumatic stress. Other than the bunk beds, there were a pair of writing desks with laptops, two closets containing more than enough NCD jumpsuits, and a single window that was too high to really see out of but let in the gray light from early morning DC.

I opened up my laptop and logged on to Facebook. Surprisingly, we're allowed to keep profiles, we're just not allowed to post anything to them. I bet there's some android in a dimly lit office in a subbasement of the Pentagon monitoring our every click. I browsed my newsfeed, filled with news and posts from kids I'd known in my old life: photographs of a hideous aquamarine prom dress, complaints about an unfair teacher, multiple invites to some stupid game where you build a farm. I wondered if any of these people ever wondered what had happened to me. Even if they did wonder, it's not like we could reconnect. There wasn't any common ground. They had school dances and term papers; I had corpses and nosebleeds.

If I was going to hang out with someone my own age, it'd have to be someone that could understand what I'd been through.

Casually, I typed JAKE STEPHENS into the search window. Just out of curiosity. About a thousand results popped up and scrolling through them just made me feel awkward and lonely, so I closed the window.

There was a rec room down the hall with a TV, a lame selection of DVDs, and a Ping-Pong table. I could go there if I wanted to kill some time, maybe make friends with some of the other telepaths, share stories about the horrible zombie massacres we'd seen over a frosty glass of Coke. No thanks. I'd always kept my distance from that place and that wouldn't change now, even if I was in a funk. This is going to sound supremely hypocritical, but the idea of hobnobbing with other telepaths gave me the willies. I didn't want anyone poking around in the sacred space of my brain.

I curled up on the bottom bunk, thinking about taking a nap even though it wasn't even noon. Isolation was one of the things they warned us about in our Coping with Telepathy orientation; it was why most of us had handlers like Tom.

Except I wasn't really isolated, was I? I could do something about this feeling.

I told myself that I was just going to take a quick peek into Jake's mind. I'd kept my mental distance since the night before, after I'd accidentally transmitted a psychic panic attack into his brain. I hoped I hadn't hurt him, although part of me wouldn't have minded if my psychic episode had disrupted his make-out session.

I found Jake sitting cross-legged on the edge of a bed in a motel room that would've caused even the cost-cutting government types I worked with to turn up their noses. He was reading a newspaper, or at least pretending to. Really, he was stealing glances at Amanda through the half-open bathroom door as she brushed black dye through her glamorous blonde hair.

So they were disguising themselves. If they only knew that I'd been hanging out in Jake's brain for the last few days. It would take more than a bad dye job to give me the slip.

Except, maybe it wouldn't. My mental connection to Jake felt more tenuous than it had the day before. It was now five days since I first made contact, and I'm sure the growing distance between us wasn't helping. I'd never been connected to a zombie this long. Usually, they were dead—like, for-real dead—within the first forty-eight hours. It was already getting harder to access Jake's mind, like that feeling you get when a word is stuck on the tip of your tongue. Today I'd found him . . . but tomorrow?

I swept through Jake's surface thoughts. He was anxious, spooked by a night of bad dreams and nervous about some plan he and Amanda were hatching. I know I should've dug a little more—found out what our priority target was up to—but I just wasn't in the mood for NCD business.

As Jake pretended to read the paper, he thought mostly about Amanda. He was doing a breakdown of every conversation they'd had yesterday post-vomit incident. Wait—vomit? Had my psychic shock wave made Jake sick?

Sorry if I screwed up your make-out, Jake. But also . . . not sorry at all.

Jake's mind was überly focused on whether or not he said the right things last night, on deciphering signals he wasn't actually sure Amanda was sending, and on not being too obvious about looking at her boobs. Is this how boys' minds work when they have a crush on a girl? It was kind of pathetic, especially considering Jake's whole flesh-eating situation. More important things to worry about, you know?

But also? Kind of sweet. Because Jake *knew* he had more important things to worry about, and he was still thinking about Amanda. I lingered in those thoughts and feelings, that wonderful, new relationship anxiety. Is it weird that I sort of let myself imagine that he was feeling that icky, gooey, lame crap about me?

As if in answer, Tom sharply cleared his throat. I hadn't heard him come in, and nearly hit my head on the bottom of the overhead bunk as I shot into a sitting position. The room spun; I'd pulled out of Jake's mind too quickly and it was disorienting seeing through my own eyes again.

Tom pulled one of the desk chairs over to the edge of my bed. "Okay," he said, "we're having a talk."

I resisted the urge to rub my eyes, not wanting to let on that I was seeing three blurry stern-faced Toms. "Um, about what?"

"Come on," sighed Tom. "I know you've been in Jake's head."

"Not really," I lied. "Just for, like, tactical reasons."

"Oh, Psychic Friend," replied Tom as he reached into his pocket to retrieve an argyle-print handkerchief. "Your little fibbing nose is bleeding."

Crap. I sniffed back a trickle of blood and guiltily took Tom's handkerchief, dabbing at my traitorous nostril. It really was getting harder to track Jake. Plus, I was psychically exhausted from the last few days. So much for keeping nosebleeds to a minimum.

"All right," I admitted. "So what if I have?"

"For starters, he's a zombie. The enemy. Our job is

to hunt them down and, well, make sure they don't eat people."

"Kill them," I said, clarifying his NCD lingo. "Or enslave them."

"Yeah," he replied firmly. "We kill cannibalistic monsters. You've seen what they do enough times, Cass. You can't start feeling sympathetic for them."

"It's not like they're doing it on purpose," I snapped. "They didn't choose to be zombies any more than I chose to be a psychic."

"Yeah, well, you have a gift that doesn't require brain-eating. It's not the same thing."

"He *wants* to stop," I said, trying to keep the justification I'd plucked from Jake's mind from sounding weak. "Or, you know, he's being selective. They're not just eating anyone."

"That makes it okay?"

"Yes." I shook my head. "No. I don't know."

"Are you listening to yourself? You're tied up in knots here, Cass. Do you see why these psychic dates you're going on aren't healthy?"

"They're not dates!" I could feel my face getting red, embarrassed that Tom had so easily made that leap about my connection with Jake. "Anyway," I added weakly, "dates need two people."

"Yeah. They do."

"But he's a normal guy," I said, sounding like I was

trying to sell my new delinquent boyfriend to my strict father. "He's funny, and he likes cool music, and he's really sorry that he ate all those kids."

Tom smiled at me sadly. I hated that look. It was like, *Oh, aren't your emotions just so teenage and adorable.*

"He can't be a normal guy. He's a zombie. Even if—and this is a monumental if—we forget about his undead status, you still don't *know* this guy, Cass."

"I do know him."

"Not really. Not like we know each other. Not like normal people that talk and share and learn things about each other do. You're cheating. I mean, how long have you spent in his mind? How much have you learned about him?"

I looked down at my hands, not wanting to dig myself a deeper hole than I was already in, unless I could crawl inside that hole and hide.

"You don't have to answer. What really matters is what he knows about you. Which is nothing, right? What do you think would happen if you met? Would you be friends?"

I shrugged, not wanting to admit that I'd thought about meeting Jake in real life and that every time I did the two of us hit it off immediately.

"He'd probably eat you," concluded Tom.

"No, he wouldn't," I mustered, cringing at how petulant I sounded.

Tom got up from his chair and sat down next to me. He put his arm around me and I leaned against him, sort of hating him right now, but also grateful for the contact.

"Do you understand why you need to stop this?" he asked gently. "It's not good for you."

I nodded, wiping his handkerchief across my eyes, feeling intensely stupid. That little nod was enough for him, thankfully, because he stopped lecturing me. We sat there like that for a while, not saying anything. Eventually, Tom stood up.

"When you're ready, Harlene wants to talk to you."

I looked up at Tom, suddenly panicked that this was only the first round of my Jake Stephens intervention. He shook his head, recognizing my terrified look.

"I haven't told her about this Jake stuff," he said. "It'll be just between us, okay? Just promise me you'll stop."

"I promise."

The main NCD building where the unit commanders keep their offices was attached to the barracks by an annex. Before I could get to Harlene's office, I had to pass through the training center. Just my luck that today was the start of courses for a new batch of future zombie killers. They cluttered the hallways, checking one another out in their newly issued NCD jumpsuits, chatting about which government agency or branch of the military they'd been recruited from.

I felt like disappearing, not faking a smile for a bunch of newbies eager to network with a veteran. Not that any of them actually approached me. I was just some kid sulking through the hallways. They probably took me for an intern on a coffee errand.

I felt like crap. Everything Tom said had pretty much been true. And it made sense to the logical part of my brain. The rest of my brain, unfortunately, wanted to go check in with Jake as soon as Tom left me alone. I was addicted to some guy that I'd met once, in passing, after he'd survived a shotgun blast to the stomach. That was abnormal. Way, way, way abnormal.

Walking those halls, I suddenly felt silly and exposed. Like everyone could see what a creepy idiot I'd been for the last few days.

I thought back to the hospital in New Jersey, the way Alastaire had manipulated the minds of those around us, convincing them not to see us. Even though it originated with a total scumbag, it was still a pretty cool trick. I decided to try it.

I glided out onto the astral plane. Not exactly an easy thing to do when you're also trying to walk your physical body down a crowded hall. I found myself goofily tiptoeing, like my mind wanted to be invisible, and my body thought it would help out. A passing trainee looked at me like I was crazy. Great. This plan was having the opposite of its intended effect so far.

On the astral plane, I could see the other minds nearby, processing all the information around them—sights, smells, sounds. I just needed to find my presence in all that psychic data and hide it from them. It was easier than it sounded—kind of like lowering your eyes when you pass by someone that you don't want to talk to.

The next recruit to walk by nearly barreled into me. He was looking straight ahead—he should've seen me—but he strolled up like he could just walk right through me. It was working!

Of course, the next recruit smiled right at me. I tried to refocus on the astral plane, but ended up tripping over my physical feet, earning odd looks from everyone nearby.

So far, I'd only managed to hide myself from one guy and I was sweating, the start of a headache coming on. I didn't know how Alastaire was able to keep up the illusion so easily, while still functioning in the physical world.

"Practice," Alastaire's voice whispered in my ear.

I spun around and found him standing outside a classroom, a newspaper tucked under his arm, getting ready to observe these new recruits and probably unlawfully probe their minds for any naughty thoughts. His bow tie was pale pink, such a gentle and soothing color. Alastaire looked like a bookish and dainty dork, which just made him scarier.

He was looking right at me, a little smile playing at his lips. Wait a minute. There's no way he'd managed to whisper in my ear and then book it down the hall without me noticing.

When he spoke again, his lips didn't move. His voice was inside my head.

Well done, my dear. Soon, you'll be strong enough for your promotion.

An image flickered across my mind's eye, unbidden and definitely uninvited. It was me, holding one end of a metal chain.

The other end was attached to a collar around the throat of a snarling Jake Stephens.

JAKE

THE ELECTRIC RAZOR BUZZED TO LIFE IN AMANDA'S hand. She waved it back and forth in front of my face menacingly.

"Are you ready?" she asked.

"Not really," I replied, shaking my head.

"Come on," groaned Amanda, tapping her foot impatiently. "We agreed."

"We agreed on disguises. Couldn't I just get a floppy hat and some sunglasses?"

I was sitting on the edge of the bathtub. Amanda was

standing at the mirror, her hair piled up underneath a shower cap. I could see smudges of black dye through the clear plastic.

When we woke up, we hit some stores in Ann Arbor. First, we stopped off at a drugstore, then went next door to one of those all-purpose preppy-tire-swing clothing boutiques to grab some college-student-style attire.

We'd even dipped into the money we'd picked up off of the trucker back at the gas station and used it to buy a cheap digital camera. For one thing, I wanted to memorialize my hair before I cut it all off. More important, though, we had used the camera to take a picture of ourselves, holding up a copy of a *USA Today* from a few days ago bearing the headline: SCHOOL SHOOTERS IN CUSTODY. Now we would be living proof that you can't believe everything you read.

That didn't make me any happier about shaving my head, though.

"Won't this make it easier for me to catch a cold?" I asked.

Amanda clicked off the razor, giving me a deadpan look. "You're a zombie worrying about the flu?"

"Okay," I said, "what if my head is tiny and/or misshapen?"

Amanda cocked her head to the side, examining me. "Yeah, that might be an issue. You do have some weird angles going on here."

"Whoa, whoa, really?"

"No. It's perfectly round, like a globe. I'm amazed you've kept such a beautiful head shape hidden from the world for so long. Stop being such a baby."

Amanda had seemed almost giddy as she squeezed the black dye into her hair, like she was happy for the change. Me, I'd had my shaggy mop since the seventh grade, ever since my dad stopped insisting that I go to the barber with him. It'd been cut occasionally, but most of those were self-administered trims. My hair was a Jake Stephens trademark. It was like my business card, if my business was being a lazy stoner, which it actually was. My hair told the world everything it needed to know about me: that I was cool, that I didn't enjoy hard work, and that I wasn't a cop. My hair was perfect.

But, it had to go.

"Okay," I said, steeling myself. "Do it."

Amanda flicked on the electric razor and took my chin in her hand. "That's a good boy. I'll give you a lollipop after."

"My barber used to give me comic books."

"I bought a *Cosmo* at the drugstore. You can have that. Now hold still."

After she was done, we stood side by side in the bathroom mirror and got used to our new looks. I ran my hand over the bristles on my scalp, my head feeling cold and about a pound lighter. Amanda had left a strip of hair in the middle of my head longer than the rest, a sort of Mohawk thing. I wasn't sure whether she'd done it on purpose because she thought it was cool or if she just really sucked at head shaving.

Meanwhile, she looked like an actress playing a punk-rock chick in some Hollywood movie about the dangers of rock and roll. She'd done a pretty good job with the dye but there were still strands and patches of blonde running through the inky black. I guess there's only so much you can do in a motel sink. She still looked like a superhot cheerleader, but now she was a cheerleader that'd had an emotional breakdown and spent some time in an institution.

"We look pretty badass," Amanda said. "No one will recognize the new-and-improved Jake and Amanda."

"These aren't the undead you're looking for," I said, doing my best Obi-Wan hypnotizing hand wave.

Amanda stared at me blankly.

So, you could dye the popular girl's hair, but you couldn't make her understand *Star Wars* references. Good to know.

We got to the student union about an hour before we were supposed to meet Kyle and backed into a parking spot close to the exit, in case we had to leave in a hurry. Then, we found a bench with a clear view of the union entrance. We wanted to see Kyle when he got there and make sure those goons in the beige sedan weren't following too close. Until then, we were just a couple college kids chilling out between classes. I have to say, considering it was the first clandestine meeting of our young lives, I was pretty impressed with us.

"I hope he shows up," I said.

"He'll show," insisted Amanda.

She was watching the entrance to the student union like a hawk, so I felt free to do a little people-watching. The day was sunny and breezy, what a poetic weatherman might describe as balmy. Kids hustled from class to class or hung out on the nearby benches, laughing, sharing lunches. It was a good scene.

"I could get used to this," I said, feeling weirdly content. "Maybe we should enroll in some classes."

"Pretty sure you need a high school diploma for that."

"Oh no," I gasped. "Are we dropouts?"

"Shh," she said. "There he is."

I glanced over to the student union just in time to see Kyle speed-walking through the front doors.

"He looks a little freaked," I observed.

"He has no idea what freaked is," said Amanda. "Yet."

We waited fifteen minutes for the beige sedan to come rolling through, but it never did. Maybe Kyle had shaken his tail or maybe they just didn't bother following him onto campus. Either way, it worked out for us.

That brief feeling of relaxation I had outside the

student union? Gone as soon as we walked through the doors of the bustling, food-court-style campus hangout. It wasn't just that Amanda and I were taking a risk being out in public like this—it's that the student union reminded me of the RRHS cafeteria. So many people milling around, talking and studying, eating their tasty, cooked meals. My stomach was quiet for now, but I dreaded its rumbling.

As we walked around looking for Kyle, I unthinkingly grabbed Amanda's hand. What can I say? Not the most masculine thing to do, but I needed something to hold on to, to reassure me that we wouldn't have a repeat of Friday. Amanda looked over at me, a grateful smile on her face—she was nervous too.

"There," whispered Amanda, nodding to a back table.

I finally got my first real look at Amanda's older brother. He was pretending to read a textbook while anxiously scanning the crowd. It looked like he hadn't slept in days, bags under his eyes, the patchy beginnings of a beard. Amanda had described him as a nerd, yet he still had that Blake aura about him, a sort of inherent confidence that seemed like it should be at odds with his oversize MICHIGAN PARANORMAL SOCIETY sweatshirt and threadbare corduroy pants, but somehow wasn't. Kyle was as blond as Amanda used to be, broad shouldered, like he could've been captain of the lacrosse team if he ever got tired of the whole slacker-geek thing. Instead, he decided to hide those amazing Blake genetics behind a pair of smudged glasses and a perpetual slouch.

As we approached, Kyle's eyes passed right over us, then snapped back in a wide-eyed double take. He leapt to his feet, chair clattering to the ground behind him. Amanda quickly wrapped him up in a hug.

"Holy shit," Kyle said, way too loud.

"Stop," whispered Amanda, trying to keep control but sounding choked up. "You need to be cool."

I felt a brief twinge of envy for the Blake family reunion. I'd never had this thought before, but man, it sure would be nice to hug *my* sister. And my mom and dad. I had to put that out of my mind, though. We were here on a mission.

I stood Kyle's chair back up, looking around. We'd gotten a few glances from the crowd, but kids probably made scenes daily in the student union. No one was paying us much attention as Amanda made Kyle sit down.

"Oh my god, you're here," Kyle said, his words coming fast, like he was about to have a panic attack. "I got the message and I thought it was like a really messed-up prank but now you're here and what the hell is going on?"

A small laugh escaped Amanda, her eyes brimming with tears. She squeezed Kyle's hand underneath the table. "I'm really, really glad to see you, Kyle."

"Yeah," he said, still talking really fast, "yeah, me too,

but also—*how* are you here? All Mom has been saying is that the cops won't let her talk to you, and they said you shot all those kids, and now—"

"We didn't shoot anyone," I interrupted. "They're lying."

Kyle stared at me, like he was noticing me for the first time. He studied me for a moment, then pointed.

"Second shooter," he declared. "Jake Stephens."

"Uh, yeah. Hi."

Kyle looked past us, searching the faces in the student union.

"Is Chazz here too?" he asked.

"Why would he be?" asked Amanda, keeping her voice neutral.

"The news said he was in on it," said Kyle. "Your shooting. That he'd lost his nerve at the school but had already killed his parents beforehand."

Amanda and I exchanged an uncomfortable look.

"No Chazz," said Amanda. "That's done."

"They're lying about him too," I volunteered. "Well, sort of. He probably did kill his parents. It just has nothing to do with us. Also he was sort of a dick, so meh."

Both Blakes were staring at me. So, brother and sister could share the same please-shut-up look.

"Chazz was a dick," agreed Kyle. "What the hell is happening, Amanda? Did you escape? Are the cops after you?"

Kyle started looking around again and this time I did too. I was pretty sure we'd gotten in unnoticed, yet I still felt exposed. I wanted to make sure those guys in the beige sedan—or really, anyone that looked the slightest bit like a gun-toting government agent—weren't closing in.

"No," said Amanda, cool as a cucumber. "The *cops* aren't looking for us because they think we're caught."

"But the dudes that set up this whole conspiracy cover-up thing?" I added. "Pretty sure they're still looking for us."

Kyle frowned at Amanda. "What's he saying?"

"You're literally not going to believe it," sighed Amanda.

I was about to point out that her brother was wearing a sweatshirt that announced his membership as one of the local ghost hunters so he should probably have an open mind, but then Amanda just launched right into our tale in her typical no-nonsense way. She started with the stomach growling, then segued into the massacre in the cafeteria, actually doing a really good job of avoiding words like *massacre* and generally glossing over the real gory details.

When she was finished, Kyle glanced between the two of us.

"Bullshit," he said.

Amanda tossed up her hands. "You believe everything

those creeps on the radio and the internet dorks say, but not your own sister?"

"I believe you. I guess. And I don't believe *everything.* Look, I'm a skeptic realist, okay? I never actually believed that crap about Aunt Ellie getting eaten. I'm sure she's fine."

"Forget Aunt Ellie. This is a little more important, don't you think? We're zombies," insisted Amanda. "Seriously."

"You don't look like zombies," Kyle said. "You look fine. Weird hair, but fine."

"We've been eating rats," I offered.

"Uh-huh," said Kyle, and leaned toward Amanda. "Look, I don't know what kind of trouble you're actually in and you don't have to tell me. But we can work it out. I'm just glad you're safe."

"We're not safe," Amanda blurted, getting annoyed. "They're hunting us."

"The government?" Kyle asked skeptically. "The men in black?"

"The same guys that have been watching your house, dude," I put in.

"Wait. There are guys watching my house?"

Amanda rolled her eyes. "Duh. For a conspiracy freak, you'd think you'd pay a little more attention to that type of thing."

"Uh. You don't think they're monitoring my, um,

internet activity too, do you?" He shot me a nervous glance.

"Look. Kyle. I think the government has more important things to worry about than your porn surfing, okay? I just need you to believe me. We're heading to Iowa," announced Amanda. "But we need your help before we go."

"Iowa?" asked Kyle, pushing a hand through his hair, mega-stressed. "Why would—? No, whatever, that's ridiculous. We're going to call Mom and a lawyer and"—he looked at me—"your parents too, I guess, and we're going to straighten this out."

Amanda slapped the disposable camera onto the table, frustrated.

"There are pictures on this that prove we're not arrested, which proves the whole cover story is crap," said Amanda. "Put them up on your message boards, send them to a newspaper, something. Just help us, Kyle."

"This isn't just happening to us," I added, thinking of Grace and Summer. "There's something big going on here. Bigger than a bunch of paranoid conspiracy nuts are going to be able to fix. We need to get this out there."

Kyle picked up the camera, turning it over in his hands.

"And I need my family to know that I'm not a murderer," I added, feeling my voice catch in my throat. Amanda looked over at me sympathetically.

Kyle was barely paying attention anymore. He hadn't

really needed to be convinced. "This is really happening," he breathed to himself.

"Yeah," said Amanda.

Kyle looked up at his sister, his eyes big with fear. Not for himself, I realized, but for her.

"I'm supposed to just sit here while you run off to Iowa for some crazy secret reason with Weirdo-Mohawk here." He glanced at me. "No offense."

"None taken," I said.

"You're going to help us expose a government conspiracy," said Amanda. "Come on, Kyle. It's your dream come true."

Kyle shoved the camera into his backpack. Then, he rubbed his hands over his face, like he was trying to shake off a bad dream or unscramble the pieces of his blown mind.

"Zombies," he said at last, with a shaky smile. "I knew it."

"Yeah," deadpanned Amanda, smiling a little too, "but the aliens still haven't landed, there's no such thing as ESP, and Bigfoot is just some fatty in a gorilla suit. So you're, like, one for one thousand."

After that, I shook hands with Kyle and then gave the siblings some space for their discreetly tearful good-bye. I was thinking about my own family again, how rad it would be to have a clandestine meeting with them. Or better yet—a normal meeting, like dinner at home, after I'd cured my zombiism and possibly overthrown a corrupt branch of government. I sort of wished I could see them now, though. For the first time ever, if my dad asked me what I was going to do with my life, I'd have an answer: I was making America safe for zombies.

Or, er, helping zombies and keeping America in the know. Or something. It needed ironing out.

Amanda left Kyle at his back table and we retraced our steps through the student union.

"So, that went awesome," I said, feeling some mission-accomplished excitement.

"That was hard," she said, glancing over her shoulder at where Kyle still sat. "So hard to just leave him knowing I might not see him again."

"Psh," I said, trying to cheer her up. "Here's what happens next. We go to Iowa and track down that creepy old guy and his elixir of life. I mean, now we have a lead. We're already better off than we were a day ago. Meanwhile, your brother exposes the government, and the people of this great nation are, like, whoa, we need to help these poor afflicted zombie children. And then we're, like—good news, everybody—there's a cure. They'll probably throw us a parade and—"

I was so focused on all the plans running through my head that I didn't see the man in the boxy black suit until I was crashing right into him, spilling his coffee onto the floor. He looked at me, super annoyed, but the whole thing probably would've just been written off as a dumb student not watching where he was going if I hadn't immediately exclaimed:

"Oh shit!"

I recognized him. It was one of the guys from the beige sedan last night. And there was his partner, a few steps behind.

They were looking right at us, recognition dawning on their faces.

"Oh shit," said the agent with the spilled coffee, apparently as surprised as we were.

I shoved the agent I'd bumped into—hard—and he slipped on the puddle of coffee, feet flying up in the air, landing right on the back of his head. Some of the students nearby started cheering and laughing.

Then they started screaming. Not because we'd gone zombie, although that's now my natural assumption for when crowds scream around me, but because the second agent had drawn a gun.

He shot at me, but Amanda shoved me down. The bullet tore through her shoulder instead. I could feel the hot spray of her blood against my cheek as I fell to the ground.

There were kids running and screaming everywhere now. Just the kind of scene I'd feared when we first entered the student union. One of the kids bumped the agent with the gun and he stumbled while trying to line up another shot.

Just like that, Amanda was on him. Her back was to me, but I could see that rotten gray color had spread up her arms, the blood dripping from the exit wound in her shoulder a black sludge. She snarled, drove both her hands into the agent's midsection, and scooped out a mouthful of fresh guts.

"Amanda?"

The student union was almost totally clear, except for a few kids cowering under tables, watching us with wide eyes. Kyle, though, he stood just a few yards away, eyes wide with horror and disbelief.

Amanda knelt over the agent, devouring him. She looked up at the sound of her name, blood smeared around her mouth, her eyes sunken and feral.

Kyle recoiled, tripped over a chair, and fell to the floor.

"Run!" I shouted, not really sure if that was for our benefit, for Kyle's benefit, or for the rest of the innocent bystanders. I guess for everybody. Everybody needed to run.

I grabbed Amanda around the waist and fled the student union.

CASS

HARLENE SAT BEHIND HER DESK, IGNORING A STACK OF paperwork in favor of a giant cup of iced coffee. The walls of her office were decorated like a time line of her awesomeness: pictures of a young Harlene posing with bouquets of roses after winning a beauty pageant right next to pictures of a more serious Harlene receiving various commendations from multiple presidents. There was even a gun mounted and framed on her wall—a lot of these military types bronzed the weapons they used for their first kills, like a warrior's lethal pair of baby shoes. I bet Harlene was the only one to have hers on display next to a tiara, though.

"There's my Sweet Pea," said Harlene, greeting me with a smile. "Have a seat."

I sank into the chair in front of Harlene's desk, making a concerted effort not to seem too sullen, which probably wasn't working at all. Harlene looked me over, frowning.

"What's going on with you, my dear?" she asked gently.

I didn't know how to even begin answering that question. How do you sum up that your freaky superior who sees you as an unwilling protégé has just promised to make a zombie slave out of the fugitive you've developed a hugely inappropriate psychic crush on?

"Feeling down," I answered.

Harlene nodded. "Tom told me you've been having a hard go of it."

Understatement of the year, maybe? I didn't reply; I felt pretty burned out on explaining my feelings. I'd done enough of that with Tom. Anyway, it seemed like Harlene was working up to something.

"I wish I could tell you it gets easier," she said. "It's never going to be pumpkin pie, hon."

Some pep talk.

Harlene reached into her desk and pulled out a roll of clean bandages and some gauze pads. She started to unwrap the bandage on her forearm from where Chazz had bitten her, but stopped to glance up at me.

"I've gotta change this," she explained, apologetic. "You're not squeamish, are you?"

I laughed, actually surprised and a little touched by the question. "I saw Jamison shoot the head off a girl the other day."

"Right. Silly question," answered Harlene. She continued to talk as she unwrapped her arm, seeming to pay more attention to the layers of bandages than her words. "You know, I've been here since they tossed this whole NCD shindig together after the first outbreak five years ago."

"I didn't know that."

Harlene nodded. "There are three kinds of people in the NCD, way I figure it. First are the soldiers—folks that're just good at doing what they're told, not asking too many questions. They're just doing a job, punching a clock, ya know?"

"Yeah, I guess," I said, although punching a clock for the NCD was a whole heck of a lot different than working a shift at a cheesy Italian restaurant.

"Second type of folks're the ones with a reason. They want to be here. Got a personal score to settle with the undead. I think we both know some people like that."

I nodded my head, thinking of sad, angry Jamison.

"Third type," continued Harlene, "don't necessarily

want to be here, and they ain't necessarily good soldiers either. They're folks the NCD feels have a use in the defense of our country, and they don't get much choice whether they want to serve or not. In case you're not following, I'm talkin' about you, Sweet Pea."

"I got that," I said. Feeling curious, I added, "What type are you, Harlene?"

"People been fooled by my pretty face all these years," answered Harlene, "but I'm just another soldier. I do what I'm told."

Harlene finished unwrapping her wounded arm and I gasped, my stomach doing a somersault. Not because the bite was hideous or ghastly, but because of what was in its place.

They'd grafted one of those feeding nozzles into Harlene's forearm, just like the one Alastaire had so proudly displayed.

Harlene smiled sadly at my reaction. She poured some alcohol onto a cotton ball and started to dab at the raw edges of the graft.

"Figured you'd already know what this is," she said, indicating the plastic tube sticking out of her. "Guess the docs decided it was a convenient time to put it in, what with part of my arm already missing."

The idea of Harlene hooked up to a zombie the way Alastaire was hooked up to Chazz, the thought of her passing fluid down a tube and into a zombie, it made me want to cry. That wasn't my Harlene. I didn't want to imagine her going along with that atrocity.

"Oh, Harlene," I pleaded. "No."

"Nothing to be done about it, Sweet Pea. I've got orders to follow, even if I don't like 'em, or if I think they push this whole operation one step closer to a royal pig-screw. You know, *if* that's what I thought was happening."

If Harlene was working her way around to telling me how important following orders was, I thought I might just make a run for it. Things could not get bleaker. Subconsciously, I'd started rubbing my smooth, non-cyborg forearms. So, maybe I was wrong and things could actually get worse. I really didn't want to find out.

"Anyhow," said Harlene, casually wrapping her forearm in fresh bandages, "I might be just a humble soldier, but I'm also a squad leader. And I make decisions about the usefulness of my squad."

Here it comes, I thought. *Harlene's going to give me the date of my zombie-slave-implant operation, introduce me to my anesthesiologist, ask if I want the traditional white forearm plate or the new hot-pink one they're rolling out.*

Harlene thumbed through one of the stacks of paperwork on her desk, tugging out a form with the fine print of an iTunes agreement. She slid it across the desk to me.

"This here is an Incapable Asset Disengagement form," Harlene explained. "I've already signed it."

I stared at the document, trying to skim over its

sections and subsections, its impenetrable text blocks of legalese. Wherever there was a blank labeled ASSET, Harlene's bubbly handwriting spelled out my name.

"What is this?" I asked.

"It says that you're no good for the NCD. That we'd be better off going our separate ways." She winked.

"Seriously?" I asked, unable to keep a rush of joy out of my voice. "I'd get to go home?"

Harlene held up her hand, trying to tamp down my enthusiasm. "Well, it's not as simple as all that. You can't just walk away, seeing what you've seen. They'd put you in a room full of psychics and they'd go to work on you and remove the memories, like with the civilians you've gotten so good at wiping."

"My memories . . ." I mumbled, considering this. I tried to think of something from the last year and a half that I couldn't live without. Truth be told, I hadn't really been keeping a mental scrapbook of all the nasty crime scenes I'd witnessed. Wouldn't it be kind of nice to just hit the RESET button?

"Not just your memories," added Harlene. "Your momma's, too. Anyone outside the NCD that knows about your government hookup."

"My mom," I repeated, trying to wrap my head around this. "What would she think? What would I think? What would I remember?"

"Not sure," Harlene answered. "Whatever the psychics

can make work. Maybe you spent a year at some swanky private school in the mountains? Who knows?"

I flipped to the last sheet of the paperwork. There was an empty line waiting for my signature.

"This could happen?" I asked, still not quite believing. "I could go back to normal."

"Normal as it'll ever get," Harlene replied, her voice lowering. "Truth is, Sweet Pea, I think things are going to get worse around here."

"In Washington?"

Harlene shook her head. "Everywhere. Just between us girls, the Control part of NCD isn't exactly going gangbusters. I told you once that one day we'd kill them all and everyone'd get to go home with a medal and a grin. I don't know anymore if that's happening."

After everything that'd gone down in the last week—heck, just the last couple hours—a huge part of me so badly wanted to sign that paperwork, declare myself incapable, and forget about the whole zombie-huntress thing. But another part of me thought about that initial pride I'd taken in being the youngest-ever member of the NCD, of doing good, making a difference.

"I could help," I said weakly. "I could stay with you."

"And I'd love to have you, darling, if that's what you want," said Harlene, giving me that sad smile again. "But maybe, instead, you might want to go back to your family. Spend some time with the people you love instead of the people that eat people you love."

Maybe I was reading too much into it, but there was a distinct note of doom in Harlene's words. Zombie apocalypse was just something they said in direct-to-video gore flicks, yet I felt suddenly like we were just a few more fugitive zombies away from barricading the doors and rationing food. Where did I want to be when that went down? On the frontlines, hooked up to a dead boy on a leash, buddying up with Alastaire? Or watching movies with my mom until the electricity went out and the end came?

I hesitated, looking Harlene in the eyes. "Does it make me a coward if I want to go home?"

She shook her head. "No. It makes you smarter than the rest of us."

Harlene held out a pen. I took it, hovering over the place where my signature would set me free.

"There's just one more thing," said Harlene. "I can't let you go if you're still in possession of actionable intelligence."

I knew immediately what the military jargon meant. "Jake Stephens," I said.

Harlene nodded. "We need you to help us catch them. Just one last mission, Sweet Pea."

Harlene gave me the rest of the afternoon to think it over. I scurried back to my room, clutching my stack of life-changing paperwork.

I climbed into bed and pulled the covers over my head. I was trying not to overthink it, but that's what I do. Overthink things. By signing, I'd basically be trading my life for Jake's. And Amanda's, but whatever. I'd also be signing away a year and a half of my memories. All the good things I'd done, the successful operations I used to be proud of—could I live without those memories? Wouldn't it be worth giving them up if it meant being normal again, just a kid ignorant of all the horrible monsters lurking out there?

My mind searched for a *good* memory, something from my time in NCD that I cherished. I thought back to my first day on the job.

There was no ceremony for graduating from the government's zombie-killing university. Most of the people in my training class just shuffled off back to the barracks, marching orders in hand for whatever unit they were supposed to join up with. Because of my underage-telepath status, my situation was a little different. I was met at the classroom door by the best-dressed man in the metro DC area.

"Hey," he said, "my name's Tom."

We shook hands and Tom smiled, quickly putting me at ease. I'd spent weeks around stiff government types and fidgety scientists in coffee-stained lab coats who taught our classes. I hadn't expected my handler to be so young and normal.

"So," Tom said, putting his index fingers to his

temples, "what movie am I thinking of?"

"NCD psychics are to refrain from making unnecessary telepathic contact with their team," I recited directly from the handbook.

"Good answer," he said, and winked at me. "It was *The Notebook*, by the way."

"Blah," I replied, remembering how my sister watched that movie four times in one weekend following a breakup, huddled under a blanket on our couch next to a pile of snotty tissues.

Tom drove us out of DC proper and into one of the swankier sections of the suburbs, where the fancier government types kept quiet homes on clean, tree-lined streets. We parked in front of a salmon-colored house, a lush flower garden lining both sides of the cobblestone walkway that led to the front door. It was such a sweet, lovingly decorated place; the scary-looking hulk sipping iced tea on the front porch looked totally out of place.

"That's Jamison," explained Tom as we approached the house. "He's our muscle."

Jamison was wearing a tank top that showed off his not-kidding-around muscles and the faded Marine Corps tattoos that covered them. He eyed me with no shortage of skepticism as Tom led me up the front steps.

"Jamison," announced Tom, "allow me to introduce our new psychic friend."

"Her?" he grunted, then looked at me. "Jesus, what are you? Thirteen?"

"Sixteen," I corrected.

"Oh, in that case . . ." He snorted, shaking his head. "Have you ever even seen a dead body, little girl?"

"Have you?" I replied, deciding to stand my ground with this brooding tough guy. "Because you kinda look like the fainting type."

Tom stifled a laugh as Jamison stared at me, his mouth open to form a comeback that never took shape.

"Oh, Jamie," said a laughing Harlene as she emerged through the screen door, drying her hands on a towel. "Stop trying to scare the new girl. It clearly ain't working."

Harlene's hair was piled on top of her head in the most immaculate-looking bun that I'd ever seen. She had a flour-spattered apron tied around her waist. This was even more surprising than having a well-coifed Gosling superfan for a guardian; Harlene reminded me of a southern version of my mom, the way she'd go out of her way to cook a fancy dinner whenever she knew my sister was coming home from college for the weekend.

"Here's the boss," said Tom.

I extended my hand to Harlene, feeling more timid around her than I had around Jamison. She brushed my hand aside and swept me into a warm hug.

"I hope you like biscuits," she said, holding me out at

arm's length. "What am I saying? You've been eating that nasty barracks food. I'm sure you're more than ready for some good home cooking."

We didn't have a ton of downtime in the NCD, but whenever we did, Harlene would insist we all get together at her place for a family dinner. It was nice. Normal. And though he never said much at the table, I think even Jamison liked it. He sure ate enough.

Amanda sure ate enough too.

I must have dozed off under the covers, or maybe I was just so emotionally exhausted that my mind sort of got away from me. Half aware of what I was doing, I drifted across the astral plane. Into Jake. But if my mind had gotten comfortable seeking him out, this was not the Jake I expected or wanted to find.

He was pulling a thrashing, zombied-out Amanda away from a guy that looked an awful lot like one of our government agents. He paused for a moment, not even thinking as he tore off a chunk of meat from the agent's side. He shoveled that bloody handful into his mouth and went back to dragging Amanda away from the body.

I woke up still shaking from what I'd just seen. I'd gotten so used to thinking of Jake as a nice boy from Jersey that I'd forgotten that he and his girlfriend sometimes killed people.

Tom stood over me, just about to wake me up.

"There's been an incident in Michigan," Tom said gravely. "Stephens and Blake were involved."

"I know," I said grimly. There wasn't anything more to say than that.

"One dead," said Tom. "A team is mobilizing. They're going to need you to track him."

I nodded, getting out of bed and crossing to my desk where I'd left the Incapable Asset Disengagement paperwork.

Incapable was right. I'd gotten all screwed up while stealing into Jake's mind, and now more people were dead. Because of Jake. Because of *me.* They'd killed others too along the way, and I'd rationalized those. What had I been thinking?

All this was definitely a memory I could live without.

I thought about Tom's lecture that morning, how my whole relationship with Jake Stephens had taken place inside my head. That I even thought of it as a relationship was a joke.

I'm sorry, Jake, I thought, *but I don't even know you.*

I signed the paperwork.

JAKE

WE DROVE OUT OF ANN ARBOR IN WHAT I'D LIKE TO coolly describe as a hurry, but was really verging on panic. It took all my self-control not to floor it, knowing that speeding would only attract more attention. I heard the distant wailing of sirens when we first skidded out of the university, but we were ahead of them. I stuck to back roads, sleepy streets in the suburbs—avoiding highways, commercial areas, anywhere the cops might be floating around. I kept an ear peeled for the *chop-chop-chop* of a helicopter.

It never came. With all the mayhem back at the student union, it'd probably take the local cops some time to figure out who they were looking for. By then, hopefully, we'd be out of Michigan. And, as for the government guys, it seemed like there were only two of them.

Well, there was only *one* of them now.

I wasn't really paying attention to where we were going. All I wanted to do was put some distance between us and our latest crime scene. I tried to keep the sun in front of us, knowing we wanted to head west, putting my four months of Boy Scout training to good use.

Amanda was camped out in the backseat. She'd come out of zombie mode, the digested parts of the agent enough to heal the bullet wound in her shoulder. She was still scrubbing herself with baby wipes. She was shuddering.

"You all right?" I asked her, trying to keep my voice steady even though I didn't feel particularly all right myself.

"We need to switch cars," she said.

We dumped the car in the parking lot of some big apartment complex, I think somewhere in Indiana. Amanda picked out a dark red Chevy whose owner had left a back door unlocked, hot-wiring our latest ride with shaky hands. While she was doing that, I ate a rat, then a second one when my stomach rumbled disappointedly. I hadn't gotten much of the secret-agent buffet back in

Ann Arbor and, with all the stress of the last few hours, I was starting to feel it. When I was finished, there were just five little rodents left on death row. I hoped we could ration them.

Rat-tion. That was clever. I turned to Amanda to share my latest bit of wit, but she had this distant look on her face.

"Seriously," I asked again. "You all right?"

She shook her head. "I ate that guy. I shouldn't have eaten that guy."

"He tried to shoot me," I replied. "Thanks, by the way. Anyhow, I know we didn't vote, but I think anyone trying to kill us is fair game. Retroactively, I'd vote to eat him."

I actually didn't feel so sure about any of this. But what else could I say?

"It's not that," she said. "It's that I was, like, more aware this time, while it was happening. I had the hunger and all that, but a part of me was still thinking, still paying attention. I saw Kyle when he shouted my name. . . ."

She trailed off as I pulled out of the apartment complex, heading west again, not sure where to go or what to say.

"He was terrified of me, Jake," she said at last. "He was terrified of his own sister."

"Well, you did look kind of scary," I offered, figuring humor might be the best medicine.

Amanda stared at me for a second, then cupped her face in her hands and started to cry. Big, racking sobs that shook her whole body. It was like, thanks to my stupid quip, the strong-willed Amanda I'd gotten to know had collapsed all at once.

Way to go, Jake.

By nightfall, we were on the back roads of Illinois. This was the country now: high speed limits, winding roads, more grain silos than there were houses. A few other cars passed us, their high beams flashing in greeting. We zipped by, like, a dozen different deer, all of them toeing their way toward the road, eyes reflecting our headlights, waiting to make a break for it.

Eventually, all the radio stations got swallowed up by static except for one gravel-voiced old man giving lethargic gardening advice probably from within the depths of his tomb.

"What's a ball weevil?" I asked Amanda, breaking the silence that'd hung between us since she stopped crying.

"Boll," she clarified simply, and clicked off the radio. I'd never get to find out what common household item to mix with my discarded orange peels to keep pests from nibbling my baby cucumbers.

We drove on in silence once again, our headlights reaching across miles of what would've been paradise if you were a grazing cow or a tractor aficionado. Me, I found it kind of eerie out here in this wide-open empty space, especially now that the radio was off.

"Look," I said, not able to handle any more quiet.

"I'm sorry for what I said before. It was a stupid joke."

Amanda waved me off. "Let's forget it, okay? You being a totally insensitive dick, me breaking down. It was just a really hard day."

"Okay," I mumbled, feeling like we shouldn't just be brushing the whole incident off, but not knowing what else to say.

Amanda was back to business. In the pale yellow dome light she pored over our road atlas, dragging her finger across a mostly empty patch of land on the Illinois/Iowa border.

"I think we're around here," she said.

I pushed the road atlas away, catching her eye.

"Look, I know you want to just forget it and that's fine," I rambled, picking up steam as I went along, "but you need to know that what your brother saw, that wasn't you. Not the real you anyway. He'll realize that once he calms down. And even if he doesn't—he totally will, but *even if he doesn't*—you need to know that there's at least one person in the world that will never find you terrifying or gross."

Amanda looked down at the road atlas, silent.

"That one person is me," I clarified.

"Yeah, duh," she said, and leaned over to peck me quickly on the cheek.

I thought about turning to give her a kiss of my own. A real kiss. But she was crying again.

CASS

MY FINAL MISSION AS A NOT-SO-PROUD MEMBER OF the Necrotic Control Division began late that afternoon.

Tom and I stood in the hangar, not much use as usual, watching a bunch of Jumpsuits load equipment onto the chopper we'd be flying to Michigan. Jamison stood nearby, supervising them while absently cleaning his shotgun.

I told myself that I'd made the right decision, the only decision I could really make. Still, I didn't feel good about it.

"He's going to die because of me," I whispered to Tom.

Of course, Tom knew exactly who I was talking about. "That'll be hard," he said. "The good news is, you won't have to remember it."

I guess that's some consolation, knowing that maybe the worst thing you've ever done will soon be wiped from your memory.

Tom squeezed my hand.

"Home soon, Psychic Friend," he said.

"I won't remember you either."

"No," replied Tom. "But whenever you see a handsome and fashionably dressed man, you'll probably have an unexplainable feeling of great joy."

I laughed, even though I felt like bawling. "Not so fashionably dressed now."

Tom grumpily tugged at the collar of his stiff new NCD jumpsuit. Apparently, word had come down from on high that his tailored suits weren't combat appropriate. "No," he said, "I guess not."

Both of us fell silent as a crew of nervous-looking agents wheeled a dog crate toward the helicopter. Inside was Chazz Slade, looking and smelling more rotten than when I'd last seen him. He was bent over in the crate, on his hands and knees. His face was pressed right up to the grating on the door, teeth gnashing ineffectually at the metal.

"Someone's excited to go on a trip," joked Alastaire, following a few steps behind his caged pet. The guys wheeling the crate forced some laughter. Alastaire hadn't donned an NCD jumpsuit like the rest of us, even though he was technically leading this mission. He wore a stupid paisley bow tie, a black suit, and his usual aura of sliminess.

"Aren't you going to miss this?" asked Tom.

I sat between Tom and Harlene in the chopper as we flew toward Michigan. Jamison sat across from us, leaving some space on the bench between him and Alastaire. Chazz flew in the cargo hold with the rest of the gear.

It was too loud to talk, so we passed the flight in silence. Harlene pored over a digital map of the area where I'd last pegged Jake and Amanda. Tom played BrickBreaker on his phone. Jamison puzzled over one of the new stun guns he'd been cajoled into carrying after blowing that other zombie's head off, probably looking for a way to make it lethal. I stared into space and tried to ignore the way Alastaire was studying me.

I found myself daydreaming about the deal I'd made with Harlene, about what I might do once I returned to my normal life. What grade would I be in? I'd missed all of sophomore year and most of junior year now too. Was I going to be one of the kids that was very obviously held back, like Felix from middle school that everyone was scared of because he had a full mustache?

I shouldn't be thinking about this stuff—not so close to Alastaire. I was pretty sure Harlene went over his head on my deal. I didn't want to give anything away, so I pushed the thoughts down, imagining them getting locked up in my mental vault made of psychic douche-bag Kryptonite.

I felt it then, like that tickle you get in the back of your throat when you're just starting to get sick, except in my brain. Alastaire's mind reaching out to mine.

Why the sad face, peanut? It's going to be a wonderful night.

Peanut? I thought back, sending a wave of revulsion along with it.

I'm trying it out. Everyone else has nicknames for you.

His thoughts were like an oil slick on my brain. I couldn't suppress a shudder. But I figured this little psychic chat was off the record. Might as well express myself.

I pictured a watermelon exploding. A watermelon wearing a paisley bow tie.

Alastaire smiled.

Not very nice, he thought, and broke contact.

Five black SUVs met us at the Michigan landing strip. Two of them were for our squad, and the other three were filled with NCD agents. After losing agents in Pennsylvania and Michigan, they weren't taking any chances. All told, there were more than a dozen of us.

"Remember," Alastaire told the assembled group of

hard-looking badasses, and me and Tom, "we intend to take these two alive."

He looked over at me.

"Now, where can we find them?"

Amanda and Jake were leaving Michigan, heading west. They were still on the move, but Jake didn't know where they were going. They were driving through the country, sometimes in circles, lost. It was almost too perfect—wherever they ended up would be the middle of nowhere, no civilians to worry about.

They didn't stand a chance.

It was a long drive to catch up with them. Thankfully, Alastaire rode in a different car. Harlene, Jamison, and Tom were all silent, thinking about the mission, or maybe about their own futures in the NCD. I stayed out of their minds, not wanting to know.

Every few miles, I updated our direction. We were getting close.

It was after midnight when we caught up to them. All the headlights in our caravan of zombie killers were turned off as we wended our way down a back country road. They'd holed up in a farmhouse just a mile or so off.

We pulled over. The military types fanned out into the woods around the farmhouse, setting up a perimeter. They seemed confident, like this was just another night at the office. As per usual, Tom and I stayed out of the way.

Harlene and Jamison gathered around me. Jamison was giving orders into a walkie-talkie, telling the other agents to hold their positions.

"What's our target's status, Sweet Pea?" Harlene asked.

I slipped into Jake's mind. It was easier than ever because we were so close together. It was sort of nice, having him nearby. Ugh, I felt guilty even thinking that. I needed to toughen up.

I gasped and broke contact almost right away, embarrassed by what little I'd seen. I was grateful no one could see my face flush in the darkness.

"They, um, won't see you coming," I said quietly.

"Good," said Alastaire. He was standing a few yards away from the others, keeping his distance because a snarling Chazz was crouched at his feet. He'd hooked up The Pavlov at some point and I was glad it was too dark to see them sharing fluids.

Alastaire bent down and unhooked Chazz. He grabbed the zombie by the hair and looked him in his eyes, the dead milky whites standing out in the dark.

"Go fetch," said Alastaire.

JAKE

THAT NIGHT, OUR STERLING NAVIGATION SKILLS LED us down a dead-end dirt road that broke off at an abandoned farmhouse.

"We're lost," I announced.

"No kidding."

I started to put the car in reverse, but Amanda stopped me.

"I don't see how more aimless driving through the dark country is a good idea," she said, and nodded toward the farmhouse. "This is as good a place as any to hide out for the night."

I looked at the ramshackle farmhouse, taking in the sagging roof and partially collapsed wood porch from the safety of our car. It's totally played out to describe broken, empty windows as looking like eyes but, man, if those farmhouse windows didn't look like some serious-ass evil eyes, just daring us to enter.

"This is some *Scooby-Doo* shit right here."

"Too bad we cut that hair. You'd have made a perfect Shaggy," Amanda said, opening her door. "Come on, I don't want to sleep in the car again."

"You sure about that?"

"Don't be a wuss, Jake," teased Amanda. "I'm sure the ghosts don't mean us any harm."

The front door of the farmhouse hardly qualified for door status; it was just a cracked piece of old wood dangling listlessly from a single surviving hinge. We pushed it open and, of course, it let out a loud and sustained creak. I shuddered, but I don't think Amanda noticed in the dark. I hoped not; I didn't want her to think I was chicken.

In the farmhouse's living room was nothing but dust, the broken-down remains of some old furniture, and a stone hearth stained black with ash.

More notable were the dozens of crushed, red plastic cups and the lingering smell of beer hanging in the air.

Amanda picked up an abandoned keg tap and held it

up for me to inspect.

"Party ghosts?" she asked.

I felt more at ease now that it seemed the farmhouse was a destination for country-style wild ragers. Clearly, we weren't the first kids to drive out here for a place to hide.

We cleared some space in the center of the room. Dust kicked up, swirling through the moonlight that poured through the windows. Amanda poked around the broken furniture and the remains of the kegger while I spread our blanket out in the cleared space. It looked like we were about to have the gloomiest picnic ever.

We lay down, side by side. I closed my eyes but, as tired as I was, they didn't want to stay shut. They just kept fluttering back open. I was wired. Too much had gone down today. I needed some rest, but it was impossible to relax.

"Hey," I said. "Can you, like . . ." I felt stupid even saying it. It made me sound like a total pussy. But I needed to be close to her right now. Seriously, masculinity aside, I totally wanted a hug.

Before I could finish my sentence, Amanda had already curled up against me, her head on my chest. I stretched my arm out and pulled her closer.

"I need you, Jake," she said quietly. "I'm not going to be able to make it through this without you. I'm so happy you're with me."

"Yeah," I said awkwardly. "Ditto."

"Sometimes when we're driving, I think, like, about how horrible all this is. About how fucked up everything's gotten. And then I realize that if none of this had happened, I probably still wouldn't know you."

"You knew me," I said. "I was in your English class."

"You know what I mean."

"Yeah," I said. "I do."

"Are you going to puke on me again?"

That was all the invitation I needed. This time when we kissed it was different than in the gas-station bathroom. Better. For starters, our mouths weren't smeared with some trucker's viscera. The kiss was less intense, well, less like we were trying to devour each other anyway. It was more intense because it felt like we both really meant it.

It was like that for a while: breathless, kissing noises, you know the drill. Then Amanda rolled on top of me, straddling my body.

"Oh my," I said before I could stop myself.

"Seriously?" laughed Amanda. "Oh my?"

"Whatever," I said. "I'm overcome with feelings."

Her hands on my chest, Amanda sat up straight, pulling back her hair, and I watched her with an expression that was probably like wonderment, this being the endgame of so many fourth-period fantasies.

"What?" she asked, suddenly self-conscious.

"Nothing," I said, and then kept talking because I'm

a well-documented moron. "Just sort of amazed this is happening, that's all. Is it, like, an end-of-the-world sort of thing? Like we might die tomorrow, so what the hell?"

Amanda stopped. "We're not going to die," she said firmly. "We're going to be okay. Do you always talk this much?"

"Okay, okay, I'm shutting up."

When Amanda leaned down and put her mouth on mine again, it seriously stopped mattering whether this was a one-time thing or some act of desperation or pity on her part, because why spoil the idea of making out with Amanda Blake by thinking too much about it. I should be devoting any excess mental energy left in my blown mind to committing every moment of this to memory.

My hands slid up Amanda's sides toward her boobs and, as they did, I swear there was a crescendo of trumpets and harps playing somewhere, the kind of triumphant orchestra that I bet mountain climbers hear in their heads when they reach the summit of Everest.

And, just as my hands reached that most sacred of destinations, the front door of the farmhouse banged open, startling both of us, our foreheads painfully knocking together.

I could see the doorway from beneath Amanda. Standing there was a hulking silhouette, shoulders heaving as it breathed raggedly.

"Angry ghost farmer!" I shouted.

The room suddenly smelled like a deli during a power outage. The silhouette staggered forward a step into a pool of moonlight. It took me a second to recognize him; he was practically falling apart, decomposed, his trademark glamour muscles gone sinewy under saggy dead flesh. A long, metal chain was dangling from a collar around his neck, like a leash. But wherever his owner was, it wasn't here.

"Chazz?!" I exclaimed.

"Oh my god, you psycho stalker!" Amanda shouted, not exactly a reasoned reaction, but I think we were probably both remembering Chazz's promise to beat up anyone new Amanda tried to date. I certainly was. I didn't have time to get over the initial shock of Chazz's untimely arrival, to wonder just how the hell he'd gotten here, because he was charging forward.

Chazz was on us before Amanda could fully get to her feet, dropping his shoulder and driving it into her like a football tackle. She flew toward the fireplace, cracking her head hard against the cobblestone hearth.

I was still on my back, Chazz staring down at me. His eyes were wide and feral—I didn't see even a glimmer of human Chazz in there.

"Hey, dude," I said. "Could you possibly come back in an hour or two?"

"Graaahhhh," replied Chazz, and reached down to wrap his hands around my throat.

Chazz lifted me up like that, my feet kicking in the air. He slammed me against the wall, his teeth snapping just inches from my face, even though he didn't seem to want to bite me. That was zombie instinct; I wasn't a meal, just something to be torn apart. I cried out as his fingers punched into my neck, digging toward my throat. It hurt at first, but then the zombie numbness took over and it just felt cold.

For a second, I felt like I was back at Ronald Reagan High and I'd finally gotten into a scrape with Chazz that I couldn't joke my way out of. Except this wasn't Ronald Reagan High and I wasn't just some nerd to be picked on. I was a fucking zombie now.

I shoved my hand into Chazz's snapping mouth, feeling his teeth dig into my knuckles. I clenched my fist and yanked back, a rotten-tooth smell filling the air as I ripped Chazz's jaw off his decaying face.

Chazz let me loose, staggering backward and slapping confusedly at his face. Rage was filling me, that zombie-killing instinct, but I had to control it. Channel it like one of those anime characters would, a big ball of cannibalistic chi stored up in my core, ready to hadouken the shit out of my enemy.

I tackled Chazz. He was weaker than me now, decaying fast. I pinned him down and grabbed the sides of Chazz's face, slamming the back of his head into the floor. There was a loud metal clang as something on the back of his head struck the hard wood.

"Jake! Stop!"

Amanda knocked me off Chazz before I could finish smashing out his brains. She had a jagged cut on her forehead, the blood oozing out of it a viscous black.

"You're going to kill him!" she shouted at me.

"Why are you sticking up for him?" I croaked back, breath whistling out of the finger holes in the side of my neck.

"I don't know!" she kept shouting. "He's—he's one of us, I guess. Do we have to talk about this now?"

She had a point. Chazz was already staggering back to his feet, his head rolling at inappropriate angles on his shoulders. Thick tendrils of greasy slobber curled down his neck, no longer contained by his jaw.

"Chazz," Amanda tried to address him rationally, like that was going to work. "Did you follow me out here?"

"Oh, how romantic," I groaned, squaring up in case talking failed and we had to rumble again. I was rumbling!

Wait, literally. My stomach rumbled violently.

Chazz had hurt me and now I needed to feed. I couldn't keep the hunger back for much longer. And—wait, whoa—I could smell them. Their scent was in the air, causing another growl to rattle my abdomen.

Human meat.

"Shit," I said to Amanda. "He's not alone."

CASS

WE HID IN THE DARKNESS, ALL OF US TENSE FROM THE sounds of fighting inside the farmhouse. It was the back line as usual for Tom and me, watching from behind an SUV that'd been quietly parked behind Amanda and Jake's stolen car, cutting off their escape. They'd left one of the NCD soldiers with us, a young guy that looked disappointed to have drawn babysitting duty.

I was nervous, my hands and feet tingling. I couldn't take my eyes off the farmhouse.

"It'll all be over soon," whispered Tom, his hand laid

protectively on my shoulder.

"Shh," snapped the agent.

The farmhouse had gone quiet. A gentle breeze blew across the overgrown wheat field that stretched out behind the house. Tom's hand tightened on my shoulder.

This was it. The moment right before something big happens.

The zombie dove out of one of the farmhouse windows, rolled across the grass, and staggered to his feet.

My heart was in my throat as the air sizzled with electricity. Three cobalt-blue electric blasts fired from NCD stun guns sliced through the air and right into his chest, on target. A spasm shook his entire body and he collapsed back to the ground just as the metallic *thwap* came from someone's net-chucker. He was pinned to the ground beneath a blanket of heavy-duty mesh. Captured.

"Hold your fire!" I heard Alastaire screech from somewhere nearby.

I breathed a sigh of relief as I realized that it wasn't Jake that'd come flying out the window.

It was Chazz.

"A diversion," murmured Tom.

I nodded. I didn't have to be in Jake's mind to see their desperate plan. Toss Chazz out the window, let the bunch of trigger-happy NCD hunters blast the ever-loving crap out of Alastaire's pet zombie and then . . .

"They're going for the back door," I said.

We had the whole place surrounded. There were at least six highly trained NCD agents hidden from view in the wheat field behind the house. The rest of our forces were concentrated in front, on account of Alastaire being convinced Chazz would just drag Jake and Amanda through the front door. A part of me—no, all of me—was thrilled that his disgusting science project had totally failed.

"There go our heroes," said Tom, pointing.

Not all of our force had been fooled by Chazz's swan dive out the window. I watched Jamison and Harlene hustle around the corner, headed for the back of the house. Jamison was on point, his stun gun leveled in front of him.

"Help me with him, damn you!" Alastaire shouted at one of his underlings.

If this wasn't such a life-and-death situation, I would've laughed at Alastaire and one of the other agents sprinting across the lawn toward Chazz and struggling to free him from the net. The rest of the crew at the front of the house just watched, not sure what to do. Alastaire was supposed to be giving the orders, but he was too worried about the big, rotting professional failure pinned down by one of his own men's nets.

"Disaster," observed Tom. "Of the unmitigated variety."

They managed to free Chazz and he came up

thrashing. He would've taken a bite right out of Alastaire's frightened helper's face if not for the fact that his jaw was missing.

"Down, Chazz!" shouted Alastaire, and for a moment Chazz swayed back and forth, like he might attack or just drop fully dead. But then, with a guttural moan, he dropped onto one knee and waited for his next order.

Something wasn't right. The men at the front of the house shifted anxiously, guns still leveled at the front door, even if most of the agents were paying more attention to Alastaire's humiliating scene than the farmhouse. The night was quiet, still.

"Where's all the shooting?" I asked Tom.

If Jake and Amanda had gone out the back door, the guys in the back should've had them by now. Harlene and Jamison should've gotten there and—

As if on cue, from behind the farmhouse, Harlene screamed.

I slipped into Jake's mind for what I swore to myself would be the last time. It wasn't just my abnormal infatuation this time—it was imperative to the mission, serious NCD field business. I needed to know what was going on behind the farmhouse. At least this time I wouldn't catch him and Amanda about to do it—God, horny teenage zombies, don't you have anything better to do?

No—I was pretty sure this time, whatever I'd find

would be way worse than a make-out session.

His mind wasn't so easy to get into this time; it was lukewarm, part Jake and part hungry eating machine. He'd started to turn full zombie. I forced myself into the part of Jake that was still capable of rational thought.

Holy shit, it's that big, black dude from New Jersey trying to pin me down. What the hell is he doing here? What the hell, in general?

Eat him. I should eat him. Eat him, eat him, eat him.

No—stay in control, Stephens.

God, my chest. What the hell did they shoot me with? It's all singed and tingly.

Amanda! Where is Amanda?

Eat him, eat him. Just one bite. One bite will be okay.

BITE HIM.

Aghh! No meat. Metal. What the fuck is he wearing? Some kind of gauntlet? No good. Harder to eat.

Wait. What was that cry? Sounds like food. And the big guy is heading toward it. Now's my chance.

EAT.

No. Focus. Sit up.

Amanda. There's Amanda, on top of that lady. What is she doing? Biting?

Eating. Mmm, eating. She's so lucky.

Whoa. That big guy just kicked Amanda right in the face. Not cool, dude. Knocked her off the lady, ruined her dinner. I'm going to defend her honor! By devouring his stupid face.

Wait. Shit! Who are these guys? Are they shooting nets? Who shoots nets?

"Jake!" I heard Amanda scream. "Run!"

I broke contact and ran, tripping over my feet, disoriented from moving so quickly after severing my connection with Jake. Tom tried to grab me, but I shook his hand off. I sprinted for the back of the farmhouse. NCD agents with their guns leveled were running right in front of me.

"Oh no, oh no, oh no," I kept repeating, feeling like the words were coming out of someone else.

Tom was right behind me, shouting my name. I ignored him.

Why were Harlene and Jamison alone back there? Where were the agents assigned to guard the back? This couldn't be happening.

I rounded the corner of the farmhouse just in time to see Jamison go barreling into the wheat field. Chasing Jake, probably. That didn't matter now.

The NCD agents who had gotten here first stood around Amanda Blake, their guns aimed at her as she struggled under the net. She had the imprint of Jamison's boot on the side of her face but otherwise looked pretty as ever, damn her.

There was color coming back to her face slowly. She'd just eaten.

I slid into the dirt next to Harlene's body, scraping

my knees. The ground around her was wet with blood.

There was a huge chunk missing from the side of Harlene's neck. Blood bubbled up as she tried to breathe. Her face was ghostly pale in the moonlight, her eyes staring up at nothing.

"Oh no," I said again. "Oh no."

Tom crashed to the ground next to me, shoving me out of the way. He tore the sleeve of his jumpsuit off and pressed it to Harlene's neck, cradling her head.

"Harlene," he was saying, "you stay with me. You hold on."

I stood up woozily, not really sure what I was doing until I was doing it. I shoved through the NCD agents and punched that stupid zombie bitch in the face.

It probably hurt me more than it hurt Amanda, the netting slicing through my knuckles. I didn't even feel any better. Amanda just stared at me, looking confused. Before I could even contemplate another swing, one of the NCD guys grabbed me by the shirt and flung me backward, away from Amanda.

"You're awful!" I screamed at her, not caring about the tears rolling down my cheeks, or all the NCD guys staring. "This is why your dad's a convict and your brother's terrified of you! Because you're—so—fucking awful!"

Amanda just kept staring at me, dumbfounded, a fresh welt forming underneath her eye.

"Cass!" Tom shouted at me. "You have to help me over here!"

I turned around. The cloth Tom had pressed to Harlene's neck was already dark with blood. She was looking at me, though, her mouth half-open like she was trying to say something.

She was still alive.

Tom took my hand and pressed it to the warm, damp cloth on Harlene's neck.

"Pressure," he said sternly. "Keep the pressure on."

I did as I was told. Tom got on his walkie-talkie, radioing in for a chopper, for a medical team.

Weakly, Harlene took my hand that wasn't pressed to her wound. She squeezed.

"It's going to be okay . . ." she told me.

I sniffed back tears and nodded.

I could tell she was lying.

JAKE

H-U-N-G-R-Y

Keep it together, Jake. Keep it together harder than you've ever kept it together before.

I booked it through the wheat field, the stalks tickling the bruises on my face and the holes in my neck. It was like a commercial for healthy cereal out here, amber waves of grain and all that shit. New, from General Mills, Honey-Coated Fleeing Zombie with Shotgun Marshmallows.

That's good. Keep thinking, even if it's about stupid made-up cereals. Breathe deep, just like Summer said. Don't think about—

EATING.

One of my eyes was swollen shut. The view out of the other one wasn't looking so good, tinged red around the edges. The zombie in me was banging the dinner bell. So much tasty human meat back there, just begging to be EATEN.

Rip them out of their little suits and crack them open and suck out their guts and smash open their faces and chew on their brains.

Stop.

The zombie in me had really terrible impulse control. I knew that if I lost my grip, I'd go racing back toward the farmhouse and try to snack on those heavily armed government dudes. The zombie in me only saw meat, not guns, not the freaking high-velocity nets, not my inevitable capture or killing. Practical thinking wasn't really a strong suit of the undead.

Shit, I couldn't believe I'd left Amanda back there. I mean, she'd yelled at me to run with the net pinning her down, but it wasn't really heroic of me to actually listen, was it? We were supposed to be a team. Running away while she was trapped with government assassins was in strict violation of the buddy system.

I should go back for her. Get all Zombie–Jason Bourne on these government jerk-offs.

I SHOULD GO BACK AND EAT.

I didn't have to go back. They were coming for me.

I could hear him crashing through the field behind me. I knew who it was without turning around—the big dude that I'd tangled with twice now. The only reason he hadn't caved in my skull back at the farmhouse was because Amanda had distracted him. He had that sort of grim and steely look about him that all the antihero types in comics had, the ones like Batman and The Punisher who are just bordering on criminally freaking insane.

EATMAN AND THE YUMISHER.

I knew this dude wasn't going to quit chasing me. Not this time.

But he was alone. The rest of his squad hadn't followed him.

I could eat him. Just him. Then I'd be able to think straight again, maybe put together a plan to go save Amanda.

My stomach rumbled. It liked this plan.

Before I could skid to a stop and face my pursuer, I heard the *chick-chick* of a shotgun cocking.

Uh-oh.

Boom.

My legs exploded like a couple of pins struck by a bowling ball, splaying and twisting in different directions as I flew through the air.

I landed on my back. He'd shot my legs out from under me. They were still attached, but felt longer somehow, probably because they were just hanging on to the rest of me by strips of skin and muscle. It hurt like crazy for a second, but then the red around the edges of my eyes soaked through my entire vision and I could hear myself snarling, feel my teeth gnashing.

EAT NOW.

I struggled to hold on. Knew he would kill me for sure if I didn't. But I couldn't get up and run. Legs not working and all. I needed to drag myself away from him. Hide in the wheat field somehow.

But instead, I dragged myself toward him, snapping at his ankles. Drool and slime dripping from my face.

I heard the shotgun cock again.

"This is for Harlene," he said. I looked into the barrel of his shotgun.

I snarled. Then everything went red.

I didn't die.

Instead, I came to with my arms around a severed piece of half-chewed leg, cradling it like a teddy bear.

The red had cleared from my vision. I felt full, content, maybe a little bloated. I wasn't sure how long I'd lost control for; it felt like I'd just woken up from a dream. Not one of those full REM sleep dreams, though. One of those starter dreams, when you're first drifting off to sleep and then suddenly jump back awake because, in your dream, you tripped and fell or went over the handlebars of your bike. Somehow, I knew I hadn't been out for long.

Just long enough to eat somebody.

My jeans were all torn up from where the guy with the shotgun had blasted me, but my legs felt fine. The holes in my neck had closed up too.

I tried to think back to the chase through the wheat field, to remember what happened. Mostly, I remembered snarling and biting. Everything else was fractured pieces, snatches of memory. I remembered the shotgun's muzzle exploding. I felt the air from the shell hot against the side of my face.

Somehow, the big guy had missed.

Something had knocked his point-blank kill shot off course.

Dark shapes had emerged from the wheat field, converging on the big dude with the shotgun. He fired at them, but they overwhelmed him.

Two of the shadows detached from the others and stood looking down at me.

"What do we do with him?" asked a male voice I didn't recognize. "He's not one of ours."

The shadowy corn-people reached down and grabbed me by the wrists. I couldn't remember much more, but one weird detail stuck out to me.

I didn't want to eat them.

I lay still as I tried to piece together my memory. I

wasn't sure if I was still in danger and didn't want to make any sudden movements. I slowly swung my head around.

There was Captain Twelve Gauge. He was sitting right behind me, about five yards away. He'd been stripped down to his boxers, that crazy armor of his gone. One side of his face was covered in blood from a serious gash on top of his head. His feet were bound together with those plastic zip-tie things and, although I couldn't see his hands on account of them being behind his back, I assumed those were tied too.

Seated in a line next to the big guy were five other agents, all of them tied up. Except for hard-ass Roadblock, they all looked scared out of their wits. One of them retched into the dirt in front of him.

"What the hell happened out there?" the big dude whispered gruffly to the agent sitting next to him.

"We were watching the back," said the agent, sounding increasingly terrified. "They came out of nowhere, Jamison. There were only supposed to be two of them. Command said there'd only be two!"

"Calm down," hissed the big guy, Jamison.

He looked over at me and our eyes met. It was awkward.

I sat up, shoving the severed leg aside. There were still tattered pieces of jumpsuit sticking to it. I guess it was a pretty safe bet that I'd just eaten one of their coworkers right in front of them. I felt suddenly ashamed.

"I didn't know him very well," Jamison said to me, his voice measured, "but the man you just ate was named Nick Thomas. He was in his late twenties. From down south somewhere. I think he was engaged, or maybe married." Jamison stared me down, his gaze hard and full of hatred. I don't think I've ever had anyone look at me like that before. I had to look away.

"I wasn't the one chasing *you guys*," I said quietly.

"Uh-huh," replied Jamison, not interested in my excuses. "Untie me and let's finish this up."

Hey, here was a good question: Who had tied all these government agents up in the first place?

I stood up unsteadily and looked around. I was in a clearing near the wheat field. I couldn't be that far from the farmhouse, although I wasn't totally sure which direction to head in. Was there a way to use the moon as a compass? *Don't worry, Amanda, I'm coming to save you just as soon as I figure out how to navigate by the stars.*

"Hey, jerk," said a voice from behind me. "You owe us for that guy you ate."

There were about twenty of them watching me when I turned back around. They weren't ghosts, or soldiers, or some local militia come to sort out who'd been screwing with their wheat field. Maybe it was the fact that some of them had skin that swampy gray color, or maybe it was the bloodstains they proudly wore, or maybe because the guy addressing me was wearing a belt lined with human scalps, but I knew right away what they were.

Zombies. An army of zombies.

They looked like something out of Mad Max. Lots of leather, piercings, and creative hair choices. They were all youngish, most of them probably around my age or just a little older, and they were all seriously thin, which is maybe just a side effect of being undead that I hadn't yet discovered.

Behind them was a line of cars, mostly old junkers but also a huge conversion van and one of those black SUVs that the government guys loved to roar around in. All the cars had been transformed in some way to look like something a zombie road gang would drive; the SUV had what looked like an antelope skull tied across its hood, a large upside-down American flag mounted on its roof. A beat-up El Camino with a spray-painted skull on its hood had its headlights on and aimed at me and the prisoners.

And then there was the guy addressing me. He was tall, lean, and in case you couldn't tell by the vulture-feather headdress and tomahawk on his belt, very Native American. But not like a real Native American—more like the kind you'd see in an old Western movie. Except a zombie. (I don't know.)

He'd done something crazy to his mouth; cut the skin up one side of his cheek and inserted rows of little wooden picks to keep the incision from closing up, so you could always see to his back row of teeth.

"Uh, hey," was pretty much all I could manage while taking this in.

"Uh, hey," mimicked the leader in a high-pitched voice. "Seriously, buddy, if we wanted these guys eaten, we would've done it ourselves. And as if sampling our provisions wasn't uncool enough, you didn't even offer to share any of what's-his-name."

He looked past me, eyeballing Jamison.

"What'd you say his name was, big boy? Your now digesting compadre?"

"Fu–"

Before Big Shotgun could really start whatever colorful insult he had queued up, the zombie swung one of those stun guns from over his shoulder and blasted him with a bolt of electricity. Jamison fell backward, convulsing.

"WOO!" shouted the zombie, some of his friends laughing and clapping. "Ride the lightning, bitch!"

I started to inch my way toward the wheat field, this being the kind of situation that I felt it'd probably be good to extricate myself from. Seeing me move, the lead zombie aimed the stun gun in my direction. Why was it that every new zombie I met had to point a weapon at me?

"Whoa there, partner," he said. "We're still not done talking about you raiding our food stores. Lots of hungry bellies back in Des Moines, you know what I mean?"

"Yeah. Uh, sorry?" I stammered, glancing at the severed leg. "My bad?"

"My bad?" echoed the zombie.

"Jesus, Red Bear," interrupted one of the other zombies, a bored-looking girl with dreadlocks. "Didn't you learn anything from Plymouth Rock? Share the bounty and shut up already."

"Relax. I was just having some fun," sneered Red Bear, although he looked penitent and immediately lowered the stun gun. "We've met our quota for Lord Wesley with these prisoners. He'll be pleased."

"Lord Wesley?" I interrupted, thinking of that weird message board post from the so-called Lord of Des Moines.

Red Bear looked at me. "Our leader. He'll be excited to meet you. Any enemy of the NCD is a friend of ours."

"NCD?"

"Necrotic Control Division," Red Bear explained, wiggling his fingers sarcastically. He looked over at the cowering agents. "Do we look like some controllable mother fuckers to you?"

I shook my head and glanced back to the wheat field, to where the farmhouse waited. "I've gotta go back. They've got my, uh, girlfriend."

Red Bear seemed to consider this. "There's more of them, huh?"

Another zombie spoke up. "We've got our prisoners. That means the rest of the humans are fair game. That means we can *eat*."

The rest of the zombies roared, "Eat! Eat! Eat!"

Clearly, they were getting antsy.

That was all it took for Red Bear to make up his mind. "Who's ready to storm the gates?!" Red Bear howled. Then they were all howling. I might have too. It seemed like a good idea to try fitting in.

Seconds later, I was running with a pack of zombies through a wheat field, feeling more alone and confused than I'd felt all week, hoping like hell that I'd find Amanda alive.

CASS

AT SOME POINT, TOM STOPPED RADIOING FOR THE medical team. He'd been desperate at first, shouting at them to move their asses, that we had a squad leader down. Eventually, he'd stopped. There was no point.

Harlene was gone.

They moved her body inside the farmhouse, put her on top of the blanket that Amanda and Jake left behind. I sat with her there, holding her hand as it slowly cooled.

This could've been just another day at the office. The inside of the farmhouse could have been any of the NCD crime scenes I'd been assigned to over the last year and a half.

Just another dead body, right?

But of course, it wasn't.

I could still sense Harlene's psychic residue, even if it was fading fast. If I wanted to, I could slip into the dead synapses of her mind, fire them up again, and relive her last moments. If this really was a crime scene that's exactly what I would do, and pretty soon I'd have a bead on the zombie that killed her.

Except I didn't need to play psychic detective because the zombie that killed Harlene was in the room with me.

Amanda Blake lay on her side next to the fireplace where one of the NCD agents had dumped her. They'd snapped some heavy-duty shackles around her wrists and ankles, thick steel things that probably weighed twenty pounds each. Even with a rush of hungry zombie adrenaline, Amanda wasn't breaking out of those cuffs. They'd also strapped a muzzle across her face, pretty much exactly like what they made Hannibal Lecter wear when they transported him in *Silence of the Lambs*.

She was all trussed up, ready to be taken to Washington and have a hole drilled in her pretty head, so she could live the rest of her life in a perpetual state of zombieness, bonded by blood to an NCD agent so that she could be dragged around on a metal chain and used as a human weapon until someone finally killed her for good.

I didn't support the whole zombie-enslavement

initiative. I think it's fair to say that it grossed me out on ethical and physical grounds. But at that moment, I couldn't think of anyone I'd rather see at the end of a leash than Amanda Blake.

Was that harsh? Cruel? I didn't care. I wasn't really in a mood for introspection. I wanted someone else to hurt.

I caught Amanda watching me. I felt embarrassed that she was allowed to see me like this, kneeling next to Harlene's body and holding her hand. She shouldn't have been in here with us. This should've been private.

"What are you looking at?" I snapped.

Amanda flicked her eyes away like she didn't want any trouble, but her gaze gradually drifted back in my direction, like she couldn't resist.

"How did you know that stuff about me?" she asked, her words muffled by the muzzle.

"Don't talk to her," snapped Tom. I wasn't sure which one of us he meant, but both Amanda and I shut up. I'd never heard Tom's voice so authoritative, although I'd also never seen him so on edge.

Tom stood at the window, watching the activity around the farmhouse. Some of the remaining NCD agents had formed a perimeter out front. The rest had gone into the wheat field, looking for Jamison and the other agents who were supposed to be guarding the back of the farmhouse and had disappeared out there. Tom shook his head, looking freaked.

"This isn't safe," he announced, and turned to me. "We're getting out of here. As your guardian, I insist we do so immediately."

"What about Harlene?" I asked, still holding her hand.

"Cass," Tom said, softening a bit, "nothing bad can happen to her anymore. You and I, on the other hand, need to be getting away from this shit-show posthaste."

"The mission isn't over, Thomas."

Alastaire strode through the front door. Actually, he strode *over* it, Chazz having knocked it off the hinge and onto the ground during his grand entrance earlier. Chazz trailed along after him, looking worn out even for a mostly decomposed zombie. His knuckles almost dragged on the floor as he shuffled after Alastaire, back hunched, arms limp.

Amanda struggled into a sitting position when they entered. Her eyes widened with confusion as she saw that Alastaire had Chazz on a leash.

"Chazz?" she asked quietly. "What did they do to you?"

Her ex-boyfriend's only response was to loll his head back and forth on his shoulders. Even if Chazz had the mental capacity to answer, he wouldn't have found it easy with his jaw laying discarded a few feet away. I'd been pretending not to notice that thing ever since we came in here. It looked like a piece of sparerib that a dog had chewed on.

Alastaire glanced at Amanda, annoyed, and then looked over at Tom, who hadn't budged from his spot by the window.

"Why didn't we gag her?" asked Alastaire.

Tom ignored his question. "This mission *is* over," insisted Tom.

"I only see one prisoner," said Alastaire, waving at Amanda. "I assume you can count as high as two?"

"And how many dead agents do you count?" Tom seethed.

Alastaire looked at Harlene's body for what I thought was the first time. He frowned.

"Yes, that's . . . unfortunate." He paused, seeing something. "Oh, hello, here's this."

Alastaire bent down and picked up the bottom part of Chazz's jaw. He snapped his fingers in Chazz's eyes until the zombie straightened up and looked at him. Then, like an artist sizing up a sculpture, Alastaire steadied Chazz's head by grabbing his hair and shoved the jawbone back onto his face. There was the grinding of bone on bone and when Alastaire took his hands away, Chazz's jaw hung half-open and crooked.

"Well, it's a start," muttered Alastaire.

"This is so fucked," declared Amanda.

I'm not sure I can put into words how much I hated Alastaire at that moment. He was more interested in putting his pet back together than he was in Harlene.

I would've never mistaken Alastaire for a good guy, but now I was convinced there wasn't even a shred of human decency in him. He was as much a monster as Amanda or Chazz.

"I'm sorry to leave you here," I whispered to Harlene. "You were so kind and wonderful."

No one heard me say my good-bye because Amanda had started trying to get Chazz's attention.

"Help me, Chazz," she said. "I don't know what they've done to you, but we can fix it." Chazz snarled and began to strain at his leash.

Alastaire just wiggled his finger. "No, no, Chazz." Chazz looked into his eyes and gurgled happily. Amanda's eyes widened, but she kept right on going.

"You aren't just going to let them take me, are you, Chazz?" Amanda pleaded. Her dumb ex-boyfriend was her only hope. "Help me get out of here!"

I'd had enough. I set Harlene's hand down gently on her stomach and stood up, looking at Tom.

"Okay," I said. "I'm ready to go."

"Good," said Tom, pointedly ignoring Alastaire. "Race you to the SUV."

Tom and I started for the door. Behind us, I heard Alastaire mutter something, followed by the metallic click of his leash disconnecting.

Before we could go another step, Chazz had positioned himself between us and the door. He watched us, eyes wide and hungry, more attentive now than before.

"Fight them, Chazz," Amanda kept on. "Please, fight them!"

I intended to march right through Chazz, to call Alastaire's bluff. Tom put a hand on my shoulder, though, stopping me before I got too close. We turned to face Alastaire together.

"You can't do this," said Tom, but Alastaire waved him off.

"Thomas, your insubordination has been noted. You can expect a transfer after this mission." He looked at me, smiling patiently. "As for you, just tell us where to find the boy and you can head back to Washington. Spend some quality time thinking about how to improve your performance for the next mission."

"No," I said, squaring my shoulders. "I'm done."

Alastaire's smile was unflappable. His thoughts, however, hissed across my brain with the heat and force of steam bursting out of a boiling teakettle.

I'm losing patience with you, child. Tell me where the boy is or I'll just rip it out of your little brain.

My body shook with the force of his thought, but I tried not to let it show.

I don't think you're actually stronger than me, I thought back. *You're just a coward that hides behind soldiers and zombies. You know I'm stronger than you. If I weren't, you wouldn't need me. You wouldn't have needed me to bring you here. I'm stronger than all of you, and that's why you're so obsessed with me, you sick freak.*

Alastaire straightened his bow tie. A nanosecond later, it felt like my brain had been locked in a spike-covered vise.

Really misjudged that one, Cass.

The pressure was sudden and sharp: behind my eyes, in my ears, down through my sinuses. I felt my nose turn on like a faucet, blood pouring out, but that was a distant thing. More present were the claws in my brain—Alastaire rummaging through my thoughts, my memories, every part of me.

My body must have wobbled because I felt Tom's hand on my arm, heard him shouting for Alastaire to stop whatever he was doing.

Alastaire broke into the place where I'd hidden away the memory of that afternoon's meeting with Harlene when she granted me my release from NCD. I could feel his psychic laughter.

It was so trivial to him, so amusing.

Do you honestly believe I'd ever let you go? One day, you'll appreciate what I've done for you.

I felt trampled by the force of his mind. I'd never so completely lost control of my being before. I was like a passenger or, worse still, a prisoner inside my own body. I couldn't think, unless he allowed it. Every memory I had, every secret, was at his psychic fingertips.

Only seconds had passed outside my body since Tom and I first went for the door. Distantly, I could hear Amanda still trying to convince Chazz to be her knight in shining armor.

"We can find Jake, he's cooler than you think," was Amanda's latest pitch. "We're going to Iowa, Chazz. You can come with us. They say there's a cure there."

And just like that, my mind was once again my own. I felt violated and weakened and disgusted, but he was out. Something had distracted him.

Alastaire rounded on Amanda.

"What did you just say?" Alastaire barked.

Whatever she'd said—something about Iowa and a cure—it had gotten Alastaire's attention. That usual façade of condescending politeness was cracked. She'd freaked him out.

Amanda just stared at Alastaire, eyes narrowed above her muzzle.

"What did you say about a cure?" he practically shouted.

I wobbled in place. Tom put his arm around my shoulders to steady me. Chazz groaned plaintively from behind us, his jaw clicking as he snapped at the air, testing it. Apparently, the zombie could bite again.

I wish I could say that I thought about all the disturbing things Alastaire had done since I met him. The severed hand in NCD training, kidnapping Jake's sister, his complete apathy toward Harlene. The way he just forced himself on me, forced his way into my mind to prove a point.

I wish I thought about all those things, but I didn't. Alastaire was distracted, so I acted. That's all there is to it.

I forced my way into Chazz's mind, not bothering to be gentle. I'd been there before. The cold and alien feeling of a zombie mind wasn't so bad after having Alastaire shove himself into my brain.

I sent Chazz a mental picture, hoping that his low-functioning zombie mind combined with the NCD tech enhancements that made him so susceptible to suggestion wouldn't know the difference between my psychic nudge and a real order.

The mental picture was of Alastaire.

In the mental picture, Alastaire said, "Eat me."

With a guttural moan that sounded almost grateful, Chazz shoved past Tom and me. Alastaire turned away from Amanda just in time to see his pet zombie bound forward.

Alastaire threw an arm up to defend himself, but Chazz bit down on him right at the elbow, hard, and twisted his head back and forth like you see those attack dogs do when they get their teeth in the big foam man pretending to be a burglar.

Alastaire fell backward and Chazz fell with him,

biting through tendons and bone. Alastaire was screaming for Chazz to stop, and Amanda was screaming for Chazz to keep going, convinced she'd made this happen through her desperate wheedling.

I just stood there, not saying anything. Not looking away.

Tom, very calmly, pulled his gun, took two steps forward, aimed, and shot Chazz in the back of the head.

Now Amanda flipped out. She tried to lunge at Tom, but her shackles got in the way and she ended up just falling on her face. Tom sidestepped her, moving quickly back to me, looking shocked at his own man-of-action routine.

"Why'd you stop him?" I asked Tom quietly, ignoring Amanda's shouted threats.

Tom studied my face, must have read in it what I'd just done. He shook his head, disapproval mixing with resignation.

"Oh god, Cass. Did you make him attack?"

Before I could answer, there was a shout outside followed by a volley of stun-gun fire. That wasn't right. Come to think of it, it was kind of strange that no agents had come running when Tom fired his pistol.

What was going on out there?

Tom pushed me toward the back of the room and walked, gun still drawn, to the farmhouse window.

"What the he—?" was all Tom managed to say before a pair of zombie hands reached in the window and grabbed him by the front of his shirt. His legs banged painfully against the window frame as a leather-clad zombie dragged him through the window.

I heard gunshots. Tom screamed.

"Tom!" I shouted and tried to run toward the door, but I was too dizzy and weak from telepathically pushing Chazz. I fell onto my knees.

Amanda had gone quiet. We listened and watched together; the night outside was lit by blue electricity fired off from a dozen stun guns. Agents were yelling, sounding desperate and afraid. Over their cries came the fierce snarls of zombies. I could hear them running by outside, the haggard way they tried to breathe through dead lungs, and the wet ripping sounds they made when they fell upon one of the agents.

Tom. Not Tom too.

I jumped when Chazz's body moved. It was Alastaire, crawling out from beneath him. He'd gone deathly pale, the lower part of his arm hanging on by just a strip of exposed muscle.

"Well played," he said to me, groaning as he tried to sit up. "Do you know how to tie a tourniquet?"

I looked at him with disbelief, sitting there expecting me to help him. Then I looked over at Amanda, her eyes wide above the muzzle, waiting for her zombie friends to come rescue her. I felt nothing but disgust for both of them.

"We can still make it out of here, Cassandra," Alastaire groaned, groping for his gun with his working hand. "Tonight will be a story we laugh about one day."

I got my legs under me, ignoring him. Harlene was dead, Jamison was missing, and Tom had been dragged into the night screaming.

There was nothing left for me to do but go.

Alastaire was still calling my name as I walked out the front door of the farmhouse.

JAKE

THE ZOMBIE RUNNING NEXT TO ME TOOK A BLAST OF electricity to the chest. His skin sizzled and popped like cooked meat as he flipped head over heels and crashed down in the dirt. Before the agent could get off another round, he was sideswiped by a zombie with dreadlocks. She tackled him, biting down hard on his shoulder. The agent screamed and that was like a dinner bell, two other zombies running over to help the girl with the dreadlocks divide him up.

I kept running.

I remembered this stupid game they made us play on spring days in elementary-school gym class. It was called Red Rover. The phys ed teacher would take us out to the grass field behind the school and divide the class up into two lines, all the kids in the line holding hands. Then, kids would take turns yelling, "Red Rover, Red Rover, send blah-blah right over," and if you were the person named, it was your job to charge that other line and try to break through. I think the only reason we played Red Rover was because our gym teacher had a sick fascination with watching little kids clothesline each other. I bet that did look pretty funny, actually.

This one time when my name was called, instead of running at the opposite line, I took off sideways. I ran down the middle of the field and took the long way around the other line until I was behind them, the gym coach blowing his whistle and looking confused.

Anyway, that's what it was like in the field outside the farmhouse, like the most intense game of Red Rover ever, with no one following any of the rules.

The government dudes tried to keep a line, standing shoulder to shoulder, firing their stun guns at us zombies as we came cheering and howling from the wheat field. It just took one agent getting pulled off from the end of the line, though, dragged down screaming by a zombie with huge steel gauges through his ear lobes, for the whole thing to become chaos. These NCD guys might have been zombie hunters but, by the looks of things, they hadn't trained for a massive pack attack.

The Iowa zombies, man, they'd done this before. They were gleeful and whooping in those last seconds as they descended on the agents, sank their teeth into them, and came up snarling greedily and gnashing their teeth.

I watched an agent toss away his stun gun and pull a real pistol from a hidden pocket in his jumpsuit. He shot the first zombie that came close, but there was another one right behind him. The second zombie grabbed the agent by the arms and wrenched him backward, biting down on his neck.

I got lower, running with my head down. I was trying to keep my distance from the agents, not attacking any of them so they wouldn't shoot me, yet somehow I didn't think they'd see the difference between me and the other zombies. Still, I didn't want to get shot in the head before I could find Amanda. Or after, for that matter.

Amanda. I didn't see her anywhere. I really hoped they hadn't killed her. They wouldn't do that, right? Why go through all the trouble of capturing us if the plan was just to blow out our brains?

I skirted around a burly NCD guy using one of their big net cannons to bash a zombie down to the ground. If you've got a big weapon, use it for blunt force. That made sense. The whole capturing thing? Not so much. Why would they bother with all that?

Then again, I was pretty sure they'd sent Chazz after us. Clearly, there was a lot I didn't understand.

There was too much to think about. Besides all this mess with the government, who may or may not have been cultivating their own zombie slaves, there was also this insane gang of zombie warriors to consider. They were disturbingly gung ho about eating people. It seemed like a no-brainer that these were the kinds of bad zombies Grace and Summer had warned us about. Sure, they'd helped me and all, but I didn't really want to get mixed up with them.

I could sort all that out later. I just wanted to find Amanda and get out of here.

There was Red Bear, standing over a dying NCD agent. He had his tomahawk out, eating a slab of flesh he'd cut from the NCD agent right off the blade. When he saw me, he held out the tomahawk, the fatty part of a thigh glistening tastily at me.

"Bite?" he offered, his voice husky and wet, like we get when we're feeding.

I hate to admit that it looked appetizing. Luckily, I'd just eaten, so my zombie urges were under control. I shook my head. "No thanks."

Red Bear shrugged and went back to his meal, the agent managing a weak scream as Red Bear raised the tomahawk above his head.

There was a gunshot and Red Bear pitched forward,

staggering. Another agent a few yards away had shot him in the shoulder. Red Bear let out a frustrated groan and charged the second agent.

I ran in the opposite direction, not waiting around to see if the agent's aim was better than Red Bear was quick.

There were bodies everywhere; agents and zombies fighting. I didn't see Amanda outside. I figured she must be in the farmhouse and started that way, taking a looping route away from the action.

I wanted to call Amanda's name, but thought that might attract too much attention. When I found her, I was definitely going to teach her a birdcall or something. We needed a signal for future hell-on-Earth situations.

I skidded to a stop. A few yards in front of me, a couple zombies had overwhelmed an agent and thrust their hands into his stomach, pulling his guts out, looking like a morbid version of *Lady and the Tramp* as they gnawed on the same section of intestine. Gross, yeah, but it wasn't what made me stop.

It was the brown-haired girl I'd seen in the back of the SUV chasing us in New Jersey, the same one that appeared in that wacked-out dream I had. She looked pale and shell-shocked, which I guess was a normal reaction to a scene like this, and it looked like she'd just had a rock-star nosebleed.

Weirder still was that she walked right by those two zombies and they didn't seem to notice. She stopped for a second, letting a screaming NCD agent run by with a zombie hot on his heels, and then kept right on walking, her hands shoved deep into her pockets.

She looked up, noticing me noticing her, and her face scrunched in confusion. Then, she walked over and hugged me, squeezing me tight, her blood-covered face pressed into my chest. I think she was crying a little bit.

"Jake," she said, her voice distant and lost like she'd just woken up from a dream. "You're here."

I patted her back awkwardly, not really sure what to do with this NCD creeper that had very clearly lost her marbles.

"Uh, hey," I said.

She peered up while still holding on to me and it was like something clicked in her mind, like she'd suddenly remembered where she was and realized we were, like, ankle deep in a bloodbath. She dropped her arms down to her sides, looking embarrassed.

"Sorry," she said hesitantly. "I'm Cass."

"Hi," I said, awkward because I didn't know the protocol for meeting someone in a situation like this. Not to mention, even though she wasn't shooting guns or flinging nets, she was very clearly part of the NCD. Should I ask her what school she went to, maybe make some small talk about hunting zombies?

Gunshots. Like, right next to my ear. An NCD agent with a pair of guns fired action-hero style at a trio of zombies, pushing them backward. One of the zombies fell to the ground, a smoking hole in his forehead.

The agent was within arm's reach of me. It would've required less effort on his part to turn and shoot me than it would've to tie his shoe.

But the agent didn't even look at me. He just kept on shooting at the other zombies, marching in their direction like the definition of going out in a blaze of glory.

"They can't see us," explained Cass. "Not if I don't want them to. I'm psychic."

Okaaay.

"But wait," I said. "Why can I see you?"

Just then, a zombie detached from a nearby agent and charged right at Cass. He was within inches when an agent, bleeding out on the ground ten yards away, shot him in the back of the head. The zombie dropped dead at our feet. Cass looked down at him.

"I haven't quite mastered it yet," she explained.

A bullet whizzed by my face. That dying agent had taken a shot at me too.

Before he could take aim again, I grabbed Cass around the shoulders in an awkward hug-like move and dragged her toward the farmhouse. She didn't put up a fight; she was like a rag doll in my arms.

"I'm not going to eat you," I told her, feeling like I should reassure this glassy-eyed space case.

"I know," she said.

"Because you can see the future?"

"That's not how it works. I just, uh, have a good feeling about you, okay?"

On our right, Red Bear leapt on top of the agent that had taken a shot at me. He looked over as he gulped down a bite of the agent, and waved.

"That's the spirit, new guy!" Red Bear shouted, apparently assuming Cass was my dinner selection and approving.

I ignored him. We were only a few yards away from the farmhouse, most of the fight now behind us.

"I can help you get into Iowa," said Cass, her face in my armpit. "If you help me get out of here. And promise not to eat me on the way."

"But you work for the scary government."

"I quit tonight."

If the plan was still to go find that old man in Des Moines—and I seriously didn't have any better ideas right then—my options were either join up with these crazy, scary zombies or trust in this fragile, seeming way-too-familiar psychic.

I looked over my shoulder. Red Bear dragged the struggling NCD agent along by his ankle. He brought the agent to where the zombie girl with the dreadlocks waited, smoking a cigarette. Red Bear stepped on the agent's neck so that he couldn't squirm away while he and the girl kissed, all tongue and hair pulling. Then, they started eating the guy. Was that the kind of zombie life I wanted to lead?

No way. I'd take my chances with the psychic.

"Deal," I said. "But I'm not leaving without her."

Cass didn't reply as I dragged her into the farmhouse, letting her go once we'd crossed the threshold.

There was a dead lady inside, laid out on the blanket Amanda and I had spread with such care, like, an hour ago. Chazz Slade was there too, or what was left of him, most of his head missing, his body looking like it had been rotting for weeks.

Amanda was lying next to Chazz, not moving, so at first I thought she was dead too. For a moment, my heart dropped. She stirred when the floorboards creaked under my feet and looked up at me. Her hands and feet were shackled, half her face hidden behind a muzzle. She breathed a long and shaky sigh of relief.

"You came back," she said, a note of wonder in her voice. "You're alive. I knew you wouldn't leave me."

"Of course," I said, my voice cracking right when I was trying to be all macho. "We're a team. I don't know how we're going to make it out of this, but I know there's no way we're doing it alone."

I knelt down and helped Amanda sit up. I pulled at the shackles, but there was no give at all.

Cass kept her distance. She looked obsessed with this huge trail of blood on the floor. It started near Chazz, then continued all the way to the back door of the farmhouse. Cass followed it, peering out the back door, maybe searching for one of her government pals.

Cass crouched down and picked something up from where the blood trail met the back threshold. I couldn't really make out what it was; it looked like a piece of blood-spattered fabric. Maybe a bow tie? Cass looked it over for a moment, then tossed it aside.

"What's she doing here?" hissed Amanda.

"Helping us," I said.

"Fuck that. They killed Chazz. They'll kill us too. Or worse, do to us whatever they did to him."

I glanced over at Chazz's body. Did it make me a total dick that I didn't feel anything that Chazz had gone and gotten himself shot in the head? I guess it was different for Amanda; they'd actually had a relationship and all that. Even if they'd broken up, seeing him killed had to be a shock. I tried to look solemn for her benefit.

"I'm sorry," I told her, tugging at her shackles again to quickly change the subject. "How do we get these off you?"

"Check her," said Amanda, jerking her chin toward the dead lady on the blankets. "She was some kind of boss."

"*Don't* touch her," snapped Cass, returning from the back door, looking more pale than before.

I held up my hands like, *Whoa, calm down.* Cass

crouched over the dead lady, gently rifling through the pockets of her uniform. After a moment, she tossed me a ring of keys. Then she neatly folded the lady's hands across her chest.

The third key I tried unlocked Amanda's shackles. They clattered to the floor, Amanda rubbing her wrists. She unstrapped the muzzle on her own.

She stood up and looked me in the eyes. She didn't blink and she didn't look away. Her eyes were glittering with rage.

"We are going to make it," she said in a low, hoarse voice. "We'll eat every fucker who stands in our way. What we can't eat, we'll burn to the motherfucking ground. I don't care anymore. I don't care what we have to do or how we have to do it. We're going to make it. And we're going to make it together."

My heart was thumping in my chest. She was right. The only direction we could move was forward. But we would get there. "I love you," I said, caught up in the moment, sure, but it was true.

Kissing her zombie mouth, I felt as alive as undead gets.

When I broke away from her and turned around, Cass was gaping at us in horror. Amanda stared daggers at her.

"Okay," I said, using that calming tone of voice the school guidance counselor trotted out during peer mediation. "I'm feeling some tension."

Amanda strode toward Cass, glaring at her. I'll give the little psychic some credit; she stood her ground. Back at school I'd seen plenty of freshman girls and even some dudes turn into blubbering idiots in the face of that white-hot Amanda Blake stare. But Cass looked more tired than frightened as she used her sleeve to wipe dried blood off her upper lip. She returned Amanda's gaze impassively.

"Amanda," I said, not sure what I'd do if she started attacking our new best hope for Iowa, really not wanting that to happen. "Come on. . . ."

Amanda shoved the muzzle into Cass's chest, forcing her back a step.

"I should make you wear that," said Amanda, sounding hard and bitter.

Cass didn't make a move to take the muzzle, just let it fall to the floor. She didn't say anything back, which was probably a wise move and, after staring her down for another couple seconds, Amanda flipped her hair dismissively and walked over to the doorway.

"Jake," she said. "Let's go."

I joined her and we watched in silence as the NCD made their last stand. The few remaining agents had hunkered down back at the cars—our car included—using the doors for cover, keeping their backs to the vehicles. The zombies had them surrounded like a pack of jackals, one occasionally darting in to snap at an agent and being driven back by gunfire. The zombies were toying with them.

"Who are these guys?" asked Amanda.

"They're from Iowa," I answered.

"Why can't we just go with them? What do we need *her* for?"

An NCD agent made it inside an SUV, trying to start it. There was Red Bear, leaping onto the hood, smashing the windshield with his tomahawk.

"I don't think we want to be friends with them," I answered, looking away as Red Bear dragged the agent, screaming, out through the windshield. "I'm pretty sure they're the *bad* kind of zombies. And Cass says she can get us to Des Moines."

"You believe her?"

"I do," I said.

Amanda nodded, sweeping her gaze over all the mangled bodies outside.

"Okay," she said, grabbing my hand. "I trust you. But, for the record, *I'd* eat her."

I looked over my shoulder. Cass had sat down next to the dead lady, in her own little world. I felt sorry for her.

"I wouldn't," I replied.

We couldn't go back to our car, and I didn't want to go back through the wheat field to where some of the Iowa zombies had stayed behind to guard Jamison and their other NCD "provisions," so we went sideways, into an endless stretch of tallgrass field. I figured if we just headed in a straight line, we'd find civilization eventually and there'd be a car for Amanda to use her master criminal skills on. Then we'd be on our way. No problem.

We walked along in silence. Amanda made Cass walk a few steps in front of us, treating her like a prisoner. I wasn't worried that she'd run off, though; she looked like she barely had the energy to keep walking.

We passed through a field where a couple of bored-looking horses grazed. I'm not sure if they were wild or if that meant there was another farm nearby. I stopped walking.

"Want to ride these horses?" I suggested.

Amanda looked at me, rolling her eyes. "You can't ride a horse."

"I don't *know* that I can't ride a horse."

"Okay," she said. "*I* know you can't ride a horse."

"Oh, come on. I've seen people in movies do it. You just hop on and go, 'Yah yah!'"

Amanda opened her mouth to pour more rain on my horse parade, but was cut off as gunshot thundered through the night air. We both flinched, spinning around to see who'd shot at us.

Twenty yards away across the open field, a lone NCD agent stood with his gun pointed in the air. He didn't look like much. Not like one of the hardened soldiers from back at the farmhouse; he was way too skinny and polished looking for that, even if he was covered in blood from a bite wound on his shoulder, another one on his calf, and probably others I couldn't see. Maybe he was the guy that got coffee for the real soldiers. He'd straggled far from the chaos back at the farmhouse, though, so props for that, dude.

"Tom?" shouted Cass with disbelief, the first words she'd spoken since the farmhouse filled. Then, she repeated herself, disbelief replaced by joy. "Tom!"

This Tom guy looked like he was one strong breeze away from falling over. He pointed his gun at us, at me specifically, his hand shaking.

"Get away from her," he shouted across the field.

I held up my hands. "Okay, man, calm down."

"Tom," said Cass, taking a shaky step toward him. "You're alive!"

"I'm hanging in there, Psychic Friend," he said. "You okay?"

"I'm okay." Cass nodded. "I thought you were . . ." she trailed off.

"O ye of little faith," replied Tom. Then he looked at me. "She's coming with me and we're getting out of here. I don't care what you do after, just don't hurt her."

I looked at Cass and shrugged, because at this point I just wanted to take a break from having guns pointed at me.

"Yeah, dude. Whatever."

But Cass didn't move. I'd felt Amanda tense up next to me when Tom first started talking. Now, she walked sideways, slowly, her body hunched over, giving Tom as little target area as possible. She looked ready to pounce.

Tom swung his aim from me to Amanda, then back to me.

"Stop moving or I'll shoot," Tom shouted.

Finally, Cass stepped forward and at first I thought she was going to walk to Tom. I didn't plan to stop her. Instead, she planted herself between me and Tom's gun.

Amanda kept circling, getting closer to Tom as she did. It was getting harder for him to keep us both in his sights.

"Amanda!" I yelled. "What the fuck?"

"He's the one, Jake," she seethed. "He's the one that killed Chazz."

"Oh, come on, so—" I cut myself off before I finished the big *so fucking what* I had for Chazz's untimely demise. "You—we killed people too, Amanda."

"It's not the same!" she barked. "They did something to him, and when it went bad, this guy just shot him in the head!"

Now Tom was aiming exclusively at Amanda.

"I got pretty good with this thing tonight, sister," he said, shaking his gun at her. "Don't try me."

"I'm not going back, Tom," interrupted Cass, the

words bursting out of her like she'd just come to a major decision. "I can't go back there."

Tom tried to look at Cass out of the corner of his eye, still watching Amanda prowl closer.

"We can fix things," Tom pleaded. "I promise I'll fix things, Cass. I saw what Alastaire did. We'll file a report."

Cass shook her head manically, her hair falling across her face, catching in the dried blood.

"You can't protect me," she said shakily, like she regretted the words as soon as she'd said them.

Now Tom swung his gun back in my direction. His eyes were wide, hurt, maybe a little panicked.

"And *he* can?" yelled Tom, pointing at me. "He is *not* your friend, Cassandra."

As soon as Tom took the gun off her, Amanda charged. She didn't have far to go, yet it was just long enough for Tom to jumpily point the gun at her.

"Shit! Stop!" I screamed, feeling helpless.

I felt it then, like a shock wave in the air, and Cass was the epicenter. It's hard to describe because I couldn't see it. In fact, I couldn't even feel it like you normally feel things. It was like that dizzy feeling you get when you stand up too fast, except this time it came on with the force of a wave crashing on the beach—and it all happened inside my brain.

Amanda fell on her face, midcharge, like a puppet with the strings cut.

Tom collapsed too, the shot he had meant for Amanda flying wild into the night.

I was stunned silent. Well, for like half a second.

"Holy fuck! Did you just kill them?!"

Cass turned to me, looking groggy, a fresh and thick trickle of blood pouring out of her nostril.

"Knock–knocked them out," she stammered, and then collapsed into my arms. "I managed not to hit you. We need you to help us. To help me. Promise not to eat Tom. Promise, promise, promise. . . ."

And then she was out too.

"Okay, I promise," I said, and set her down in the grass.

I looked around. Three passed-out bodies in the middle of nowhere; one the beautiful undead girl I was nurturing a raging crush on, one a psychic chick that I'd made multiple promises to tonight, and then that Tom guy.

Well, Jake. What now?

CASS

I'M NOT SURE HOW LONG I WAS OUT FOR. IT HAD TO BE a while. I'd never pushed myself like that before.

I didn't dream. I was glad for that, worried what I might see.

Jamison running into the wheat field, never to return.

Harlene's cold body, forgotten on the floor of the farmhouse.

The pained look in Tom's eyes when I told him that he couldn't protect me.

Alastaire. Anything involving Alastaire.

I woke up in a tight space. It was hot and smelled like gasoline. I was thirsty, my mouth like a desert, the back of my throat sore. My tongue was like a dried sponge in my mouth and yet I could still taste blood.

My clothes felt stiff and gross. I was sweating and my head was throbbing like it had never throbbed before. I tried to reach out to the astral plane, to find the minds around me, maybe get some clue where I was, but it hurt too much. I had a migraine and my migraine had an ax and my mind was made of wood.

I was in the trunk of a car. That much I had worked out.

That was a bummer. Still, I felt lucky to be alive.

I bumped along for a while. The ride didn't do my head any favors.

Eventually, the car pulled over. I couldn't hear any other cars nearby. Wherever we were, it wasn't populated.

Two car doors opened. Slammed closed.

"How long are we going to keep checking on her before we just dump her somewhere?" I heard Amanda say, her voice muffled by the trunk.

"Until she wakes up, I guess," Jake replied. Keys jingled, clinked in the lock. Amanda threw open the trunk, sunlight pouring in. I had to shield my eyes, it hurt so bad, new, tiny spears of pain spreading from behind my eyes and into my brain.

"Oh, look," said Amanda. "Sleeping Boring awakens."

I sat up, my back cracking, my cramped muscles joining my brain in its chorus of agony. I was still in my NCD jumpsuit. Bloodstained and filthy.

I pushed my hand through my knotty hair reflexively as my eyes adjusted to the daylight and I saw Amanda. It looked like she'd just had a shower.

"Hey," said Jake, trying to sound chipper as he sidled up beside Amanda. "You're okay! We thought you might be in a coma or something."

"Hoped," clarified Amanda.

"Water," I croaked.

"Oh shit, right," said Jake, darting off to rummage in the car's backseat. Amanda just stood there, watching me. So, this was going to be a fun trip.

I guess I sort of *was* one of them now, right? I mean, not a zombie, but a fugitive.

Jake returned, handing me a bottle of water. I chugged the entire thing, then felt like I might puke, so I lunged out of the trunk, shoving past Amanda. I staggered to the side of the empty country road we were parked on and wetly heaved into the grass.

"Gross," Amanda observed.

"Would you be a little nicer?" I heard Jake whisper.

"No," said Amanda, and went back to the car.

Jake walked over and stood next to me as I finished retching.

"Are you okay?" Jake asked.

"Yeah," I said, working moisture into my mouth. "But can I ride in the car from now on?"

Jake snorted, glancing over at Amanda. "I'll see if I can swing that."

There was an awkward silence. I stretched my legs, not sure what I should say or do. Thank him for keeping his promise and not eating me while I was passed out? Apologize for spending so much time uninvited in his brain?

Right then, if my psychic powers hadn't been totally burned out, I would've slipped into Jake's mind. Just to see what I should say next.

"So," he said finally, "I'm glad you're awake."

"Really?" I asked, looking at him, wishing I could change out of this disgusting jumpsuit and into something even half as heinous.

"Yeah," he replied. "I think you can help us. Maybe we can help you. I don't know. We've been driving for a couple days—"

"Days?" I asked, my eyes wide.

"Yeah," he said, recognizing my shock. "You were really out of it. All you missed was a lot of driving in circles. It's all roadblocks and ominous black patrol cars out here. We've been afraid to get too close."

"Where's here?"

"We're just outside Iowa," said Jake.

Iowa. I remembered what I promised him back at the farmhouse. That I could get them into Des Moines. But

I didn't have any idea how to do that, or what was even there, not to mention at the border. All I'd heard were the rumors that the place was overrun, but our superiors never let on if they were actually true.

I glanced back at the car. Amanda was leaning against it, peering down at a road atlas. Pretending to read. Really, she was watching me. I was pretty sure she'd take any excuse to eat me.

I should've let Tom shoot her. Oh, Tom! What about Tom?

"That guy back at the farmhouse—" I began hesitantly. "My friend Tom, did you . . ."

"I left him there," Jake said. "I don't know what happened next."

I nodded. Jake had kept his promise. I hoped Tom had made it back to Washington safe. And I hoped Jamison was safe too, wherever he'd ended up.

As for Alastaire, I hoped he'd bled to death in that wheat field.

Amanda approached with the road atlas.

"All right, Magellan," she said, pointing on the map to an empty spot of country on the southern border of Iowa. "We're here. Where's the secret entrance?"

"Guide us," said Jake, lowering his voice conspiratorially and looking right at me. "We have no idea what we're doing."

That made three of us.

DATE DUE
DISCARDED
Rochambeau Branch